PRAISE

A Crafty

(Best of 2011 by *Suspense Magazine*)

"Fun plot, fanciful characters, really fabulous crafts . . . Bartlett put her art and soul into this mystery!"
—Laura Childs, *New York Times* bestselling author of *Scones & Bones*

"Bartlett combines murder, a touch of romance, and a lot of intrigue in this charming story. With a cast of personable characters and a lively, fast-paced story line, readers will be enthralled and delighted with this fresh new series."
—*Fresh Fiction*

"A fun new mystery with a cast of charming characters . . . Readers will look forward to more with Katie and the artisans from Artisans Alley." —*The Mystery Reader*

"A sweet new mystery series by a top-notch author who writes under a few pen names. Katie is a likable heroine, fallible yet strong, tough but tender. A great book for readers looking for something light—and who also look for happy endings. I expect this series to go on for a long time."
—*Cozy Library*

"[A] fantastic start to a new cozy series . . . *A Crafty Killing* kept my attention from the very first word until I turned the last page. The red herrings were aplenty, and the killer a complete surprise. Ms. Bartlett has created a crafty tale that must be read." —*The Best Reviews*

"This opening tale in a small-town amateur-sleuth series is a terrific first act." —*Genre Go Round*

The Walled Flower

LORRAINE BARTLETT

BERKLEY PRIME CRIME, NEW YORK

THE BERKLEY PUBLISHING GROUP
Published by the Penguin Group
Penguin Group (USA) Inc.
375 Hudson Street, New York, New York 10014, USA
Penguin Group (Canada), 90 Eglinton Avenue East, Suite 700, Toronto, Ontario M4P 2Y3, Canada
(a division of Pearson Penguin Canada Inc.)
Penguin Books Ltd., 80 Strand, London WC2R 0RL, England
Penguin Group Ireland, 25 St. Stephen's Green, Dublin 2, Ireland (a division of Penguin Books Ltd.)
Penguin Group (Australia), 250 Camberwell Road, Camberwell, Victoria 3124, Australia
(a division of Pearson Australia Group Pty. Ltd.)
Penguin Books India Pvt. Ltd., 11 Community Centre, Panchsheel Park, New Delhi—110 017, India
Penguin Group (NZ), 67 Apollo Drive, Rosedale, Auckland 0632, New Zealand
(a division of Pearson New Zealand Ltd.)
Penguin Books (South Africa) (Pty.) Ltd., 24 Sturdee Avenue, Rosebank, Johannesburg 2196,
South Africa

Penguin Books Ltd., Registered Offices: 80 Strand, London WC2R 0RL, England

THE WALLED FLOWER

A Berkley Prime Crime Book / published by arrangement with the author

PRINTING HISTORY
Berkley Prime Crime mass-market edition / February 2012

Copyright © 2012 by Lorraine Bartlett.
Cover illustration by Chris Beatrice.
Cover design by Annette Fiore Defex.
Interior text design by Laura K. Corless.

ISBN: 978-0-425-24616-0

BERKLEY® PRIME CRIME
Berkley Prime Crime Books are published by The Berkley Publishing Group,
a division of Penguin Group (USA) Inc.,
375 Hudson Street, New York, New York 10014.
BERKLEY® PRIME CRIME and the PRIME CRIME logo are trademarks of Penguin Group (USA) Inc.

PRINTED IN THE UNITED STATES OF AMERICA

10 9 8 7 6 5 4 3 2 1

For my dear friends
Leann Sweeney and Jennifer Stanley

Acknowledgments

Welcome back to lovely Victoria Square in the village of McKinlay Mill, New York. I had such fun writing *The Walled Flower*, and had lots of input from my wonderful critique partners and first readers who entered the story at various points in its creation. My thanks go to Gwen Nelson and Liz Eng; Sandra Parshall, Krista Davis, Avery Aames, and Janet Bolin; as well as to Janette McNana and readers of the 13th Precinct.

Thanks also go to my wonderful editor, Tom Colgan, and the world's best agent, Jessica Faust. Most of all I'd like to thank my husband, Frank, who supports me in everything I do.

To learn more about the series, I hope you'll visit my website, www.LorraineBartlett.com, and will consider signing up for my periodically e-mailed newsletter.

One

Steam seeped through the airholes in the Angelo's pizza box, along with the aroma of melted mozzarella, pepperoni, sauce, and spices. Katie Bonner clutched the twenty-first-century equivalent of "cake on a plate" that housewives once brought to welcome new neighbors and approached the Webster mansion on the east end of Victoria Square. The day was cool, bright, and beautiful. Perfect weather for early spring in Western New York, but Katie felt anything but cheerful, despite her mission to welcome the newcomers.

She opened the sagging gate and stepped into the small front courtyard, which was littered with rocks, weeds, and remains of rusty old garden urns. As she mounted the rather rickety wooden steps, Katie noticed the mansion's heavy oak door stood ajar. Katie paused in the doorway, squinting into the darkened interior. Yup, it was definitely *ocupado*. Using her elbow, she knocked on the doorjamb, its blistered, peeling paint just another job awaiting completion on the list of renovation and restoration that was taking place at what was soon to be an upscale bed-and-breakfast.

"Anybody hungry?" Katie called.

A dirt-smudged face appeared around the door. Dusty blond bangs hung over a pair of light blue eyes. More wisps had escaped the faded red bandana that was supposed to protect the rest of the woman's hair. Clad in a grubby T-shirt and jeans, she held a claw hammer in one hand, the knuckles on her other hand oozing blood.

"Pizza?" the woman said hopefully.

"The best," Katie assured her, proffering the box. "Where can I set it down?"

"On any flat surface you can find."

Katie entered and stepped over a fallen two-by-four, tracking through plaster dust to set the box on a makeshift table of boards on sawhorses. "Do you need a Band-Aid?"

The woman sucked at the abrasion. "Not for this."

"Janice," came a male voice from the room beyond.

Katie glanced in that direction. The owner of the voice, a dark-haired man in his late thirties, stepped through the doorway, just as dirty as his counterpart. Not surprising in the ruin of what, one hundred years before, had been a lovely home.

"Hi, I'm Katie Bonner. I manage Artisans Alley on the other end of the Square, and I'm president of the Victoria Square Merchants Association. Welcome to the neighborhood."

"Thanks," the man said and moved to stand by the woman.

"I've seen you working here for the last couple of days and figured you might need a break," Katie said.

"Do we ever." The woman moved closer, setting the hammer down and offering Katie her hand. "Janice Ryan. And this is my husband, Toby."

Katie shook both their hands, then pulled a sheaf of paper napkins from the back pocket of her jeans. "Please, help yourself."

"Thanks," the couple chorused, and each dove for a slice.

Katie took a long look around the cavernous space. Bare

studs gave the room a skeletal look. Lath and chunks of plaster from the ceiling filled plastic buckets, waiting to be emptied into the commercial Dumpster out back. A bare lightbulb hung from a cheap 1960s fixture. That, too, would eventually have to go.

"Wow, I can't believe how much you've already accomplished," Katie said.

Janice swallowed, her mouth flattening into a frown. "Sounds like you've been in here before."

Many times, Katie was tempted to blurt. She and her late husband, Chad, had tramped through the cold, uninviting place on dozens of occasions during the four years they'd saved to buy it. Then Chad had impulsively invested instead in Artisans Alley, a going concern quickly going downhill. Chad had passed away the year before—the victim of a car accident—and Katie was now the owner and manager. So far she hadn't made a nickel of the money back either.

"Once or twice," Katie said, forcing a smile. "What are your plans?"

Janice beamed. "We hope to open the Grand Victoria Inn in about three months."

A very ambitious plan, considering the state the building was currently in.

"We'll have seven guest rooms to start. The property comes with plenty of acreage to add guest cottages if we do well."

Katie had planned an extensive garden refit, perfect for outdoor weddings and corporate picnics. And if the weather didn't cooperate, she figured she could always tent such affairs. And she'd wanted a white-painted gazebo at the far end of the yard, flanked by a lovely cottage garden, with lots of pink and white cosmos.

Janice's eyes glowed with pride. "The entryway will be totally restored," she said, taking in the space with a sweep of her hand. "As you can see, we've just got that wall over there to remove. They divided the place into apartments, but that's good in a way, because we won't have to replumb the whole house for the guest rooms."

That was one of the things Katie had counted on, too. Her plan had been to renovate the old mansion and open the English Ivy Inn. Chad was to be the host, and Katie would manage the kitchen and the financial end of things. It was a solid plan. It was her life's dream. And now it was forever out of her reach.

"Toby's good at carpentry and has plans for a lovely oak check-in desk, over here," Janice said with a wave of her hand. "We've got wood salvaged from another site that'll be just perfect."

Katie already had a lovely oak reception desk sitting in a storage unit waiting to be stripped and refinished. She'd collected brass headboards, Oriental carpets, dressers and nightstands, pedestal sinks, light fixtures, dishes, and silverware, too. Every month she wrote out a check to keep her treasures warehoused, and every month she debated getting rid of it all. Owning all that stuff was just another painful reminder that life wasn't always fair.

Katie's anger flared as she noted the sledgehammer resting against the wall. "Are you doing all the work yourself?"

"Just the preliminary demolition," Toby said, reaching for another pizza slice. "It'll save us three or four grand that we can better use elsewhere."

"There's a certain satisfaction in taking down a wall, especially when you can already visualize how perfect the space will be," Janice said. She laughed. "I've spent the last few months decorating this house in my mind. I can't wait until opening day when I can show it off to the world."

Katie, too, had imagined exactly how she'd renovate the old house. Replacement newel posts for the staircase, frosted glass sconces on the walls, delicate rose-patterned wallpaper, chair rails and crown molding. For years she'd longed to swing a sledge and take out an extraneous wall or two.

She picked up and hefted the tool, nearly staggering under its weight. "Would you mind if I took a whack at that wall—just for fun?"

"Go for it," Toby said, grinning. He put down his pizza, grabbed a pair of work gloves, and accompanied Katie to the wall.

"I'd better cover the pizza," Janice said.

"We're taking down the plasterboard first, then we'll yank out the studs. It's not a load-bearing wall," Toby said, handing Katie the gloves and a pair of safety glasses.

That she already knew. Many an evening she'd pored over how-to books in anticipation of applying her own brand of sweat equity to the place.

Toby or Janice had already removed the baseboard molding at the bottom of the wall, leaving a three-inch gap that had never seen a coat of paint. An odd, gummy dark stain marred the middle of that section of pristine plasterboard.

Katie donned the gloves and glasses, grasped the sledge firmly, swung it high, and let its weight slam against the wall. *Bang!* A circular dimple marred the surface, but not enough to make a break in the drywall.

"Put your weight into it," Toby encouraged with a smile.

Clenching her teeth, Katie hauled off and swung again. *Bang!*

The anger blossomed inside her, threatening to engulf her.

This should have been *her* house!

Bang!

It would have been hers if Chad hadn't invested—without her knowledge—in that money pit, Artisans Alley.

Bang!

The sledge careened through the air, smacking hard into the wall, taking a jagged hunk of plasterboard with it.

Katie swung again and again, her biceps complaining at the strain. Clouds of dust swirled in the air.

Hands on hips, Toby watched from her left. "You're

doing great, Katie." He didn't sound as pleased as he had a few moments before.

Katie took another mighty swing, sending a fragment of plasterboard flying. She paused to yank a loose piece from the studs.

Janice gasped behind her.

Katie lost her grip on the sledge, nearly crushing her toes. She turned to see what Janice was fussing about.

Openmouthed and panting, a wide-eyed Janice frantically pointed at the gaping hole in the wall.

Confused, Katie turned to see the source of her distress.

Behind a heavy layer of plastic, empty eye sockets gazed at nothing; the jaw hung open as though in a scream. The remains of long blonde hair were suspended like Easter grass among the bones, and a shiny silver locket dangled from the proximity of its neck.

Katie swallowed, her mouth going dry. "Well, this could ruin your day."

~~~~~~~

Yellow crime tape barred the mansion's entrance. The east end of the Victoria Square parking lot was clogged with squad cars scattered with no regard to the orderly lines painted on the asphalt. Katie leaned against a paint-flaked column on the wide veranda, noting the rain damage at its base. It would be expensive to replace.

"This is a bad omen," Katie heard Janice complain for the hundredth time from inside the house. "Who'll want to come to the inn knowing we found a body in a wall?"

The poor woman had no concept of marketing, Katie thought with a rueful shake of her head. A ghost was a great draw . . . if you had a good story to go with it.

She'd been glad to escape the crowd inside. As a material witness, Katie was compelled to stay until the law said she could leave. She glanced at her watch. It was going on two hours now.

She sighed, unsure why she hadn't felt as shattered as Janice and Toby at finding a skeleton walled up in what once might've been her home. Maybe because it *wasn't* her home and never would be. Then again, she'd seen Artisans Alley's former owner/manager dead in a puddle of his own blood. She'd found one of the vendors dead with a broken neck from a fall. An anonymous skeleton wasn't half as scary. Or maybe she was just in denial. But it was obvious the person behind the wall had been dead a long—well, reasonably speaking—time, and it sure hadn't been an accident.

A crowd of rubberneckers ringed the cordoned-off area. Katie looked up to see her friend and Artisans Alley vendor, Rose Nash, among the crowd, clutching a card or paper, madly waving to her, trying to get her attention. Dyed blonde curls bobbed around her anxious, wrinkled face. Katie took a step forward, but a hand on her shoulder made her turn.

Detective Ray Davenport of the Sheriff's Office homicide detail was once again on-site, looking just as formidable and bad-tempered as the other times Katie had interacted with him.

"You seem to attract death, Mrs. Bonner," the balding, middle-aged cop said.

Katie straightened indignantly. "Me, attract death? Detective, that poor woman's been dead for decades."

"And how do you know it was a woman?" he asked suspiciously

Katie frowned. "Long blonde hair, a locket—it doesn't take a genius to figure out the gender."

Davenport glowered. "Just what were you doing here anyway, Mrs. Bonner?"

"Paying a friendly visit to my new neighbors on behalf of the Victoria Square Merchants Association. Believe me, I didn't want to find the remains of that . . . that poor person."

"Detective! Detective!" Rose called, elbowing her way through the crowd. "I heard they found a body."

"You'll have to read about it in the paper, ma'am," he said, ignoring the agitation in her voice as he turned back toward the mansion entrance.

"Was it a woman?" Rose persisted. "Blonde hair, brown eyes? Did she have a locket?"

Davenport stopped dead, turned. "Locket?"

"Rectangular, sterling silver. Rhodium plated with a bright-cut floral design," Rose cried in desperation. She held out a wallet-sized photo, waving it at him.

Davenport trudged down the steps, took the picture from her, studied it, and frowned. Then he lifted the crime tape, motioning her forward.

Katie hurried to meet Rose, steadying the elderly woman as she climbed the six shallow steps into the mansion.

Portable work lights illuminated the crime scene. The room seemed claustrophobically small with so many deputies and technicians crowded in. As the trio entered, they stepped back, quieting as Davenport approached.

The wall had been taken down in one piece, thanks to a reciprocating saw, and now lay flat on the floor. The rest of the drywall had been removed, revealing the earthly remains—just bones—in situ, wrapped in clear plastic sheeting and lying on a fluffy pillow of faded pink fiberglass. A petrified black substance—rat or insect dung, Katie surmised—was also visible. She shuddered at the thought of how it had gotten there and turned her attention to the wooden studs, which were twenty-four inches on center—not a lot of room. The body must have been wedged in at an angle, the shoulders cocked, the wrists crossed in front of the pelvis. No remnant of cloth or flesh remained.

Rose blanched, and Katie felt her friend wobble in her grasp.

"Do you recognize the locket?" Davenport asked the older woman.

Tears filled Rose's eyes and she nodded, the movement causing her to sway. "It belonged to my niece." She took a shuddering breath and choked on a sob. "Oh, Heather, everyone thought you'd run off to New York—and you were here all along," she said, and collapsed in a dead faint.

Two

Detective Davenport turned the still-shiny locket over and over in his stubby fingers while a shell-shocked Rose gripped a cup of, by now, cold coffee and stared into space.

Katie felt like an intruder, yet the two of them were using her office at Artisans Alley as a makeshift interrogation room; Davenport sat at her desk while Rose was planted in her guest chair.

Katie leaned against the battered, buff-colored file cabinet, looking over Davenport's shoulder. Surely the lab team had dusted the locket for possible fingerprints before releasing it to the detective.

Katie twisted the wrapper from a peppermint. The sound of crinkling plastic drew a pointed glare from the detective. As an act of defiance, Katie popped the candy into her mouth and crunched it between her molars.

"This isn't a conventional locket," Davenport said to Rose. "It's too fat."

Rose sniffed. "Actually, it's a pillbox. Heather had epilepsy. She was always forgetting to take her medication. I modified it myself, so she could wear it on a chain. She was ashamed of her health problem."

"How often did your niece have fits?" Davenport asked.

"Detective!" Katie admonished. This guy could use a session or two in sensitivity training.

"Quite frequently, I'm afraid," Rose answered matter-of-factly. "She wasn't even allowed a driver's license."

Davenport scowled. "And why did you say you thought she'd run off to New York?"

"I *never* thought that," Rose snapped. "That was what the Sheriff's Office decided when we reported her as missing."

Davenport bristled at the implied criticism. "There had to be a reason for that opinion."

Rose frowned. "Heather *did* want to be a model. In fact, she'd even had a few assignments at fashion shows in Midtown Plaza in Rochester."

That *was* quite a while ago. The state's first enclosed mall hadn't been a shopping mecca for years.

Davenport didn't seem the least bit interested in Heather's career aspirations. "Explain to me again why you immediately assumed the remains *might* be that of your niece," he said.

Rose sighed. "No one else in McKinlay Mill has ever gone missing—at least not for more than twenty years. Part of me wants closure. A bigger part hopes it isn't Heather so I can go on pretending there's still a chance she might one day come home."

Davenport pursed his lips, continuing his inspection of the locket. "Why isn't this thing tarnished?"

"It's chemically treated to resist oxidation," Rose explained.

Davenport's eyes narrowed. "How do you know so much about it?"

"Rose deals in jewelry," Katie said, exasperated.

Davenport pried off the locket's lid, which made a soft

popping sound. "No pills here," he said and, using the tip of a sharp pencil, pried out a small black-and-white photograph, which had been wedged into one side of the locket. "Who are these people?"

"That's my sister and brother-in-law, Iris and Stan Winston. I took the photo back in the 1960s." Rose swallowed. "They're both dead now. Stan died about eighteen years ago, and Iris a year after—of a broken heart. Detective, how—how did Heather die?"

Davenport shot Katie an evaluating look, as though asking if she thought Rose could handle the truth. She nodded ever so slightly, then moved closer to Rose, resting a hand on the old woman's thin shoulder.

"Probably strangulation, ma'am. The medical examiner will be able to tell us for sure, probably tomorrow. We'll probably have to get a forensic anthropologist in, too."

"Then she wasn't put there . . . I mean, was she already . . . ?"

Davenport nodded, his voice softening. "Yes, it looks like she was dead when they nailed up the drywall."

Katie raised an eyebrow. Maybe Davenport had more compassion than she'd given him credit for. And yet something didn't add up. She worried at her lip, thinking back to what she'd seen at the crime scene. It would eventually come to her.

Rose's gaze focused on the locket once more. "Detective, do you think I could just . . . hold it . . . for a minute?"

Davenport stared possessively at the still-gleaming metal box, seeming to weigh the request. Then, with a shrug, he handed Rose the locket.

Rose's trembling bony fingers wrapped around the little silver cask. Katie's heart ached as Rose raised it to her lips and kissed it. A tear leaked from the old woman's eye, falling to soak into her pale blue slacks.

Davenport picked up the creased wallet-sized high school

graduation picture of the pretty young woman with the silver locket decorating her throat. "Tell me about Heather,
Mrs. Nash."

Rose let out a long breath. "When she disappeared,
Heather was a sophomore at the community college, but
she missed a lot of classes. Transportation from McKinlay
Mill to Henrietta was a bit of a problem. She rode with a
local girl for a while, but they had a falling out and my
sister, Iris, had to drive her to and from her classes."

"Did the girl live at home?"

Katie bristled. *Girl?*

"Yes," Rose answered with a nod.

"Did she have a job?"

"No. It would've interfered with her schoolwork," Rose
said, her voice faltering.

Davenport remained ever the cool, calm detective, completely unmoved by her growing distress. "Did Heather
have a boyfriend?"

"Jeremy Richards. He wasn't from McKinlay Mill. I
don't know what happened to him. He left the area soon
after Heather disappeared. Stan always thought the boy was
responsible for her disappearance."

Rose toyed with the locket, lovingly rubbing the etched
decoration with her right thumb, letting the chain dangle
from her fingers. "Heather liked silver better than gold," she
said to no one in particular.

"When did Heather disappear?" Davenport asked.

"November seventeen, twenty-two years ago."

Davenport's eyes widened as though the date held some
significance, but then he seemed to shake himself and
turned his face aside.

Antsy, Katie shifted her weight from one foot to the
other. "Perhaps you ought to go back to headquarters and
review the old case files," she suggested, hoping he'd take
the hint and vacate her office. Instead, he seemed to have
grown roots.

"Can I keep this locket, Detective?" Rose asked.

He shook his head and held out his hand. "I'm afraid it's evidence, Mrs. Nash."

Again tears filled Rose's eyes as she reluctantly relinquished the treasure she'd thought forever gone. "When will I get it back?"

"When our investigation is complete, and it's established that you *are* the deceased's next of kin."

"Oh, come on, Detective. Rose identified the locket, plus the picture of the people in it. What more do you need?" Katie asked.

"Dental records will confirm whether or not the remains are Heather Winston's," he reaffirmed.

"Heather and everyone else in town went to Dr. Elliott. He's been dead for years. His daughter was—"

"I'm sure we'll locate the records, ma'am," Davenport said, cutting her off, "although it may take some time."

"But I want to give Heather a decent burial! She deserves that," Rose insisted.

"That can happen, *if* we establish that this *was* your niece."

Rose's tears had dried, and her eyes now blazed with anger. "Of course it's Heather. The locket proves it."

Davenport shook his head. "For all we know, your niece might've been present at the time of this person's death, put the locket on the body, and stolen the victim's identity. As we speak, Heather Winston could be a forty-year-old woman living in Flagstaff, Arizona—if not Timbuktu."

"That's preposterous," Rose blurted. "Heather was a good girl. She wouldn't have disappointed her parents like that. She'd never—"

Davenport abruptly rose. "I'm afraid this interview is at an end, Mrs. Nash. I'll be in touch." He tucked the locket into his suit coat pocket and strode from the room without a backward glance.

Rose stood, too. "That—that man!" she exclaimed and

turned to Katie. "Did he treat you as shabby after Ezra's death?"

Katie sighed. "I tried to tell myself it was job burnout. After all, the poor man recently lost his wife and has three teenaged daughters to deal with. That's a job in itself. But now I'm beginning to think he's just a grump."

"And he didn't do much to solve Ezra's murder, as I recall. It was you who figured out who killed him."

That was true, but spreading that opinion wasn't going to win Katie friends with the Sheriff's Office.

Fists clenched, Rose paced the tiny office. "I suppose he'll drag his feet working on Heather's murder, too. Well, I'm not going to stand for it."

"Rose, he probably isn't eager to work on a cold case that will be difficult to solve. There really can't be many clues after all this time."

"Katie, I'm seventy-five years old. I haven't got years to wait for him to *get* motivated. It looks like I'm going to have to take matters into my own hands."

"Now, Rose—"

Rose turned, facing Katie. "Will you help me?"

Katie started. "Me?"

"Well, you did solve Ezra's murder."

Katie raised a hand in denial. "That was a fluke. I didn't set out to do it."

"But you *did* do it!"

"Rose—"

"Please, Katie? This is important to me. Please, *please* help me!"

Rose had that same look of determination in her eyes that Katie's aunt Lizzie MacDuff often adopted when she wanted some unpleasant task done, like cleaning the toilet or emptying out the gutters. Katie felt her resolve melt. Her soft spot for elderly people made her a pushover, especially with Rose.

"Well, I suppose we could ask a few questions, poke

around a little bit. But Detective Davenport won't like it, and he'll do everything he can to stop us."

"Heather was my niece. It's my duty to my sister, and as her aunt, to find out what happened to her and make the person who killed her pay."

Katie sighed, reaching out a hand to rest on Rose's shoulder. "You've had a traumatic afternoon. You should go home and rest."

"How can I rest when Heather's murderer is out there somewhere, running around free?"

Katie could only nod. "Would you like me to drive you home?"

Rose pursed her lips. "I may be old, but I'm not feeble."

"I didn't mean to imply—"

Rose's expression softened. "I know." She clasped Katie's hand. "Thank you, dear. Together we'll find out who killed Heather. Even if I have to die trying."

~~~~~~

Katie didn't like to feel rattled, but if she was honest with herself, despite her outward appearance of calm, she was definitely in a state of denial. Finding what was likely Heather Winston's earthly remains had indeed left her feeling decidedly unsettled. She had too much on her mind to allow herself to dwell on the whole subject. And yet . . . she knew Rose would keep pushing.

Katie fought to concentrate on the printed spreadsheets before her. Artisans Alley's bottom line had improved considerably since she'd taken over its management some six months before, but there was still so much to do if she was going to drag it completely out of the red and into solvency.

She thought she heard a noise off to her right, but it really didn't register, so she paid no attention to it. She shook her head at the expenses column. There wasn't much she could do about the escalating utility costs. Sales had dropped considerably since the holidays. Taking ten percent of her rent-paying vendors with it. With Easter right around the corner, it was time to put another ad in the Rochester newspaper. Not too big an ad—and only if she could convince the Merchants Association to go in on it.

"Ahem."

This time Katie turned at the interruption, and found Gilda Ringwald standing in the doorway of her office. Gilda, of Gilda's Gourmet Baskets on the south side of Victoria Square, was the Victoria Square Merchants Association's PR director—and she'd arrived just in time to receive Katie's ad pitch.

"Gilda, I was just thinking about you," she said with a smile in her voice and rose from her chair.

"Do you have a few minutes?" Gilda asked sheepishly, her shoulders rounded as though she were trying to look smaller than her five foot four inch height.

"For you, always. Can I get you a cup of coffee?" Katie asked and ushered Gilda into one of her shabby guest chairs. A trip to OfficeMax was in the offing—she really should replace the chairs with something more comfortable and stylish. One day . . .

"Oh, no," Gilda said and sat down, resting her empty hands on the knees of her navy slacks. Katie always found Gilda's jet-black pageboy haircut to be a bit disconcerting on a woman her age—late fifties or early sixties. But she had no complaint with Gilda's efforts on behalf of the Merchants Association, of which Katie was the reluctant head—voted in after Ezra Hilton's untimely passing the previous fall.

"What brings you to Artisans Alley? Something for the Merchants Association?" Katie asked, almost dreading the answer.

"Actually, I'm here on some personal business. I want to ask a favor of you."

"If I can help—I'd be glad to."

Gilda's cheeks blushed. "Conrad and I are finally going to tie the knot."

"That's wonderful," Katie said with genuine surprise. She understood that Gilda and Conrad Stratton, who owned the Square's wine shop, The Perfect Grape, had been a couple for a long time. Decades, in fact. For them to suddenly marry . . .

Gilda smiled and nodded. "We never thought we'd need that piece of paper—but we're getting on in years, and if something happened to either one of us, it would be better to be married in the eyes of the state than to be considered just good friends."

Katie nodded. "I understand completely." But what kind of favor could Gilda have in mind that involved Katie—or did she want Artisans Alley to play a part in the proceedings?

Gilda continued to smile, looking somewhat dreamy.

"You said you needed a favor?" Katie prompted.

Gilda shook her head as though to clear her mind, and giggled. "I'm sorry, I just never thought I'd get to be a bride. I've had so much fun this past week making plans."

"What have you done so far?"

"I've settled on a dress, and called Judge Hart—she's a dear, isn't she? And we're making the final arrangements for the reception at Madison's on the Canal in Spencerport."

Swank!

"When *is* the wedding?" Katie asked.

"A week from Saturday."

Whoa! That was sudden.

"Oh, my," Katie said, taken aback.

"I know it's rather short notice, but I was wondering . . . that is, if you had the time . . ."

"Do you need a place to have the actual wedding?" Katie asked, thinking of Artisans Alley's large, and frequently empty, lobby. It could probably hold fifty people and had served as a gathering place after Ezra Hilton's funeral service back in October. Of course, for a wedding it would need to be repainted, but that could happen before the big day.

"Actually, we're planning on getting married at the restaurant with the reception immediately afterward. It's just so much easier to do on such short notice."

"I see."

"But if you're not doing anything—"

"I would *love* to attend," Katie said, genuinely pleased.

Gilda gave an embarrassed laugh. "I was hoping you'd do more than just attend. I wondered—would you be my matron of honor?"

Katie's jaw dropped. *Matron of honor?* Was she kidding?

She closed her mouth, unsure what to say. "I'm—I'm— flattered," she finally came up with. *Matron of honor?* she thought again with dread. The timing was not good. She had to be out of her apartment the day *before* the wedding. There was no way she could move *and* participate.

Gilda didn't give her a chance to speak. She clasped her hands together. "Oh, good. Then it's all settled."

"But, Gilda," Katie protested, thinking of her promise to Rose to help find Heather's killer and the rest of the things on her list of things to do during the coming week. But Gilda seemed so excited about the impending nuptials. Could Katie dash her hopes? Surely she could take off one evening from work and packing to devote to helping out a friend—well, a business acquaintance—on her special day.

"I-I," Katie stammered again. "I guess so."

It wasn't exactly an enthusiastic acceptance, but Gilda hardly seemed to notice.

"Wonderful. I already have the dress—"

"Dress?" Katie asked with trepidation.

"Yes." Gilda's blush deepened. "My best friend, Cindy Marie, was all set to fly up from Brooklyn for the wedding. We picked out the dress from a catalog and she had it shipped here. But then two days ago, Cindy tripped over her dachshund, Daisy, and broke her leg. It took the surgeon three hours and several pins to put it back together again. It broke Cindy's heart to tell me she couldn't participate in the wedding, but she can hardly navigate with a hip-to-ankle cast."

"No, I don't imagine she can," Katie said, perturbed that she was second (or worse—third or fourth?) choice for the honor. Or was it just that she would more or less fit the dress already bought for the occasion?

As though reading her mind, Gilda said, "I'll bring the dress over later today. You might want to have the hem taken up before the ceremony."

"Okay," Katie agreed, disconcerted she'd have to wear something that might not be to her taste.

Gilda stood. "I'll be in touch with things as they develop. And thank you for letting me count on you."

"Oh, you're welcome," Katie said, but without much enthusiasm.

"And I'll drop off the stuff for the favors later," Gilda said as she headed out of the office.

"Favors?" Katie called after her, but Gilda was already out of earshot, heading for the exit.

Katie collapsed into her chair. If she'd felt stressed before, that factor had just doubled. Then again, how much time could it take to help Gilda with her wedding favors and have a dress altered? She'd just have to make the time.

As she turned back to her spreadsheet, she realized she'd forgotten to ask Gilda about the Victoria Square Easter newspaper ad.

Swell. Just swell.

~~~~~~

Not many hours later, Andy Rust handed Katie a paper plate laden with a slice of Angelo's deep-crust pizza, swimming in sauce, meat, and veggies. "And this body—skeleton . . . whatever—wasn't gross or anything?"

"Not really," Katie admitted. She paused to take a bite. Having a boyfriend who owned a pizzeria had been a great perk. For the first week or so. Not that Katie didn't like pizza, but she ate it more for sustenance than enjoyment these days. And because it was free.

Seated next to Andy on the lumpy lime green couch, Katie gazed around the tiny living room. The apartment over Angelo's Pizzeria had been empty since Andy evicted the former tenants for nonpayment of rent some six weeks before. It gave the two of them a quiet place to share a meal away from the watchful eyes of Andy's teenaged employees, who probably thought they used the place for romantic purposes.

As if!

Along with the former occupant's couch, the place contained only a rickety Formica cocktail table that had to be at least four or five decades old. At Katie's insistence, Andy had pulled up the stained, blue-tweed shag carpet to reveal hardwood floors in remarkably good condition. But the sickening yellow enamel walls—that had been painted years before Andy took possession of the building—would not inspire a Martha Stewart award. Maybe Martha would find it a challenge to decorate such a dingy place. The apartment was unoccupied only because Andy didn't want the hassle of dealing with tenants. Meanwhile, Katie hadn't renewed the lease on her apartment and needed a cheap place to live that was close to Victoria Square.

"Rose wants me to help her solve Heather's murder," Katie said, and took a bite of pizza, pulling the crust away while a string of mozzarella followed. She yanked at it until it broke and tossed it back on the slice.

Andy stopped chewing, swallowed, and glared at her. "And you told her no, right?"

Katie sighed. "Not exactly. The poor girl's been dead twenty-two years. The trail's cold. I'll give Rose some extra attention for a few days, and hopefully that'll be that."

Andy didn't look convinced.

"Besides," Katie said, examining a round of pepperoni on her pizza, "I need to concentrate on apartment hunting. I've got to be out of my place by the end of the month, and I haven't had any luck so far." Her voice sounded innocent, but she knew Andy wasn't taken in.

"We've had this conversation before, and I'm not renting you this place."

"I didn't ask you to. I'm just updating you on my situation."

"You can move in with me," Andy said.

"We've had *that* conversation before, too. I have two cats. You don't want to live with them, and I'm not about to give them up."

"You're using that as an excuse," he countered. "You don't trust me. Or any man."

"That's not true. It's just—" It's just that she'd trusted her late husband with their financial future, and he'd squandered their savings, and then died and left her virtually penniless.

Katie recognized the set of Andy's mouth. He was primed for an argument. Andy was right to some extent. She wasn't yet ready for the kind of commitment he was offering.

"I've got some leads," she said to diffuse the tension. "And I've got an appointment to look at a place tomorrow afternoon. That is, if I can get Vance to cover for me at Artisans Alley."

"And if you can't?"

She shrugged.

"What if you don't find a place by the end of the month?" Andy asked.

"There's always Chad's pad."

Andy scowled. Chad's pad had been a dismal, airless little room in Artisans Alley's loft. Chad had lived there illegally for two months after he and Katie had separated.

They'd been close to a reconciliation when Chad's car had careened into a tree one icy March night the year before.

"And if you do that, what happens to the cats?" Andy asked.

"They can wander around Artisans Alley."

"And if they destroy the vendors' merchandise?"

"They won't."

"You hope."

"I hope," she repeated and sighed, knowing her cat Mason's fondness for capturing and "killing" anything made of fabric. He was known to drag around pot holders, dust rags, and washcloths. In cat parlance, he was known as a "wool eater," and Katie knew if left to wander Artisans Alley, Mason would zero in on Gwen the weaver's handmade place mats, napkins, and bookmarks.

She *would* find somewhere else to live, she told herself firmly.

Andy took another slice of pizza from the box.

Katie used her paper napkin to wipe a spot of sauce from the crummy little table. Still, she wasn't about to let Andy get the last word in. "Besides, it's been proven that having a cat on the premises encourages people to spend. It makes any retail establishment more homey."

"And if your customers are allergic?" he asked.

Katie pondered another piece of pizza, decided against it, and closed the lid. "I'm not worried. I'll find a place soon, and it'll be perfect for all three of us."

Still skeptical, Andy took another bite of his pizza.

Katie again studied the apartment's putrid yellow walls. Not a chance of a skeleton behind any of them. Some peachy paint, some crown molding near the ceiling, a few plants, her overstuffed chintz-covered furniture, and two cuddly cats would make the place into a snug and comfy home.

Katie smiled at Andy. He looked wary but manufactured a facsimile of a smile.

The poor, dear boy would cave in.

Eventually.

"Anything new in pizza land?" she asked and reopened the lid on the pizza. After all, in the grand scheme of things, what was one more slice? She chose a piece with cheese that actually touched the edge of the crust and took a bite.

"I might change cheese distributors," Andy said. "I wasn't happy with this last batch."

Katie's chewing slowed and it took real effort to swallow that last bite. She looked at her slice of pizza and wondered if she ought to continue eating it. But then Andy took another bite of his own piece and she figured *what the heck.*

"Oh, something else interesting did happen this afternoon," she said and reached for a fresh napkin, dabbing it around the corners of her mouth. "I was asked to be the matron of honor at Gilda Ringwald and Conrad Stratton's wedding."

"Lucky you," he deadpanned.

"Will you be free a week from Saturday to escort me?" she asked.

"Sure. But I got an invitation, too. Probably because I'm a member of the Merchants Association."

"That makes it even better."

He squinted at Katie over his pizza slice. "You've got a lot on your plate right now. Have you got time for everything that's involved in participating in a wedding?"

"All I have to do is show up in the dress she provides, and hold her bouquet. It'll be a piece of cake." She laughed. "Wedding cake."

"I dunno," he said and shook his head. "When my cousin Diane was a maid of honor, she was expected to do all kinds of piddly tasks for bridezilla. It's been three years, and I don't think she's spoken to her former best friend since."

"What kind of tasks?" Katie asked, suspicion growing in the pit of her stomach.

He shrugged. "Girl stuff."

Katie bit her lip thoughtfully. "Gilda did mention something about favors."

"Bingo!" he said, and took a huge bite of pizza.

"Gilda knows I'm tied up with Artisans Alley, and though I didn't mention my house hunt to her before now, I will the next time we talk."

"Or you could just save time and move in with me," Andy said and waggled his eyebrows à la Groucho Marx.

"Let's not start that again," she chided and put her pizza down, completely turned off by the idea of it after Andy's comment about his cheese distributor.

"But don't you see how much easier it would be for both of us? And we could split the chores. You could do the laundry and cleaning, and I could do the cooking."

"That's hardly an even split," Katie protested.

He shrugged. "Sounds good to me. I wouldn't even ask you to contribute to the household expenses."

She shook her head. "I'm not ready for that step quite yet." And certainly not under those conditions.

Andy sank back against the couch's back, looking smug. "Suit yourself. But I predict in another week or so those terms will sound pretty good to you."

Katie frowned. *Only if hell freezes over*.

Three

Katie recognized Rose's tiny red Mini Cooper as soon as she drove into the Square's parking lot the next morning. She parked her white Focus and sorted through her collection of keys, then picked up her unread newspaper before getting out to open Artisans Alley's vendor entrance.

"Rose, what are you doing here so early?" Katie called.

Impeccably dressed, as always, in a tailored polyester suit coat and slacks, apricot today, with a rope of amber beads dangling down her white-bloused front, Rose was the epitome of determination. She held a large, flat book in one arm and a shoe box tucked like a football under the other.

"I'm here so we can start working on Heather's case. Where do we begin?"

Katie paused, brass key hovering near the lock, and her heart sank as she read a note taped to the door: *She's at it again.* Katie recognized the handwriting. She looked back at Rose. "What did you say?"

"Heather's case," she said impatiently.

"Oh, well . . . I haven't decided on an approach. Let's make some coffee and talk," she said to stall.

Katie unlocked the door and entered the ante/storeroom, disarming the security system before venturing into Artisans Alley's main showroom.

Six months before, the artisans arcade's cavernous main hub had been a depressing sea of dark Masonite Peg-Board. Katie hit the main light switch and the room came alive with beautiful displays of sparkling blown-glass goblets, vases, and bowls on a backdrop of dainty floral wallpaper, Victorian-inspired stained glass windows, cards made of handmade papers, and too much else to take in at one glance. Every day a crowd of vendors came in, changing their displays, making a walk through the aisles like a treasure hunt.

Rose headed straight for the vendors' lounge and its commercial coffeepot. That room, too, had recently undergone a total transformation. Gone were the woppy-jawed wooden table and chairs, replaced by a chrome and red Formica table for ten (complete with two leaves), straight out of the 1950s. The vendors had pitched in to paint and decorate the lounge to look like a *Happy Days* set, with appropriate 1950s kitsch for accent.

Katie went straight to her office, where she set the note down. She'd deal with it later. She stowed her purse in her desk drawer and opened the safe. She counted out the money for the tills, shut and locked it, then headed for the cash registers, placing cash in each drawer. Register two needed more quarters, she noted. She'd bring them up later. By the time she made her way to the back of the store, she could smell coffee brewing.

"There's some apple Danish in the fridge. Do you want a piece?" Rose called out.

"No, thanks. Just coffee," Katie said and took a seat at the table.

Rose had already assembled two legal pads, pencils, and pens, along with the mysterious shoe box. She plunked a steaming mug down before Katie and took a seat on the opposite side of the table.

"Looks like you've made a good start," Katie said, indicating the notes on one of the pads.

"I spent last evening writing lists and gathering some of Heather's things. This box," she said, removing the lid, "has pictures and certificates, things a young girl keeps." She pushed it toward Katie.

Katie peered inside, flipping through the assorted odds and ends. She withdrew several photos of Heather and a shaggy-haired, bearded young man.

"That's Heather and her boyfriend, Jeremy Richards. They went together for almost a year before she disappeared."

Katie replaced the photos, reaching for the creamer. "Is that a high school yearbook?" she said, indicating the tome by Rose's elbow.

Rose nodded. "From Heather's senior year. Some of her classmates still live in McKinlay Mill." Her gaze drifted. "Most of them got married and had families. I want to find the bastard who cheated Heather out of her future," she said, her voice hardening.

Katie wasn't sure how to comfort the old woman. Finally, she said, "What we need to do is backtrack Heather's last days. That'll mean locating the people she knew, which could take time—a very *long* time."

"I'll do whatever it takes," Rose said, determination once again entering her voice.

"Who was her best friend?" Katie said, and took a sip of coffee.

"Barbie Jackson." Rose opened the yearbook, flipping pages until she came to a shot of the McKinlay Mill High School cheerleading squad. She pointed to the only brunette in a sea of bleached blondes. "That's Barbie. They were inseparable as children, but I don't think they were quite as close by the time Heather disappeared. But then, I only knew this secondhand from Heather's mother."

"Seems like finding Barbie would be a good place to start."

"I'm pretty sure she married Joe Gordon. They live somewhere on the outskirts of town. I'll look in the phone book. If she'll talk to me, will you go with me to see her?"

"Of course. I've got an errand of my own to run this afternoon. If Vance will take over here, maybe we can combine them."

"Are you going apartment hunting?" Rose asked.

Katie nodded.

"Why doesn't Andy just let you live above his shop?"

"That's a good question." Katie took another sip of coffee. "I don't suppose you've heard from Detective Davenport."

"He never even took down my phone number," Rose groused.

Katie shook her head. Davenport had been just as close-mouthed during Ezra Hilton's murder investigation. Either he was the laziest detective on the planet or the shrewdest, letting others solve all his cases—and no doubt taking the credit. Katie's successful efforts to find Ezra's murderer had never made it into the newspaper or other media accounts. In retrospect, she'd preferred it that way.

Rose stirred more sugar into her coffee. "I saw Polly's note on the door. She isn't picking on Edie again, is she?"

"I'm afraid so," Katie said.

"Edie wouldn't steal," Rose declared.

Edie Silver was the first of the low-end crafters to rent space in Artisans Alley after Katie had taken over as manager. She'd convinced Katie that her type of crafts—dish towels with crocheted hangers, silk flowers, and the like—could bring in customers, and she'd been right. Since admitting Edie and her friends, Artisans Alley was averaging twenty percent higher sales per week. That average had shot up to fifty percent during the holiday buying season. But fine-arts craftsmen (and women) vendors like Polly Bremerton were averse to change, and opening Artisans Alley to the low end of the spectrum was still a bitter pill. Still, Polly's creations were dolls made with molded bisque heads, arms, and legs, with stuffed and sewn bodies, not masterpieces on canvas.

"I agree," Katie said. "Under normal circumstances, Edie would never take anything that didn't belong to her. But she might if she had Alzheimer's disease."

Rose's eyes widened with indignation. "Don't tell me Polly's spreading that vicious, ugly rumor?"

"She hinted that might be Edie's problem."

"Edie was confused when her doctor changed her medication back in January. Now she's fine. And she has never taken anything that didn't belong to her."

Katie nodded. "Shoplifting *has* increased dramatically in the past few months."

"That's because we have more customers than we ever had before. Every retail establishment has to deal with it."

"I know. But as manager, I'm the one who has to address it."

Rose straightened. "You're not going to confront Edie based on one person's accusations, are you?"

Katie shook her head. "Of course not. Not without proof, and so far Polly hasn't given me any." She rose from the table. "If you want to use the phone in my office to make your calls, you're welcome to."

"Thank you, Katie." Picking up her coffee cup, Rose headed for the eight-by-ten-foot room that comprised Katie's workspace. It would be cramped quarters for a few days until Rose realized just how fruitless the search for her niece's killer would be. Somehow she'd find the patience to stand the intrusion.

Katie lingered over her coffee and picked up the newspaper. Heather's murder was, of course, the top story. Inevitably, Ezra's murder the year before was mentioned as well. The McKinlay Mill Chamber of Commerce would no doubt see this as a public relations dilemma.

Katie's frown deepened as she scanned the story.

An unnamed source indicated the body was entombed before death.

Katie's ire flared. Detective Davenport's assertion that Heather was dead when entombed didn't match what Katie had seen for herself at the mansion. There'd been holes in the plastic where Heather's hands would have been. Grooves were dug into the drywall that had been removed from the studs. How long had Heather clawed at the drywall in a futile effort to escape before she'd suffocated—or more likely, died of a seizure? Either way, it had been pure stupidity for Davenport to lie to Rose. Katie hadn't figured the detective was that dumb. Had he actually been trying to show Rose some compassion? That stab at courtesy was bound to blow up in his face when Rose learned the truth.

Katie folded that section of the paper, tossing it aside and opening the local section. The headline read: FAMED UR ALUMNI SPONSORS HI-TECH STUDIO. She skimmed the local-boy-makes-good—remembers-his-roots—story. Well, good for him.

She studied the stock-shot handsome, lightly lined face. Gray laced the man's hair and the close-cropped beard, reminding her of a younger Sean Connery. Hot stuff. Maybe she should try to convince Andy to grow a beard. He'd make a fine Jack Sparrow wannabe.

Nah. He'd never go for it.

Glancing at her watch, Katie decided it was time to get to work. She folded the newspaper and tossed it into the recycle bin. Rose would eventually learn the truth about Heather's death, but Katie vowed she'd do her best to keep it from her until she figured out a way to break the bad news gently. That would take some creativity, and right now she didn't feel up to it. The question was, how long could she stall, and would Rose be angry with her, too?

She'd have to risk it—and suffer the consequences either way.

~~~~~~~

Cool lake air whipped through the open windows of Katie's car. Rose had tied another knot in her plastic rain bonnet, but Katie refused to feel guilty for enjoying the gale. The long, dreary winter was over and the fresh spring air revitalized her. Sunshine glinting off the car hood felt like a good omen, too. She'd find her new home soon. Maybe today. But first, they'd attend to Rose's quest.

Leaving Vance Ingram in charge at Artisans Alley, Katie had packed up Rose, her box of mementos, and Heather's yearbook, and headed for County Route 8. Ezra Hilton's house had been near the rental property Katie was scheduled to inspect. Katie had inherited half of Ezra's estate. In order to go to probate, she'd had to sell the old man's house and property, effectively buying out Ezra's nephew, Gerald, and leaving her the sole proprietor of Artisans Alley. That felt good until the realization had sunk in that all the Alley's debts fell on her shoulders alone.

Too bad Ezra's house was gone. She could've lived there temporarily. The five-acre site would soon be developed for low-income senior housing, which, as Katie was only thirty, she was ineligible for.

"It should be coming up soon," Rose said.

Katie braked, taking in the numbers on a solitary mailbox. This portion of Route 8 consisted of small farms, but McKinlay Mill and the surrounding area were not entirely immune from urban sprawl.

"There it is," Rose said.

Katie slowed even more, activating her turn signal. She pulled into the remnant of a gravel drive, now two ruts cut through a sea of long, matted grass. A single-wide trailer stood on concrete block pylons, wind-scrubbed of paint and charm.

"Oh my," Rose muttered, taking in the sight.

"And I thought I had housing problems," Katie said, cutting the engine. "Looks like someone's at home." She pointed at the rusting Chrysler K car parked at the side. It had current plates, so it wasn't just a derelict.

They got out of the car, treading carefully to the trailer's front—only?—door. The tips of several tulip points stood timidly near weathered, pressure-treated wooden steps, someone's halfhearted attempt at beautification.

Mounting the steps, Katie banged on the aluminum outer door, its window frame devoid of glass or screen. She waited for what seemed like a minute before trying again.

Thumping feet from within halted. The door was wrenched open by a prematurely gray-haired, dowdy woman, a cigarette dangling from her lower lip, a toddler in pull-up training pants and a faded pink T-shirt straddling her left hip. "Yeah?"

"Barbie Jackson Gordon?" Katie asked.

"Who wants to know?"

"I'm Katie Bonner, and this is my friend, Rose Nash. Rose was Heather Winston's aunt."

"We tried to call, but it seems your telephone has been disconnected," Rose chimed in.

"What do you want?" Barbie asked, none too kindly.

"Did you know Heather's remains had been found in the old Webster mansion?" Katie asked.

Barbie's lips pursed, but she said nothing.

"We came to ask you if you knew anything about Heather's last few weeks before she was reported missing," Rose said.

"I heard on the radio about them finding her. I guess I thought like everybody else—that she was just another runaway." As an afterthought, she said, "I'm sorry she's dead."

An awkward silence followed.

"Could we come in and talk for a few moments?" Katie asked. Barbie threw a quick glance over her shoulder, pondered the question for a moment, then shook her head. "Now's not a good time. Besides, it was a long time ago. I don't even remember what I was doing back then, let alone what Heather was into."

"Gramma, I want a cookie," the little girl in Barbie's arms whined.

Katie's mouth dropped open. Gramma? The woman before her was only eight years older than herself.

"Heather was murdered," Rose said. "I want to find out who killed her. You must remember something."

"Hey, Heather and I parted company after high school. She went on to college. I had to go to work. I don't know anything about who she hung with, where she went, or what she did."

"Gramma, I'm hungry," the tot wailed.

Katie dipped into her purse and took out a business card. "If you remember anything—anything at all—that you think might be of some help, would you please give me a call?"

Barbie took the card, scrutinized it, and shoved it in her shorts pocket. "Sure."

Katie nodded. "Thank you for your time."

Without a word, Barbie turned and slammed the door.

Rose blinked, confusion shadowing her eyes. "You'd think she'd want to help. After all, Heather *was* her best friend."

Katie sighed, directing Rose down the steps. "It was a long time ago. I'm afraid the people Heather knew have gone on with their lives."

Rose frowned, taking in the shabby trailer with a sweep of her hand. "What kind of a life is this?"

Katie was tempted to agree with her. Instead, she said, "We knew digging into Heather's past would be difficult."

Rose pursed her lips and nodded. "You're right. And I refuse to be discouraged so quickly." Straightening her shoulders, she marched for the car.

Katie looked back at the trailer. A pale face peered through the crack between the faded curtains at the window. Was it just her imagination, or did Barbie Gordon look downright scared?

Four

With her pen already poised over the lease agreement's signature line, Katie paused to read one of the document's small-print paragraphs.

The apartment—half a house, really—was absolutely perfect, and the price was unbelievably reasonable. The freshly painted, large sunny kitchen, with its sparkling clean appliances, begged to be filled with the scents of baking. The old-fashioned claw-footed tub in the spacious bathroom would be a heavenly haven to soak in while sipping wine and reading steamy romance novels. The detached garage was the icing on the cake. No more scraping snow from frozen windshields.

"I don't understand your pet clause, Mrs. Hildebrandt," Katie said. "It says here that—"

"'Pets permissible per approval of the landlord,'" the grim-faced, hefty woman recited.

Something about her starched demeanor put the fear of God in Katie. But the rental price was so attractive . . .

"I don't allow snakes or other reptiles, large-breed dogs,

ferrets, or other rodents." Mrs. Hildebrandt shuddered at the thought.

"So that leaves fish—"

"Tanks must be five gallons or less."

"Birds—"

"Small, caged only, with clipped wings. They must never be allowed to fly free."

"And cats."

"Must be neutered, declawed, and female only."

Katie straightened, knowing her cat Mason fit only one of the three criteria. "Females only?"

"Male cats stink. They spray the walls and make the house unlivable. I won't have that."

"My cat is neutered, and has always lived inside. He doesn't spray."

"That's what they all say, Mrs. Bonner. You *did* say you were a widow, didn't you?"

"Yes," Katie said.

"I prefer widows. I don't allow hanky-panky in my home. Male visitors must leave by eleven o'clock at night."

"Mrs. Hildebrandt, the apartment would be my home, not yours."

"If you'll check the lease, you'll see that you are incorrect. Paragraph thirty-four, section two, says that I may restrict visitation between the hours of eleven at night through seven in the morning."

Katie scanned the page. Sure enough, what Mrs. Hildebrandt said was true. She set the pen down on the counter. "I think I've wasted your time, Mrs. Hildebrandt. I'm obviously not the type of person you want as a renter."

Mrs. Hildebrandt threw out her ample bosom, her nose rising in the air. "I think you're probably right, Mrs. Bonner. My tenants must have high moral codes, and I see now that you don't fit that category."

Rose, who'd been quietly standing in the doorway, gasped. "How dare you!"

"Rose—" Katie cut her off. "Thank you for your time, Mrs. Hildebrandt. I hope you'll find exactly the right person to rent your apartment." *And may she be just as bitchy as you.*

Katie and Rose trundled down the stairs and walked back to the car in silence.

"It was almost perfect," Katie said, wistfully, as she got behind the wheel.

"You wouldn't want to live in the same house with that—that—" Rose paused, buckling her seat belt. "I just don't have the words."

Katie buckled her own belt and started the car.

"How soon do you have to move?" Rose asked.

"Ten days." Katie palmed the wheel, pulling onto the highway. "I've been living out of boxes and eating off of paper plates for weeks."

"If you don't find something soon, you could come stay with me," Rose offered.

"That's very kind, but I don't want to inconvenience you. I've got a contingency plan and I can put everything but the cats in storage," she kind of, sort of lied.

"Oh, yes. The cats." Katie was well aware that Rose was not a feline fan. The older woman was quiet for a minute or more. "This isn't a good time for you to help me find Heather's killer, is it?"

"It's the best time," Katie said, if only to spare Rose's feelings. Although there was that little problem of Gilda's wedding to fit into the schedule, too. "And I have a lot of ideas," she continued. "First, I want to talk to Toby and Janice."

"What for?"

"When they bought the Webster mansion, they got the property abstract. That chronicles all the past owners. We need to find out who owned the property at the time Heather disappeared, who was renting the apartments, and if Heather knew any of them."

Rose's eyes widened. "That's a great idea. Can we go there now?"

"We're on our way."

Rose settled back in the Focus's bucket seat, looking more relaxed. Meanwhile, Katie clenched the steering wheel. One apartment down—only two more prospects to go.

~~~~~~~

"That awful man wanted to *take* the original," Janice said, pawing through an accordion folder filled with papers.

"I'm assuming you mean Detective Davenport," Katie said innocently.

"He creeps me out," Janice said.

"He could at least try to be more personable," Katie agreed.

"Do you know how much these things cost? There was no way I was going to just give it to him. I made him follow me to the post office and pay for his own copy." Janice plucked out a sheaf of papers. "Ah, here it is." She handed the property abstract to Katie, who paged through it.

"Would you mind if I take it to Artisans Alley to make a copy? It will only take a few minutes."

"Sure. Go right ahead."

"I'll do it, Katie," Rose said eagerly, taking the document and heading for the door.

Katie waited until Rose was out of earshot to speak. "I appreciate your helping my friend. We're pretty sure it was her niece that was found in your wall."

"I'm willing to do anything I can to speed up the investigation." Janice collapsed into a battered, paint-speckled metal folding chair. "Detective Davenport won't let us continue the demolition until his investigation is complete."

"That could take months," Katie blurted.

From the woman's expression, Katie deduced the thought was not new to Janice.

"Toby went back to his regular day job, but I already quit mine, and we've got a deadline to get the preliminary work done before the contractor shows up next week. We really can't reschedule without throwing our whole timeline off. And all I can do is sweep the floor and strip paint."

Katie remembered from past inspection visits—when she'd hoped to buy the property herself—that the attic had contained a vast amount of junk, including cartons of papers. If the owner had lived on-site, perhaps something in those boxes, such as old tenant receipt books, might help them in their search for Heather's killer.

"If you can't do demolition, surely there are other chores that need to be done. Scraping paint and puttying the windows. Replacing the newel posts . . . cleaning the attic."

Janice looked thoughtful. "Yes, the attic is in a mess. There's tons of stuff up there. Davenport didn't say I couldn't empty it. The ceiling is too low to make it into guest quarters. We were thinking of making it into a study for Toby. Would you like to see it?"

Katie smiled. "I'd love to."

She followed Janice up the creaking staircase, past the empty bedrooms, their painted doors off the hinges waiting to be stripped of multiple layers of paint.

"You can see all of Victoria Square from the widow's walk. I was thinking of putting a telescope up there," Janice said.

"That would be nice," Katie agreed. She'd had the same thought. She'd even priced the cost of a spiral staircase to reach the space.

Janice grasped a piece of rope and pulled opened a trapdoor in the ceiling. A wooden ladder unfolded. "It's a bit steep, so watch your step."

The steps were treacherous, and the rope rail was almost ineffectual. Katie steadied herself on the adjacent wall, finally hauling herself into the dim space above. Janice pulled a string hanging from the room's sole light fixture—a bare bulb. Even during daylight hours, forty watts of light couldn't dispel the gloom in that vast space.

"I'd better install a hundred-watt bulb next time I come

up here," Janice said. "Maybe I'll run some extension cords and work lights up here, too."

The attic was two years dustier than Katie remembered. Cobwebs hung from the ceiling, and spiderwebs with petrified prey inhabited the corners of the small, dingy windows. Dust motes drifted in the shafts of dull light that managed to penetrate the grime. Clustered around the edges of the room were cartons filled with the debris from past tenants, old chairs, their caned seats rotted and sagging, a box of chipped dishes. There was no treasure here.

Katie lifted the folded-in lid of a box marked "receipts." Her heart picked up speed when she saw the year written on the top—a three-year span surrounding Heather's disappearance.

"It's all junk," Janice said. "It'll have to go. I may as well toss it now, since I've got to pay for the Dumpster anyway."

"Don't be so hasty," Katie warned, hoping she'd kept the excitement of her find out of her voice. "You ought to get a professional up here to give you an estimate of what everything's worth. There're several vendors at Artisans Alley who also deal in antiques and offer that service."

Janice bent down to open a box. She withdrew a yellowed magazine that otherwise looked brand new. "Look at this. It's dated 1947."

"See, that could be worth a few bucks."

Janice's eyes widened. "Do you think so?"

"Sure. Rose is very knowledgeable about ephemera."

Janice frowned. "How's that?"

"Old paper products. If you're short of money, selling some of this stuff could improve your bottom line. You might even make enough to pay for some of the demolition you're unable to do yourself right now. It could help you with your tight deadlines."

Janice flipped through the old magazine. "I'd welcome anything about now."

"I'd be glad to give you a hand taking some of this downstairs."

"Thanks," Janice said. "I guess we'd better start by the ladder."

Katie grabbed her box and made for the makeshift stairs.

Within five minutes, she knew her seemingly altruistic offer to help had been a big mistake. Janice seemed determined to make up for lost time. Stationed on the wobbly ladder, Katie staggered beneath the weight of the boxes Janice handed down to her. She carried them into the first empty room she found and dumped them. Then it was back to the ladder, grab something, and repeat the process. Soon she was sweating and her hands and clothes were covered with grime.

They worked steadily for over twenty minutes, and Katie wondered just what was taking Rose so long to make those copies.

As though in answer to her silent pleas for release, a voice called up the stairs. "Yoo-hoo, Katie—Janice!

"Up here! Janice, Rose is back." Katie hoped Janice would take the hint and knock off for the day.

Rose appeared in the open doorway and did a classic double take at Katie's rumpled and dirty clothes. "What happened to you?"

"I'll explain later," she whispered. "I think I found something we can use to track Heather's connection with this house."

"I did, too," Rose said. "Wait 'til I tell you—"

"Katie!" Janice called.

"Shhh! Go along with everything I say, will you?" Katie hissed.

Before Rose could answer, Janice popped up behind her. Somehow she didn't look half as grubby as Katie felt.

"Here you are," Rose said, handing Janice the property abstract. "Fascinating reading. The house was built in 1897.

For nearly five decades, the surrounding land was a peach orchard."

"Interesting. I'm looking forward to reading it myself later. Rose, I told Janice that you were a bit of an expert at ephemera and that you'd be glad to take a look at some of the papers here and give her an estimate on their worth."

"Er . . . yes," Rose said, sounding quite unsure of herself. "Of course."

"Would you mind if we took a couple of cartons to Artisans Alley to study the contents?" Katie asked.

"I don't know," Janice said, sounding suddenly wary.

"I assure you, I've dealt with hundreds of customers when liquidating estates," Rose said. "It's standard procedure to have time to study the goods when trying to estimate the value of the property." She sounded so sincere, even Katie wanted to believe her.

"Well, maybe if you just took one carton and we could talk about the other stuff later."

"Certainly," Katie said. "We'll just take—" She bent down, picking up the carton she'd chosen up in the attic. "This one."

Katie bent her knees as she hefted the box, wishing a few longshoremen had perched in her family tree. Of course, Detective Davenport would probably wring her neck if he found out what she was up to, but she was willing to take the chance.

Feeling smug, Katie forced a smile as she faced Janice. "We'll let you know tomorrow morning if there's anything of material worth in here."

"I'll be here all day," Janice said with resignation.

Katie nodded and headed for the stairs, with Rose following in her wake. She passed through the soon-to-be-restored entryway, stepped over the threshold, and stopped dead. A sharp-eyed Detective Davenport was making a beeline for her, his gaze focused on the box.

Five

<tt>~~~~~</tt>

"What are you up to, Mrs. Bonner?" Davenport demanded as he charged up the Webster mansion's wooden porch stairs.

Katie swallowed. The detective's normally ruddy complexion had darkened considerably. "Just visiting Janice—Mrs. Ryan," she amended, hoping her voice didn't convey the guilt she felt.

Davenport eyed the box in her arms. The very heavy box, which she was sure must contain lead ingots. She shifted its weight, leaning the carton against the doorjamb to ease the ache already building in her arms.

"And what have you got there?"

Katie worked at a bland expression. "Just some ephemera. Janice needs a quote on their value." She leaned closer, whispering to Davenport, "You have no idea how much antique Valentines can be worth. Especially if they're three-dimensional."

"I'm not that stupid, Mrs. Bonner. That looks like papers to me. Papers that might be instrumental to my investigation."

Katie glanced at an agitated Rose standing beside her. She shifted her gaze back to Davenport. "Do you really think you might find something of use in this old box of junk?"

"I won't know that until you hand it over." He held out his arms.

Katie gave him the box, hoping its dusty surface would leave indelible marks on Davenport's raincoat. "We've got first dibs on buying them, so please handle them carefully," she admonished, but Davenport wasn't taken in by her innocent act.

"I always handle evidence carefully." He turned to glower at Janice. "Mrs. Ryan, don't let anything of this nature leave the building without the Sheriff's Office's permission."

Janice's cheeks flushed. "Well, you might have said so before this, Detective. And I want a receipt for anything you take."

Good for you, Katie silently cheered. She glanced at her watch. "Artisans Alley closes in half an hour. We'd better get back, Rose. See you later, Janice."

Rose glared at the detective and obediently followed.

They were halfway across the lot before Rose spoke. "Bad luck, him showing up like that."

"Yes. We'll have to concentrate on the property abstract for now."

"It's a gold mine of information, too. One of the former owners was Burt Donahue."

"Who?"

"Just the biggest auctioneer in the county. I had no idea he'd dabbled in real estate all those years ago."

"Tell me more," Katie said as they entered Artisans Alley via the back door into the vendors' lounge.

Before Rose could utter another word, Polly Bremerton's shrill voice cut the air. "Katie!"

Katie didn't even slow down, continuing straight to her

office. Rose was smart enough to head in the opposite direction. If Polly didn't rant and rave over some imagined slight or petty infraction of Artisans Alley's loose set of rules, she'd harp about Edie, and Katie was determined to keep Polly's gripes behind closed doors and beyond customers' ears.

But before Polly could corner her, Vance intercepted Katie in the vendors' lounge. "Gilda Ringwald stopped by while you were out. She left a box on your desk," he said with disdain.

Katie's heart sank. No doubt the favors Gilda had mentioned. And what was she supposed to do with them anyway?

Katie approached the cardboard carton as though it were filled with deadly rattlesnakes. She disentangled the interleaved flaps and looked inside. Nestled on top of a big wad of lilac-colored tulle was a roll of ivory satin ribbon and two large bags of deep purple Jordan almonds. Katie frowned. She'd never been fond of the candy-covered nuts—especially after cracking a tooth on one several years before. And purple?

She dug through the box, looking for some kind of list or instructions. Nothing. How many little sachets did Gilda expect her to make? It was then she caught sight of the plastic-enshrouded garment that hung from the pull on the top drawer of her file cabinet.

"Purple?" she cried, horrified. "The dress I'm supposed to wear to this wedding is purple?"

"Oh, yeah," Vance said, standing in the doorway. "I forgot to mention she dropped off something else, too."

Katie lifted the dress from the pull and whisked off the plastic to gaze at the monstrosity. First of all, it was sleeveless—and this was April in Western New York. She'd surely freeze to death wearing this. The color—that of a ripe eggplant—was bad enough, but while the front was scoop-necked, the back of the dress was entirely missing. The skirt seemed to go on and on and on. Had Gilda's friend with the broken leg been a giantess?

Before Katie could make sense of this new development, Polly stormed into her office and bellowed, "She's at it again!"

"Please close the door—and lower your voice," Katie said, then returned the dress to its makeshift hook and opened her desk drawer, pawing through the contents until she found a small bottle of liquid hand sanitizer. She should've thought of using the cleaner before she touched the dress—not that any dirt would show on the deep purple color.

The door banged and an impatient Polly stood before Katie, her face twisted in a scowl.

Katie took her time, rubbing the solution into her palms. It was then she noticed the property abstract on the blotter and wished she could examine it instead of listening to Polly vent her paranoia. Taking a Kleenex from her desktop box, she wiped off some of the dirt before tossing the tissue into her wastebasket.

She pulled her chair away from the desk, sat down, and studied the stern, solid woman before her. In a crisp white blouse, dark wool skirt, heavy support hose, and brown, lace-up sensible shoes, Polly probably would've made an excellent librarian—half a century ago. She prided herself on her knowledge of dolls, the arts, and anything to do with the craft and history of sewing, looking down on anyone who wasn't as savvy. Katie counted herself among that crowd.

"What can I do for you, Polly?" Katie asked at last, using every ounce of patience she could muster.

"It's that *crafter*. She's stealing my merchandise again!"

Katie sighed and grabbed a toffee from the jar on her desk. "What's missing?"

"Several vintage darning eggs, antique pincushions, antique buttons—"

Sewing items! Polly could sew.

Katie glanced at the dress that needed to be shortened—thought about asking Polly for a favor, and then abruptly changed her mind. Polly might ruin the dress out of spite . . . and then she'd be forced to wear something different at the wedding. Ah, a plan! But Gilda probably loved the dress. Why else had she picked it? Or did she want to make sure that her matron of honor couldn't take center stage on *her* special day?

Buttons, buttons, Katie reminded herself. "Were these buttons on cards or loose?"

"On cards, of course. They're handmade and *very* expensive."

Katie frowned. "The items you've mentioned are all small, things that can easily be concealed in a pocket or purse. It sounds more like a shoplifter to me."

"I *know* it's that Silver woman," Polly asserted.

"What's your proof?"

Polly straightened in indignation, as though her word alone should sentence poor Edie to years in the slammer. "She's always hanging around when I come in to straighten my booth."

Katie unwrapped her candy. "Well, her booth *is* next to yours."

"And I'd like that to change. I've been a vendor here ages longer than Edie—"

"According to Ezra's records, your booth was assigned only three months before Edie came in."

Polly's eyes bulged. She hadn't expected to be caught in a lie. "My merchandise is superior quality goods. Handcrafted bisque and fabric dolls of exquisite quality, not crap from China."

"Now, Polly, you know why we had to let crafters into Artisans Alley. It was either that or raise the rent so that nobody made a profit. Or I could have let the business go under. Since those crafters came on board, Artisans Alley has averaged a substantial increase in sales, for the fine-arts pieces *and* small craft items. Almost everyone has made more money in the past six months."

"I haven't!"

"Have you considered lowering your prices or participating in the sales events we've held?"

"I want a new booth location," Polly demanded.

Katie forced herself to keep a level voice. "As I've explained in the past, there's a waiting list. Vendors who've been here a lot longer want the same thing."

"Are they willing to pay extra for the privilege?"

Katie raised an eyebrow. Giving Polly preferential treatment, even for a fee, would cause an uproar with the rest of the Artisans Alley dealers. It wouldn't be worth the hassle.

"I'm sorry, Polly, you'll just have to be patient. In the meantime, I'll ask those walking security to pay special attention to your booth."

Polly's face flushed with anger. "It's not fair. It's just not fair!"

"I'm sorry, but that's all I can do without proof."

"You've bent over backward to accommodate those new people. You could do a lot more for those of us who've been here for the long haul."

Katie sat back in her chair, folding her arms across her chest. "I'm open to suggestions."

"Invite someone famous in to give a free talk. Some of the professors from the Rochester Institute of Technology."

"That's a bit beyond our budget—unless they're willing to do it for free."

"Then call in an appraiser who'll tell customers what their works of fine art are worth."

Katie thought about it. "That might be workable."

"We could also do special displays out in the lobby, showing customers how to decorate their homes with our products."

"Another good suggestion. Thank you, Polly."

Polly scowled. "I see no reason for you to patronize me, Mrs. Bonner."

Katie's jaw clenched. "I'm serious, Polly. And I'll do what I can to make your suggestions happen."

Polly's mouth tightened, but before she could speak, a sharp, insistent knock sounded—just the disruption Katie could've hoped for. She abandoned her toffee, and rose, sidling past Polly to open the door. Standing with a hand poised to knock again was Edie Silver. A marked contrast to prim and proper Polly, Edie looked like somebody's grandma, from her pink polyester pantsuit to her Velcro-clasped sneakers. Only now her face was twisted with agitation.

"Oh, Katie—it's Rose. You've got to do something!"

"What's wrong?"

"She found this morning's newspaper and . . ."

Katie had forgotten all about the headline story indicating Heather had been alive when she'd been entombed in the old Webster mansion's walls. "Where is she?"

"In the cloakroom crying her eyes out." Edie caught sight of Polly standing behind Katie, and her cheeks reddened.

Before Polly could explode, Katie placed a hand on Edie's shoulder, turning her around. "Come with me," she said, and hurried the older woman along.

"We haven't finished our conversation," Polly called after them.

As ever, the cloakroom's brown-painted walls exuded a depressing aura. The sounds of racking sobs did nothing to lighten the gloom. Rose sat hunched over, elbows on the card table, her head resting on her hands, the morning newspaper spread out before her.

Katie paused in the doorway, unsure if she should venture farther. "Oh, Rose, I'm so sorry. I was hoping you wouldn't see the newspaper article."

The older woman raised red-rimmed eyes toward Katie.

"You knew? All day long you knew about this and said nothing?"

"How could anyone tell her friend news like that?" Katie said, braving a step forward. But she knew, hard as it would have been, that she should have somehow found the courage to do so.

"I'm so sorry," she said again, stepping forward to rest a hand on Rose's shoulder, knowing her excuse was as inadequate a defense as she'd ever heard. "But I promise we'll find out why Detective Davenport misled you."

Anger tightened Rose's face. "Do you think he's still over at the mansion?" she asked, pushing her chair from the table and rising. "Let's go confront him now."

"That mean old cop is gone," Edie said. "I saw him dump some boxes in his car and take off a few minutes ago. Must've left half an inch of rubber on the tarmac."

"Perhaps tomorrow," Katie suggested.

Rose wiped her eyes, then gathered up the newspaper, folding it. Mouth slackening, she stared at the teaser photo in the upper-right-hand corner. "I don't believe it," she whispered.

"What is it?" Katie asked.

Rose pointed to the picture. "That man, he's—he's—"

"He's that famous movie director, Rick Jeremy, who's giving money to the university," Edie said.

"Oh, no, his name's Jeremy Richards—he was Heather's boyfriend!"

Six

Katie bent down to take a closer look at the muddied color photograph. "Are you sure?"

"See for yourself," Rose said, and rummaged through the box of mementos she'd shared with Katie that morning.

Katie thumbed through the newspaper until she found the feature story with a larger version of the director's portrait. She placed it on the card table. Rose selected a photograph from the box—Heather and Jeremy smiling—and set it next to the newsprint picture.

Edie crowded in. "Looks like the same guy to me."

She was right, although the man in the newspaper photo was twenty years older, with a neatly trimmed salt-and-pepper beard. Still, there was no mistaking the sharp cheekbones and piercing blue eyes. Rick Jeremy was Jeremy Richards.

Katie remembered what she'd read earlier that day, and an idea blossomed in her mind. "The article says he's holding a press conference tomorrow afternoon in downtown Rochester. We're going to be there, too."

"Do you think he'd admit to knowing Heather?" Rose asked.

"It can't hurt to ask," Katie said.

"What about Artisans Alley?" Edie asked. "We need you here."

"Vance can babysit, right?" Rose asked.

"Well, if he can't . . ." Katie's gaze slid to Edie, who blanched.

"Me?"

"Sure. You can fix a tape jam in the register. You're practically a fixture here. You pretty much know how everything runs."

Edie seemed to think it over, and then straightened with pride. "I'd be glad to help out."

"Great. And as long as I'm asking for favors . . . Gilda Ringwald from Gilda's Gourmet Baskets is getting married next week. She's asked me stand up for her."

"Oh, so that's why she brought over that dreadful purple nightmare," Edie mused. "Why is it brides choose the ugliest dresses for their wedding party?"

Katie forced a smile. "I have no idea. And it's miles too long for me. I was wondering if I could pay you to adjust the hem."

"I mostly work with terrycloth and cotton, but I'd be willing to give it a try."

Uh-oh. Had she made a mistake trusting Edie with the dress? Katie's forced smile resurfaced.

"And you don't need to pay me," Edie said. "When do you want to have me work on it?"

"Whenever it's convenient. The wedding isn't until next Saturday."

Edie nodded. "We've still got plenty of time."

"Thanks. And since we're on the subject, do you know anything about making wedding favors?"

"Are you kidding? I've made so many over the years, I could probably write a book on it, why?"

"Gilda left a box of stuff. Apparently I'm in charge of making them, and I have no idea where to start."

"Leave it to me," Edie said with a nod.

"Thanks." She was starting to sound like a broken record. "The box is in my office. I'll be more than happy to turn it over to you."

"How many do you need?"

Katie took a wild guess. "Fifty."

"That won't take long."

"Great." Katie glanced at the clock on the wall. "It's time we locked up for the night."

"Maybe I should practice closing down the register." Smiling broadly, Edie bustled from the cloakroom.

Katie glanced back at Rose, who'd been silent during the last exchange. Her lips were pursed, and Katie could see she looked hurt. "I'm surprised at your insensitivity, Katie. You were the one who found Heather's remains right here on Victoria Square, and now you're going to participate in a wedding?"

"It's not until a week from Saturday. And believe me, it wasn't *my* idea," Katie muttered. "But, Rose, would you deny Gilda and Conrad the chance to celebrate what could be the happiest day of their lives?"

Rose seemed unmoved by her words.

She tried again. "You've told me how much you loved your husband, Howard. Well, Gilda loves Conrad. It's taken them decades to come to this point in their lives."

"I know," Rose said, defeat coloring her voice, "but did they have to do it *now*?"

"A week from now," Katie reminded her. "Were you invited to the wedding?"

Rose shook her head. "Why would I? I don't know them."

"But *I* do. As the leader of the Merchants Association, I work with Gilda and Conrad and the rest of the merchants on a regular basis. We've all gotten to be friends." Okay, that was stretching the truth just a bit. "Please don't ask me to choose."

Rose hung her head. "I'm sorry. I wasn't thinking. Of course you should be in Gilda's wedding. Just because Heather is dead and can no longer experience joy doesn't mean others should be miserable. I don't know what I was thinking."

"You were thinking that Heather was cheated out of a beautiful wedding day, and the joys of motherhood, and maybe a wonderful career—everything her parents and *you* had wished for her. I don't think that's too hard to understand."

Rose nodded and looked back down at Jeremy's photograph, worry creasing her already lined face. "What if the security people at that press conference tomorrow won't let us in?"

Katie picked up a steno pad from the table, handing it to Rose. "We'll pretend to be reporters. If you put a pencil behind your ear, the disguise will be complete."

"What about you?" Rose asked.

"With Chad's Nikon camera slung around my neck, I'll look just like any other press photographer."

Rose picked up the newspaper, folding it carefully. "I'm sure Jeremy knows something about Heather's death. He's just got to!"

Katie studied her friend's face. "I'm so sorry I didn't tell you about the other news article. Can you ever forgive me?"

"I'm still angry—but not at you."

Katie let out a breath. Thank goodness.

Rose's mouth settled into a determined straight line. "In fact, I'm so angry at Detective Davenport, I'm going to call a lawyer."

~~~~~

"I want to sue!" Rose declared, and paced two steps and back in the confines of Katie's tiny office.

"Now, Rose, please be reasonable," said Seth Landers, McKinlay Mill's only lawyer. He'd taken a position on the edge of Katie's desk, as far away from Rose and the door as he could get.

"I'm tired of being reasonable," Rose ranted. "I want an apology from Detective Davenport—in writing—and I want damages. Lots of them. Punitive, monetary, and any others you can think of. I don't care what it costs."

Katie shrugged as Seth's handsome face collapsed into a frown. At Rose's insistence, Katie had called the small-town attorney, knowing he'd give Rose his best counsel.

"Why would Detective Davenport lie to me about Heather?" Rose said for at least the tenth time. "Why?"

"Perhaps to spare your feelings?" Seth suggested, giving Katie a sidelong glance.

"Yes, but he had to know she'd find out the truth eventually," Katie said. "It's extremely unprofessional behavior on his part. Can't Rose at least complain to his superior officer?"

Seth sighed. "I'll tell you what; tomorrow morning I'll make a couple of calls and see what I can find out. It may just be that the detective is drowning in casework and was simply having a bad day. It happens."

"I don't trust that man," Rose said. "He wasn't that motivated to solve Ezra's murder, and I'm afraid he'll show the same lack of interest in Heather's case. I can't have that. She was like my own child. I have to make sure that the person or persons who killed Heather are brought to justice."

Seth let out another sigh. "I'll do what I can. In the meantime, how would you ladies like to accompany me to Del's Diner for dinner? There are no two people I'd rather be with tonight." When Rose gave no answer, he added in his most sincere voice, "The special tonight is chicken and biscuits."

Rose glanced at Katie, her expression one of defeat. "All right. I'll get my coat." Rose exited the room, leaving Katie and Seth alone.

Katie strained to look around the door to make sure Rose was out of earshot before speaking. "You're a peach, Seth."

"Hey, I gotta eat, too," he said, rising. "And why shouldn't I have the company of the two prettiest women in town?"

Katie raised an eyebrow. "Do all lawyers lie as sweetly as you?"

"Only the good ones," Seth admitted, smiling.

Ahh, that gorgeous smile. Months before, Katie had nearly fallen for Seth. His good looks, his kindness, and his charm made her feel giddy with infatuation. It was only when Andy informed her that Seth found guys more attractive than gals that she realized his overtures were of a friendly—not romantic—nature. In the intervening time, he'd become her best friend.

"We ought to take separate cars," Katie said, grabbing her sweater from the peg behind the office door. "Afterward we can head home without coming back here."

"Good idea," Seth agreed. "I'll tell Rose."

The phone rang.

"I'll meet you at Del's," he said, and sketched a wave as he exited the office.

The phone shrilled again and Katie grabbed it. "Artisans Alley. Katie Bonner speaking."

"Mrs. Bonner, we need to talk. Tonight."

Katie couldn't immediately place the woman's voice. "Who is this?"

"I don't have much time," the woman insisted. "Now— and not on the telephone."

"Now's not good. How about eight o'clock at Del's Diner?" What better place for a rendezvous? A public place, well lit, with plenty of witnesses. Katie shook herself. Polly's paranoia must be contagious.

"Okay, eight o'clock," the woman said.

Katie heard a click, and then silence. It was only as she put the receiver down that she realized to whom the voice belonged: Barbie Gordon.

~~~~~~

The chicken and biscuit special at Del's did not disappoint, and in fact, the portions were so generous Katie and Rose would each have enough leftovers for a hearty lunch. Katie didn't tell Rose or Seth about the phone call she'd received prior to her leaving Artisans Alley, knowing they'd both insist on staying and their presence might scare Barbie off. Instead, she surreptitiously looked at her watch at least a hundred times, hoping she could get rid of her dinner companions before the appointed hour.

Seth insisted they all have dessert—cherry pie for him, and lime Jell-O for the ladies—and over a second cup of coffee, Katie told him about her plan to attend the press conference scheduled for Rick Jeremy the next day.

Seth frowned. "You really should inform Detective Davenport about Jeremy and his relationship with Heather."

"Why?" Katie asked. "He gets paid to investigate. I'm willing to let him do it."

"That's my point. *He* should be the one to talk to the man. Especially if you consider him a suspect in Heather's death."

"We're certainly not about to accuse Jeremy of anything as heinous as murder," Rose said, although Katie doubted her sincerity on that account.

Seth wasn't easily fooled. "Are you sure showing up Davenport isn't part of your motivation?"

"Why would I want to do that?" Katie said.

"Because he's treated you, and now Rose, badly."

Betty, the portly night waitress, reappeared and hovered with a carafe of coffee. "Can I get you folks anything else?"

Rose pushed back her thick white coffee mug. "Any more and I won't sleep tonight."

"Same here," Seth said. "Can we have the check?"

Katie, too, felt bloated and ready to explode, but needed an excuse to linger. "If you don't mind, I'm going to stay for another cup." She proffered her cup as Betty handed Seth the bill.

"I'll wait with you," Seth volunteered.

"Andy said he might take a break and meet me here right about now," Katie lied.

Rose's smile was conspiratorial. "We don't want to stand in the way of romance," she said and winked at Seth as she slipped out of the booth. Seth helped her with her coat. As Rose fastened the row of buttons, he peeled several bills from his wallet, setting them under his empty water glass.

"I'll talk to you tomorrow, Katie," Seth said, and leaned down to plant a brief kiss on her cheek.

Rose waved good-bye, letting Seth escort her out.

Katie watched as her two friends left the diner, then painfully got to her feet. "I'll be right back," she told the waitress, and hightailed it to the back of the restaurant and the ladies' room.

When she returned, Katie found the table wiped clean and occupied. One of Del's large faux red-leather menus hid the person's face.

"Barbie?" Katie asked.

"Shhh!" The menu sank to half-mast, revealing Barbie Gordon's wan face. "About time. I've been standing outside for almost ten minutes waiting for your friends to leave."

Katie resumed her seat with her back to the door. "Sorry, but I couldn't exactly throw them out. Now, what was it you wanted to tell me?"

"Can I get you anything?" the waitress asked Barbie.

"Yeah. A cheeseburger and fries to go. Add a slice of pie, too—whatever travels best."

"Sure thing."

Instead of replacing the menu on the tabletop stand, Barbie raised it to cover her face up to her eyes once again, keeping watch on the door across the way.

"What did you want to tell me?" Katie repeated.

"Just talking to you could get me killed. You have no idea what I've been going through."

No doubt Barbie had read about Rick Jeremy being in town, too. Did he already know Heather's murder had been discovered? Had he contacted Barbie?

"Keeping a secret can be wearing. Especially for as long as you've carried this one," Katie said.

For a moment Barbie looked confused. "Oh, yeah, sure. I can handle being threatened, but now that lunatic says my granddaughter is in danger. In case anything happens to me, I've arranged for certain evidence to be delivered to you."

"What kind of evidence?" Katie asked.

"I'm not proud of my part in this whole mess, but I really didn't have a choice."

"No, I can see that," Katie bluffed. "Why don't you just give me the evidence now?"

"Then I'd have nothing to bargain with. I could go to jail for what I know," Barbie insisted.

Betty appeared with a brown paper sack in hand, setting it and the check on the Formica table. "I'll take that when you're ready."

"Fine," Barbie said, her curt tone one of dismissal.

Betty shrugged and walked away.

"You haven't really told me anything about Heather," Katie reminded Barbie.

Barbie tore her gaze from the doorway and for a moment looked confused. She shook her head as though to clear her thoughts. "Everybody thinks Heather was such a sweet little Goody Two-shoes. They didn't know the *real* girl. Not like I did." Barbie looked over Katie's shoulder once more. "Oh, hell." The menu popped back up to hide her face again.

Katie turned her head to see what—or who—had spooked Barbie.

"Don't draw any attention this way," Barbie pleaded.

Katie's head whipped forward again. She was tempted to

blurt that Barbie's handling of the menu had already done that, but decided against it.

In seconds, Barbie slid across the booth's shiny synthetic leather, scrambling to her feet. She grabbed the food sack and bolted for the kitchen. "Later."

"Wait!" Katie called, but the swinging door had already whooshed shut behind Barbie.

Betty reappeared and picked up the check from the table. "I have to cover for patrons who stiff on checks, ya know."

Katie grabbed her purse, dug for her wallet, and plucked out a couple of bills. "Does this cover it?"

Betty nodded. "Thanks." She stuffed the money in her apron pocket and turned away.

Katie slid from the booth and donned her sweater. As she headed for the door she passed a number of familiar faces—Artisans Alley vendors and customers—and more than a few unfamiliar ones, and wondered which of them had scared Barbie Gordon half to death.

Seven

~~~~

Barbie Gordon's frightened face haunted Katie's slumber. So much so that she hauled herself out of bed long before dawn's early light to search the stack of boxes for Chad's camera. The cats thought it was terrific fun and practiced daring dives into opened cartons filled with breakables. It was only extra rations that distracted them long enough for Katie to find the correct box. She wished she'd been more diligent about labeling each container.

Katie assessed the piles, deciding she ought to start moving some of the boxes to Artisans Alley—just in case she didn't find a new apartment and had to stay at Andy's for a while. Not the best solution, but marginally workable.

She restored order and longed for some semblance of home. The aroma of baking always did that for her, but she didn't have time for that. Instead, she rummaged through the foil-wrapped packages in the freezer. She liked to keep a couple of loaves of frozen quick breads on hand for just

such an emergency, and took out a some banana bread to
thaw while she filled the back of her car with cartons and
the things she didn't think she'd need right away.

After that, she lingered an extra five minutes in the
shower, but still ended up trucking into Artisans Alley an
hour earlier than usual. She was sweating by the time she'd
carted the boxes up to Chad's pad. She'd have to call a
couple of movers to get estimates on moving the furniture.
There was enough room in the north storage room to fit all
of it . . . she hoped.

Her thoughts trailed back to Heather. What had she left
behind? She'd still lived with her parents at the time of her
death. Did they take her belongings with them to Florida or
leave them with Rose in hopes Heather would one day return, or had they disposed of them?

On that depressing note, Katie closed and locked the
door to her husband's last place of residence and went back
downstairs.

The coffee had finished brewing and she sat down at
her desk with a mug and cut herself a slice of banana bread,
deciding to shun work for a little research. Even the old
Webster mansion property abstract wasn't enough to keep
her thoughts from straying to the bones she'd discovered
days before. Her questions about Heather's death were mul-
tiplying at an alarming rate—uncomfortable questions Rose
may or may not have answers for, and might not want to
consider.

"Hello, stranger," came a voice from her office doorway.
Andy Rust leaned against the doorjamb, looking boneless
and weary, a dark line of whiskers shadowing his jaw.

"You're up early," Katie said. Anytime before ten was
early for Andy, who often worked until one or two in the
morning.

"You didn't stop by to see me last night, so I thought I'd
bum a breakfast cup of coffee from you. I brought doughnuts." He held up a white bakery bag.

Katie rose from her chair, paused to give him a quick kiss, then ducked into the vendors' lounge to scrounge a cup of coffee for Andy and to fill her own mug. By the time she returned, Andy had planted himself in her guest chair and spread out napkins, leaving a powdered-sugar, cream-filled doughnut for her, with a couple of his favorite jelly sticks for himself. Katie was glad she'd eaten only one slice of the banana bread.

Andy pointed at the papers on the desk blotter. "What's that?"

Katie took her seat. "The Webster mansion's abstract. Janice Ryan let me make a copy. Do you know Burt Donahue?"

"The guy with the auction house in Parma?"

"That's him. He owned the Webster mansion back when Heather died. Seven apartments should have been a gold mine. I wonder why he sold it?"

"Dealing with multiple tenants probably drove him nuts. That's why I'm not sure I want to rent out the apartment over my shop."

"It's income, Andy. You really can't afford not to."

"I can manage without it," he said, and bit off the end of one of his jelly sticks.

"Your debt burden isn't anywhere near Artisans Alley's, but you still owe a lot on all that dough-making equipment."

"Look, tenants break bathroom fixtures—not to mention plugging them up every other week. They're not always good at housekeeping. They destroy woodwork, and ruin kitchen appliances. Then there're nasty cooking odors, loud sex, or arguments overhead when I'm trying to run a family-friendly business below." He paused for dramatic effect. "Do you want me to go on?"

"I've been a tenant for years, and I've never cooked a stinky meal or plugged a sink yet."

"It's not the sinks you worry about," Andy said, and sipped his coffee.

"Maybe you chose bad tenants."

He glowered at her. "It's hard to be picky what with all the antidiscrimination laws. And get this, if my tenant is a drug dealer, I could go to jail for allowing that kind of activity on my property—even if I don't know it's going on. Uh-uh, it's just not worth it."

"Seriously, Andy, you know I'd never destroy your apartment. You can trust me."

"What if we broke up?" he asked, his expression hardening.

Katie blinked. The conversation had definitely taken a left turn. "Are you planning on it?"

"No, but I figure it's only a matter of time before you get sick of us only having stolen moments together and dump me."

"Oh, Andy, do you really think that?" she asked, hurt.

"You're an attractive woman," he said, his voice softening. "You've got a business to run, and so do I. Can a relationship survive when we work opposite ends of the clock?"

"It's been almost six months. I haven't gone anywhere."

Andy reached to tuck a stray lock of hair behind Katie's ear. "I know. And I appreciate it."

"There *is* an answer," she insisted.

Andy looked away.

Katie plowed on. "Maybe it's time you hired an assistant manager."

Andy turned his sharp gaze on her. "It's my business. I need to know what's going on—all the time."

"Yeah, but you can't eat, sleep, and breathe pizza twenty-four hours a day. You're a success—you can afford to hire more help." Inspiration hit. "Otherwise, you'd have to rent out that apartment over the shop. And the perfect tenant is sitting right in front of you."

"Let's not get started on that again."

Katie shrugged. "Okay. But I'm sure your personal life"—*And mine,* she mentally amended,—"would improve immensely if you weren't always so tired. Chill out, Andy. You deserve a real life apart from work."

"That thought's crossed my mind more than once lately. And I know you're right. It's just . . . I have to do it in my own time. Okay?"

She gazed into his big brown eyes, her heart melting. "Okay."

"Thanks." Andy's gaze traveled Katie's office before returning to her face. "I kinda thought I'd be saying this somewhere more romantic, but . . ." He took a breath, as though to steel himself. "I'm, uh, pretty sure I love you."

Definitely an unexpected admission. Andy's ex-wife had left him, making it hard for him to trust as well.

"I think I love you, too," Katie admitted.

The look of relief that crossed his face brought a smile to Katie's lips. Andy reached for her hand, squeezed it, then leaned forward to kiss her mouth, his bristled chin gently scraping her own. "Wow. This is heavy talk for first thing in the morning."

"Yeah," she agreed, but kissed him again anyway.

He rested his forehead against hers, Eskimo kissing her nose. "Next time we talk about this, let's do it over candlelight with a nice bottle of wine."

"It'll have to be at your place. I'm about to be homeless, remember?"

Andy pulled back and laughed. "You got it. But that brings up another ugly subject. You keep talking about me having too much on my plate—look at you agreeing to be part of Gilda's wedding."

"Don't worry, it's manageable."

He picked up his cup. "Then how's your little murder investigation going?"

"I'm not investigating anything. Just asking some questions. Finding someone's remains is pretty gruesome. That the person was related to someone I care about makes me furious," Katie said.

Andy drained his coffee. "I guess I don't associate a pile of bones with a real person."

"I'm afraid I can—all too well." Rather than dwelling on it, though, she told him of her adventures with Barbie Gordon, Detective Davenport's most recent faux pas, and how she and Rose planned to attend Rick Jeremy's press conference later that day.

"Rose is a sweet old lady, but she can't expect you to jeopardize Artisans Alley to help her."

"She's all alone in the world. Who else can she depend on?" Katie thought of Rose's sad, determined face and hoped she would grow old with as much grace.

Andy took a huge bite of his doughnut. "In a moment you'll have me crying," he said around his breakfast treat.

Katie glowered at him, irritated that the surge of love she felt for him was tempered with the sudden urge to throttle him. She picked up her doughnut and took an equally large bite. Powdered sugar rained onto her jeans.

It was going to be that kind of day.

Like a new mom leaving an infant with a sitter for the first time, Katie spent nearly an hour jotting down emergency and other information Edie might need later that afternoon while she was in charge.

But in the midst of her parental concerns for Artisans Alley, Katie also considered how just showing up at the press conference might be construed. It wasn't her intent to ambush Jeremy Richards—aka Rick Jeremy—but to talk to him about his former, now long dead, girlfriend. Perhaps he was just a jilted suitor. If so, who might Heather have been with just prior to her death?

On impulse, Katie grabbed the phone book, found the hotel's number, and punched it in. It rang once. Twice.

"Hyatt Hotel. How may I direct your call?"

"Mr. Rick Jeremy's room, please."

"I'm sorry," said the hotel operator, "but he isn't accepting calls."

"But I really need to speak to him."

"I'm sorry, but I cannot connect you with that party. Thank you for calling the Hyatt."

The connection was broken.

Katie frowned. Rank hath its privileges, she supposed. But what if she'd been an old friend? A relative? Had Jeremy Richards forgotten his roots, or was he so insulated he didn't have a clue who might want to contact him—be it friend or foe?

Katie glanced back down at her list of instructions for Edie. Had she covered every possible contingency?

Rose's voice over the PA broke her concentration. "Katie, please come to the front counter to speak with a customer."

Interruptions were sometimes a good thing, Katie admitted, getting up from her desk. Otherwise she might have written an entire manual for Edie.

As she approached the cash desk, Katie saw a snowy-haired woman dressed in dark slacks and a hand-knit sweater wild with purple, turquoise, and green swirls. However, it was the Artisans Alley shopping bag clutched in her hand that drew Katie's attention.

"I'm Katie Bonner, the manager. How can I help you?"

"Is there a place where we could talk privately? I'm afraid what I have to say might be construed as . . . sensitive," the stranger said.

Katie's stomach tightened. *Oh, swell.*

She sighed. "Certainly. Follow me." Katie led the way to her office, offered the woman a seat, then shut the door before she took the chair in front of her desk.

"Did you want to return something? As you know we have an 'all sales final' policy."

"I understand that. But I was hoping we could talk about the selling of obvious forgeries."

"Forgeries?" Katie asked.

"I'm afraid so, dear." The woman opened her trim leather purse, took out a business card, and handed it to Katie. It read:

THE INTERNATIONAL FOLK DOLL CONFEDERATION
MRS. BONITA MEREDITH

"Our organization is dedicated to the preservation of antique dolls. We also do our best to expose counterfeits."

"We don't generally sell antiques."

"One of your vendors does," Mrs. Meredith insisted.

"And you believe something purchased here isn't the real thing?"

The woman opened the Artisans Alley shopping bag, taking out a tissue-wrapped bundle, removing the paper to reveal a handsome, naked, cloth-bodied doll with a wooden head, hands, and feet. She handed the doll to Katie, who held it reverently.

"Oh, he's wonderful," Katie said, examining the workmanship.

"Yes, he is," Mrs. Meredith said. "Such a charming face. Someone did a remarkable job carving, painting, and aging the wood to look old."

Katie examined the doll's cloth body. "The fabric looks antique."

"And it probably is. But the doll's stuffing and construction give away its true age."

A small cut along a seam in the doll's body leaked bright white fibrous material. Even Katie could tell it wasn't old. "What would've been used to fill out the body of an antique doll?"

"Excelsior."

Katie's brow furrowed. "And what is that?"

"I'm sorry. Excelsior is actually fine wood shavings. Or they might have been filled with flock—long cotton fibers. Sometimes dolls were stuffed with rags."

Katie propped the doll on her lap and stared into its painted blue eyes. "He really is a dear. I almost want to keep him myself. Did you buy him?"

Mrs. Meredith shook her head. "One of our new members did. I've had a look at the merchandise, or what I can see of it in a locked case. The dolls, all similar in appearance, are priced in the two-hundred-dollar range, which probably isn't an outrageous sum considering the materials and workmanship, but they are being advertised as antiques, and that's just not the case."

"I'll be sure to speak with the vendor to make sure he or she puts a sign up saying they're reproductions."

"That's a good first step," Mrs. Meredith said, "but the dolls themselves should be marked to let future owners know they aren't buying the genuine article. Ideally we'd like that to occur at the time of fabrication, although we know it's not likely to happen."

Katie bounced the doll on her knee, wondering what he'd look like dressed as a Victorian boy in his finest clothes—velvet britches, a white silk shirt, and a snug blue cap. "Do you have the sales receipt?"

"Yes." Mrs. Meredith produced the slip of paper.

Katie frowned. Booth one-twenty. Off the top of her head, she couldn't remember who it belonged to. She set the doll on the desk and reached for the list of vendors in her right top drawer. Running a finger down the column, she paused at number one-twenty: Polly Bremerton.

Eight

A cold wind whistled between the high-rise buildings on Rochester's Main Street, puffing up Rose's plastic rain bonnet like a balloon. Katie suppressed a smile and glanced at her watch while they walked. They were late.

"Remember, Rose, we've got to be careful what we say in front of the press. We don't want to accuse Jeremy of anything. As far as we know, he doesn't know anything about Heather's death and may be completely innocent."

"Then why did he leave town soon after she disappeared?" she groused.

"'Soon' is relative. The newspaper said he graduated the spring after Heather disappeared. That had to mean he was still in the area for nearly six months. Did your sister and brother-in-law ever talk to him?"

Rose frowned. "He was hard to track down. But I do seem to remember that Stan cornered Jeremy at the university. They had an angry exchange. Jeremy said Heather had broken up with him, and he no longer cared what happened to her."

"Didn't the Sheriff's Office think that was suspicious?"

Rose shrugged. "Apparently not."

"I wonder if we can find out who was assigned to Heather's case."

"Maybe Seth can help us," Rose said.

"I'll ask."

They entered the Hyatt's resplendent wood and marble lobby, asked for directions from the desk clerk, and headed for the Regency Ballroom.

Rose untied her rain bonnet, removed it, and began to fold it. "I don't think I can do this, Katie," she hissed.

"Of course you can." Katie eyed the burly young man in a suit and tie who was guarding the door. "Just march right up and go in. I'll be right behind you."

The bonnet couldn't be folded any smaller. Rose shoved it into her raincoat pocket with a trembling hand.

Katie took the lens cap off Chad's camera. "Remember the pencil." She watched as Rose removed it from her purse and placed it behind her right ear. Rose clutched her steno pad and took a deep, steadying breath. With a thumbs-up from Katie, she charged for the ballroom door.

The security guard straightened, blocking their way. "Sorry, ma'am, this is a private affair."

"Excuse me, but I'm Marge Cannon from *The Golden Times*," Rose said with authority.

He stared blankly at her.

She exhaled as though in exasperation. "Rochester's own senior citizens' newspaper." She rolled her eyes. "Of course I'm not surprised someone of your extreme youth and obvious inexperience hasn't heard of us. But our readership encompasses almost ninety percent of the area's mature population. Our award-winning staff—"

"Yeah, yeah. Can I see your press pass?"

Rose's mouth dropped, but she opened the snap on her purse and began to rummage through its contents. "In all the years I've covered local events, I've never—"

"All right, already," the guard said in surrender. He nodded toward Katie. "Who's she?"

"My photographer."

"But she's not old."

Rose closed her purse with a loud snap. "There are age-discrimination laws, young man. If I were to report this to your management—"

He waved them forward. "Go in. Now!"

Straightening, and with her head held high, Rose led the way. Katie followed, giving the young man a weak smile, and the heavy door closed behind them.

"That was brilliant," Katie whispered.

Rose's cheeks glowed pink. "My heart's pounding. Let's get this over with."

The news conference was already in progress. Rick Jeremy sat behind a table at the front of the room, his hands folded before him. His dark Armani suit had been tailored to fit every exquisite muscle on his lean body. Tinted glasses hid his eyes—the epitome of Hollywood cool.

Katie expected to see a mob, but although there were cameras from the five local television stations, as well as radio microphones grouped on the table before the director, there couldn't have been more than thirty people in the cavernous room.

Katie and Rose circled the left bank of chairs to take a position near a table filled with hundreds of empty glasses and five sweating water pitchers—talk about overkill. Still, their location would let them see and be seen.

"What's your next project, Mr. Jeremy?" asked a reporter from Channel 9 News.

"A film in Tuscany, starring Robert Pattinson."

"Big deal," Rose whispered.

"Do you know who Robert Pattinson is?" Katie asked, amused.

"No. Should I?"

"The budget is a hundred million, and worth every penny," Jeremy said. A laugh rippled through the newspeople.

Katie noticed a ponytailed man with a full mustache standing across the room from them. He conversed in low tones with another dark-suited man. Were they part of Jeremy's security force? The ponytailed man looked familiar. Where had she seen him before?

Rose poked Katie in the ribs. "Ask him."

"Got the pictures ready?" Katie asked.

Rose slipped them from her steno pad and held them out for Katie to see.

Katie raised her hand, waiting as the director answered another question about his latest deal. Eventually, Jeremy acknowledged her.

"Do you credit your success to your education here in Rochester?"

"Yes. The film school was instrumental in teaching me what I needed to know to get my first jobs in LA. Now it's my turn to repay this fine institution." He blathered on about the teaching staff, the grounds, and even the quality of the cafeteria food.

Shut up and let me ask another question, Katie mentally implored, waving her hand in the air again.

"Do you keep in touch with old school friends?" she tried, once he'd run out of steam.

"As much as possible. I have a busy schedule."

"Do you remember Heather Winston?" Rose called out, her voice thin and nervous.

Dead quiet enveloped the room. Every reporter spun to stare at her. They hadn't forgotten McKinlay Mill's most recently revealed murder victim.

Jeremy looked thoughtful, then shook his head. "Sorry, never heard of her."

"That's odd," Katie said, "because we have at least twenty pictures of you with her. Of course, back then you were known as Jeremy Richards. Why did you change your name?"

Reporters and cameramen swarmed to Katie and Rose, microphones at the ready. A cacophony of questions bombarded them while still and video cameras whirred. Beyond the sea of heads, Katie saw Jeremy gathered up by his entourage, including the ponytailed man, and fleeing for the room's side exit.

~~~~~~

Extricating themselves from the press had taken more than half an hour. Not content with "ask the Sheriff's Office" and "no comment" answers, the reporters had followed Katie and Rose to the nearby parking garage, still asking questions all the way. Katie was glad to steer her car toward the expressway's entrance ramp and head for home.

"Maybe crashing the news conference wasn't such a good idea," Rose said, her voice quavering, apparently still rattled by the confrontation.

"If nothing else, linking Heather to a prominent movie director will force Detective Davenport into action. He can't claim it's a cold case now."

"I suppose," Rose said faintly, turning to look out the window and the roadside flashing past.

Katie kept glancing to her right. Rose's pale, wrinkled face was reflected on the passenger-side window. Katie wondered if she ought to hold off questioning the elderly woman about Heather, but now that Davenport was sure to devote more time to the case, it seemed best to prepare Rose with the same kind of questions the investigator was likely to ask. And she couldn't forget Barbie's remark from the previous night, that Heather wasn't the Goody Two-shoes everyone thought.

"Rose, you told Detective Davenport that Heather was a

good girl. But she wasn't a girl. She was a young woman with a boyfriend."

Rose's gaze swiveled toward Katie. "Are you implying she had a sexual relationship with Jeremy Richards?"

"It's a real possibility."

Rose's pursed lips betrayed her distaste at the thought. She probably still thought of Heather as a little girl needing protection. Protection she didn't get when she really needed it.

"Rose, when I found Heather, there was no trace of fabric. That implies—"

"That she was naked?"

"It's possible she died . . ." Oh, how to put it delicately.

"During sex?" Rose asked.

Katie nodded.

"I can't deny that I haven't thought of that myself. But was it consensual or forced?"

"Either way, it's possible she had a seizure. The pillbox locket had no medication in it. It could just be that whoever she was with didn't know what to do when she lost consciousness."

"So they walled her up behind plasterboard?" Rose asked, incredulous.

"I know. The thought gives me the creeps, too."

That explanation also sounded too simple. There was malice attached to Heather's death. And yet, why hadn't the person responsible removed the locket from the body? He—and Katie was sure it had to be a he—should have known it would help identify her. Unless whoever had done it *wanted* Heather to eventually be identified.

Rose remained pensive for the rest of the ride to McKinlay Mill. Katie found her thoughts wandering to Artisans Alley and the possible consequences of leaving an inexperienced Edie Silver in charge. Those thoughts were soon eclipsed by a different anxiety when Katie saw the cluster of Sheriff's patrol cars gathered around the front of the Webster mansion once more.

"Now what?" Rose asked, vexed.

"Maybe they discovered something that will help solve Heather's murder," Katie said and parked the car close to Artisans Alley. She jumped out and jogged across the lot.

Vance Ingram, Katie's right-hand man and one of Artisans Alley's vendors, had stationed himself at the fringe of the crowd.

"More bones?" Katie asked, breathless.

Vance shook his head, smoothing a hand over his trimmed, Santa Claus white beard. "A body."

Katie's stomach lurched. "Not Janice Ryan?"

"No. Some woman named Gordon."

～～～～～

Detective Davenport's face was nearly purple with outrage. "Why didn't you tell me this before now?" he thundered, and paced the creaking wooden floors in what had once been the Webster mansion's dining room.

"When did I have the chance?" Katie asked.

"Have you ever heard of voice mail?"

"Do you ever return my calls?" she countered.

Davenport snorted, his indignation palpable.

Katie huddled in her raincoat, wishing the mansion's heating system had been first on the repair list. Fixing the loose and missing clapboards and adding insulation wouldn't have hurt either.

"When I think back on it, Barbie really didn't say much," she said at last. "Except that some lunatic had threatened her granddaughter. Barbie must've seen whoever frightened her while we were at the diner, because she scooted out the back door in a hurry."

"And she gave no indication of who that might be?" Davenport asked.

Katie shook her head. She glanced behind her to an un-curtained window. It had been almost an hour since she'd arrived. Barbie's body still lay where Janice had found it in back of the house. It looked like she'd fallen—or more likely been pushed—over the porch railing, landing on a pile of construction rubble. Had she died of a broken neck, or was she impaled on some sharp instrument?

Katie's fists clenched. She should've done something the previous evening. After Barbie had escaped from the diner, she should have called Davenport or gone to Barbie's home. Maybe if she had . . .

"When did Barbie die?" she asked, responsibility weighing heavy on her soul.

"The ME figures sometime last evening. We found your business card on the ground near her body. Since you've got your sticky fingers all over the Square, I was surprised it wasn't *you* who found her." His voice dripped with sarcasm.

"I can't be everywhere at once," Katie replied. "You knew, of course, that Barbie was Heather Winston's best friend."

"Yes. She wasn't very helpful when I interviewed her yesterday."

"Well, you might also want to know that Mrs. Nash and I found Heather's old boyfriend for you."

Davenport's bushy eyebrows nearly joined as his eyes narrowed.

"His name was Jeremy Richards. He changed it to Rick Jeremy, and he's staying at the Hyatt downtown."

"Rick Jeremy the movie director?" Davenport asked, disbelieving.

"The very same. Rose has pictures of him with Heather. I'm sure she'd be glad to give you a few." Katie told him about the press conference, and how she and Rose had dis-rupted it.

Katie frowned. "I wonder . . ."

"What?" Davenport asked.

"One of Rick Jeremy's bodyguards looked familiar to me. Did I see him at the diner last night?"

"You tell me," Davenport said.

Katie thought about it. There were a number of unfamiliar men and women sitting in booths in the diner. She hadn't noticed a ponytail at the time. Still . . .

"Maybe."

Davenport nodded and jotted down the information in his small notebook. "Mrs. Bonner, I know you think you're being helpful, but I'd appreciate it if you'd just report what you think you know and then butt out of my case." He looked up at her. "The Sheriff's Office is quite capable of solving this itself."

So far he wasn't batting a thousand. And he wasn't finished with his rebuke either.

"Mrs. Bonner, may I remind you that people who kill often kill again. Mrs. Gordon is a prime example. I don't want you or Mrs. Nash to get hurt."

Damn him for sounding so sincere. She wanted to dislike him.

"We'd hoped confronting Mr. Jeremy would push you into making Heather's case a priority."

"Mrs. Gordon's death has done that." He sighed, and when he spoke again, his voice sounded weary. "Please, *please* let me do my job. That means doing everything by the book. Screwups during an investigation can cause roadblocks for the district attorney. You wouldn't want Heather Winston's—and perhaps Mrs. Gordon's—killer to avoid prosecution because you were in a hurry to see an arrest made, now would you?"

Katie couldn't argue with that logic. "I apologize, Detective. We only wanted to help."

Davenport sighed again. "Next time, talk to me first. And try to be a little patient. I'm juggling three other homicide cases and I need my downtime during the eight or nine hours a day I'm not on the job."

Duly chastised, Katie nodded. What else could she do?

"If you'll excuse me, Detective, I need to get back to Artisans Alley. We close in a few minutes."

"Go," Davenport said with a dismissive wave of his hand. He turned and left the room to rejoin his deputies, leaving Katie standing alone in the mansion's dismantled parlor.

The sky had darkened and speckles dotting the asphalt warned Katie it had started to rain. She crossed the parking lot and entered Artisans Alley just as Rose gave the standard five-minute warning over the PA that the store was about to close.

Several customers stood at the register, baskets filled with items, ready to check out. Anne and Joan were taking care of them with friendly professionalism.

Katie saw Polly Bremerton standing at the top of the stairs to the balcony. Catching sight of Katie, the woman made an abrupt about-face, hurrying away.

Katie frowned and quickened her pace, heading for her office. She found Rose standing over a distraught Edie. "Is everything okay? Did you have any problems while I was gone?"

Edie wiped her nose with a tissue. Her usual tough-as-nails facade had cracked, and her eyes were red-rimmed and watery. "I've never met such a-a mean-spirited, terrible person in all my life."

"Polly?" Katie asked.

"She was picking on poor Edie," Rose said, "telling her she was incompetent, and how stupid you were to leave a thief in charge of Artisans Alley."

"Was this in front of customers?"

"No, at least she showed some intelligence," Rose said.

Edie sniffed. "I can handle just about anyone, but I thought she was actually going to hit me!"

At least six foot tall, Polly was an intimidating figure. Edie couldn't be more than five foot one or two. And yet,

on occasion, even Katie had been cowed by Edie's sometimes forceful presence. Still—

"I will not stand for that," Katie said, taking off her coat
and hanging it on the peg behind her door. "I saw Polly
heading for her booth. I'll take care of this. Rose, will you
help Edie cash out?" She turned her gaze back to Edie.
"That is, if you feel up to it."

Edie stood, cleared her throat, and regained her compo-
sure. "Thank you for trusting me to take care of Artisans
Alley, Katie."

Katie placed a hand on Edie's arm. "I'll be back in a few
minutes."

Katie's anger stoked itself as she headed up the stairs to
the loft, now empty of customers. She charged for the back
wall and Polly's booth.

Polly was bent over, straightening the white christen-
ing dress on one of her handmade bisque dolls that sat in a
vintage doll pram. Katie fought the urge to kick the older
woman, who was becoming a lot more trouble than she was
worth.

"Polly?"

Polly straightened. "Katie," she gushed, as though ad-
dressing a long-lost friend. "Will you look at this mess? I
don't know why customers have to leave the booths in such
a state."

Katie wasn't taken in by her show of friendliness. "I
understand you had an altercation with Edie Silver a few
minutes ago."

Polly blinked, all wide-eyed innocence. "I don't know
what you're talking about. I don't believe I've even seen her
today."

"Not according to Rose Nash."

Polly's expression hardened, a look of contempt twisting
her features into a scowl. "Are you accusing me of lying?"

"Edie has my complete trust, as does Rose, who heard
the whole conversation."

Polly pursed her lips. "That woman is stealing from my booth, and you won't do anything about it."

"I've told you that your word alone is not ample proof of anything. I'm putting you on notice: If you verbally abuse any of the vendors—including Edie—I'll have to ask you to leave Artisans Alley."

Polly's mouth dropped. "You can't do that."

"I'm afraid I can, and I will. There's also another problem that needs to be addressed. We've had a complaint that the dolls in your locked case aren't antiques—that they're reproductions."

Polly's eyes bulged. "That's impossible. My source has impeccable credentials."

"Not according to The International Folk Doll Confederation. One of their representatives came to see me this morning. She showed me the fiberfill stuffing inside one of them. It was definitely new material."

Polly flushed. "I-I don't believe it."

"The Folk Doll people want us to at least post that these are reproduction dolls."

"I'm sure these dolls are antiques and I'll prove it." She unlocked her cabinet, where an entire family of similar dolls sat primly on a purple velvet tufted cushion. Polly grabbed what looked like the mama doll. Next, she borrowed a pair of scissors from a sewing box she had for sale. She pulled the doll's clothes aside and made a small incision along a seam. A gush of wood shavings escaped the small hole. "This doll is genuine. I'd stake my reputation on it."

"The doll I saw this morning definitely was not."

"Can you produce it?" Polly demanded.

"No."

"Then it's *your* word against *mine*."

"Polly, as the manager of Artisans Alley, I cannot allow you to sell the dolls as genuine antiques. I have the reputation of Artisans Alley to consider."

"You should've thought of that before you let in crafters."

Katie ignored her outburst. "You'll either have to post a sign saying the dolls are reproductions, or remove them from your booth."

"I've never been so insulted," Polly said.

You ought to get out more, Katie thought.

Polly straightened to her full imposing height and stepped forward, forcing Katie to step back and stagger against a shelf jammed with replacement doll parts. The shelf tottered, its contents threatening to fall.

As Katie stumbled against the toy carriage, a large, bald doll's head whizzed past her cheek, crashing on the wooden floor and smashing.

"Now look what you've done!" Polly scolded. She reached out, and Katie jerked back, expecting a blow.

"What on earth is wrong with you?" Polly demanded, and picked up a jagged chunk of porcelain from the floor, holding it in her fist as though it was a weapon.

Katie swallowed and realized she was trembling. Was it her imagination, or had Polly been ready to clock her?

Nine

Vance Ingram scowled as he handed Katie a cup of coffee. "It's the dregs, I'm afraid."

Katie reached for the cup and noted her hands were still shaking. "Thanks. I need something to sooth my jangled nerves." She took a sip, feeling its warmth course through her. Hopefully the caffeine would soon kick in.

Like her predecessor, Ezra Hilton, Katie considered Vance to be her right-hand man. Behind gold wire-framed glasses, the retired gentleman's bright blue eyes took in everything that went on in Artisans Alley. And as the former manager's second-in-command, Vance knew every vendor by name and reputation.

"Strange as it seems, Edie's terrified of Polly. I have to admit, for more than a moment, I thought she was going to hurt me."

Vance leaned against one of the file cabinets. "Ezra didn't like that woman, but he needed to rent the booth."

"We're not that desperate anymore."

"I admit she's disagreeable, but she didn't cause any real trouble until just the last few weeks."

Katie nodded. "By the way, I hope my asking Edie to babysit Artisans Alley today didn't bother you. I thought she needed a shot of confidence. Polly's been riding her hard."

Vance shook his head. "It's a good idea to have more than one backup. Janey's been feeling good lately, but on her bad days I'd prefer to stay close to home."

Katie nodded. Vance's wife suffered from multiple sclerosis and, quite naturally, he was devoted to her. "I should let you get back to Janey now." Katie polished off her coffee and tossed the cup into the wastebasket. She took her purse from the desk drawer and got up to retrieve her coat from the peg behind the office door.

"I'll help you shut down," Vance offered, and the two of them split the tasks of killing the lights and setting the security system for the night, and then locking up.

The drizzle had escalated to a downpour, and Katie gave Vance a quick wave before she pulled her coat up over her head and made a dash for Angelo's Pizzeria. As she neared, Katie noticed the apartment window above the pizza shop was open. Andy had probably forgotten to close it the last time he'd been up there.

The brass bells jangled on the back of the plate glass door as Katie opened it. "Hi, Katie," chorused a couple of Andy's teenaged employees. A new face among the blue T-shirted crew tonight looked up at her.

"Hi, guys. Is Andy around?"

"Right here," Andy said, coming in from the back room with a stack of empty pizza boxes. "I'll be right with you."

Katie took one of the white plastic lawn chairs Andy kept for customers and watched as he removed steaming pizzas from the oven, deposited them in the boxes, and loaded them into the warming bags for the deliveries. The addresses were on Post-it Notes, which he stuck to each bag. "Head on out," he told the two waiting boys, who waved to Katie before exiting for their cars.

Andy donned clean plastic gloves and started on the next pie. "You're early tonight," he said to Katie.

"Aren't you going to introduce me?" she asked, indicating the tall, dark-haired boy who stood beside Andy, watching him assemble a pizza.

"Sorry. This is Richie. Richie, Katie."

They exchanged pleasantries, and Andy let the boy take over making the pizza.

"You've got a window open upstairs—in front," Katie said. "Do you want me to go up and close it?"

"Nah. I'll do it later."

"It's raining pretty hard," she said.

"Yeah, but it's coming from the west." He was right. The open window *was* on the east side of the building.

"Okay. Oh, shoot! I just remembered I was supposed to confirm an appointment to see another apartment tomorrow. Do you mind if I use your phone?"

"Sorry, but yeah, I do—this is my peak ordering time." To prove him right, the phone rang. "What about your cell phone?" Andy asked and reached for the receiver.

"I think it might need to be charged." Katie dug in her purse. She located the tiny phone, checked the battery graphic, and noticed it didn't yet need life support. She found the scrap of paper where she'd jotted down the number from a couple of days before, punched it in, and then stuck a finger in her right ear so she could hear.

The call was answered on the third ring. "Hello, Mr. Hartsfield, it's Katie Bonner. We spoke a few days ago about my coming to see your apartment. Have you rented it yet?"

He hadn't. She arranged to see it first thing in the morning, before Artisans Alley opened, so as not to inconvenience Vance, Edie, or Rose. With that settled, she folded her phone and put it back in her purse.

Andy finished taking another order, handing it to the new boy. "How goes the apartment hunt?"

"Nothing yet, and I've only got nine days before I'm out on the street."

"You have a lot of options," Andy said. "Including the one I offered you."

"Right now living with you isn't the one I'd prefer. How about offering me something to eat—that would placate me for at least an hour."

Andy smiled. "Richie, please make a small white pizza with double garlic, double cheese, and double pepperoni for the prettiest lady on earth."

"Oh, really, Andy, I'm probably only the second most beautiful woman," Katie deadpanned. "And triple the garlic, will you, Richie?"

"Then you'd better pucker up now, because I'm not kissing you after that," Andy said and laughed.

"I'll go shut the window and wait for you upstairs."

Andy shook his head. "It's Richie's first night. I don't want to leave him here alone. You don't mind, do you?"

"Not at all," Katie said, and tried to keep a frown from her lips.

"Have a Coke while you wait," Andy offered, and grabbed the ringing phone once again.

Katie took a can of pop from the refrigerated case in the corner. That was twice he'd discouraged her from going upstairs. Very curious, especially since this morning he'd again refused to rent her the place. She sniffed the air. Was that paint she smelled behind the aroma of sauce and spices? No wonder the window was open, Andy was probably trying to dissipate the fumes. He should have used a non-VOC paint. Did painting the place mean he'd changed his mind and was going to rent the place? If so, why not just own up to it?

Katie wasn't about to argue and was glad she'd made the appointment to see the half house at the edge of town the next morning. Instead, she plastered what she hoped was a genuine-looking smile across her lips and forced herself to sound cheerful. "How's that pizza coming, Richie?"

"Another fifteen minutes, Ms. Bonner."

"Thanks."

Katie choose the seat farthest from the door to wait, and sipped her Coke. She didn't dare pick up one of the well-thumbed magazines Andy kept in a stack on a small table under the front window. Who knew what kind of germs lived within the pages, and Katie's little bottle of hand sanitizer was locked in her desk back at Artisans Alley.

Not a minute passed before Sue Sweeney, owner of Sweet Sue's Confectionary—Victoria Square's heavenly chocolate shop—entered Angelo's. Katie liked cheerful, plus-sized Sue, whose personality matched her shop's name. "Hi, Andy," she called. "Is my pizza up yet?"

Andy looked at the stack of pizza boxes waiting to be filled. "Coming right up."

Sue nodded and looked around the shop, her face brightening when she spied Katie. "Hey, Katie, I heard you were arranging a bachelorette party for Gilda Ringwald?"

Katie gaped, panicked. "Who told you that?"

"Gilda," Sue said in all innocence. "I hadn't received an invitation yet and I wanted to make sure I didn't have to be elsewhere on whatever night it's planned for."

"Bachelorette party?" Katie repeated in disbelief, her voice squeaking. Where was she supposed to find time to arrange for a party with only ten days before the wedding.

"Yeah," Sue said. "So, where will it be held and on what day?"

"I have no idea. Gilda and I haven't spoken about it." But they surely would—she'd make sure of that.

"Pizza's ready, Sue," Andy called, with a large, sealed box in hand.

Sue handed him a twenty and he made change. "Thanks,"

she said and turned back to Katie. "You'd better get those invitations out in the mail tomorrow—or else you'll have to hand deliver them." She laughed and, with hands full of her purse and the pizza, she backed out of the shop. The cheerful little bell on the door rang after her.

Andy shook his head ruefully. "Katie, you're going to have to back out of that wedding. You haven't got the time for all the stuff Gilda has planned."

"I can't back out now. Edie's already started to alter the matron of honor's dress. I was Gilda's second or third choice as it is," Katie said, although she was unable to squelch that panicked feeling that continued to grow inside her.

"Then you'd better find Gilda and pin down exactly what she expects you to do and when. Maybe you can recruit one of her other friends to help you with the arrangements, although why she hasn't made them all herself is beyond me."

"Me, too."

"Pizza's ready, Ms. Bonner," said Richie, coming up behind Andy with the small cardboard box. He handed it to Katie.

"Thanks. But I think I just lost my appetite."

"Then now's the perfect time to give Gilda a call. Or better yet"—Andy gazed out the pizzeria's plate glass window—"there's a light on in her shop. You'd better go see her now."

Katie's shoulders slumped. She wanted to confront Gilda like she wanted to grow a third leg. "Yes, sir."

Andy leaned across the counter to give Katie a quick kiss on the top of her head. Then he grabbed her shoulders, turned her about, and gave her a shove toward the door. "Do it now, before you lose your nerve."

Losing her nerve wasn't what she worried about. It was more her temper.

~~~~~

On the way to Gilda's Gourmet Baskets, Katie dropped the pizza off at her car, and then hoofed it across Victoria Square's parking lot. As Andy had said, there was a light on inside the shop. With her reading glasses perched on the end of her nose, Gilda sat at the sales counter, gazing down at what looked like paperwork. Katie pounded on the door, and Gilda looked up, delight soon replacing her wary expression. She hurried to unlock the door.

"Just the person I wanted to talk to," Gilda said, and ushered Katie inside her shop.

Katie loved the heady aromas that mingled inside the shop. Chocolate, vanilla, coffee, and the background scent of the many varied baskets themselves. "I bumped into Sue Sweeney. She mentioned something about a bachelorette party."

Gilda's smile broadened. "Because there's not much time before the wedding, I thought we could combine the bridal shower and the bachelorette party into one event. Won't that be fun?"

"Bridal shower?" Katie asked, warily. She hadn't even thought far enough into the future to consider buying Gilda a wedding gift, let alone one for a shower.

"Yes. One of the duties of the maid or matron of honor is to set up the bridal shower. I'm registered at the Bon-Ton, Lord and Taylor, Bed, Bath and Beyond, and—"

"Stop, stop, stop!" Katie ordered. The panic was back. "Don't you think it's a little late to be planning all of this? I mean, doesn't stuff like this need to be done well in advance?"

Gilda giggled. "Usually. But this wedding is all such a spur-of-the-moment thing. And it *is* my first time at the altar. Don't you think I deserve the wedding of my dreams?"

Katie had been married only once, too, but she and Chad had gone to city hall, and the judge's clerk had been their only witness. She hadn't had the dress, the cake, or any of the pomp and circumstance.

"Gilda," she began, trying to keep her voice level. "You definitely *should* have the wedding of your dreams. But it takes a lot of time and, quite frankly, I don't think I'm up to the task to provide it."

Gilda's expression fell. "But you promised you'd be my matron of honor."

"I'm happy to stand up with you, it's just the rest of it I can't—"

Gilda's mouth began to tremble, and a single tear rolled down her left cheek. She sniffed. "This is supposed to be the happiest day of my life."

Katie wasn't sure what to say. She started to stammer. "Th-th-this is all so last minute . . . I wasn't prepared for . . ."

"Don't *you* want me to be happy on *my* wedding day?" Gilda asked.

"Of course I do, it's just—"

A tear dribbled down Gilda's other cheek.

"I'll do my best," Katie said with resignation. If worse came to worst and she didn't find a new apartment, she could always sleep in her car. It would be a little tight with two cats and their litter boxes, but Gilda would have her dream wedding day.

Gilda brightened, wiping a hand across her eyes before handing Katie a piece of paper. "Here's the list of wedding guests. Of course, you'll only want to invite the ladies to the bachelorette party. It's up to Conrad to figure out what he wants to do about the bachelor party." She giggled like a schoolgirl.

Katie scanned the list. There couldn't have been more than twenty or so people on the list, and many of them were members of the Merchants Association. Hopefully that would make the preparations easier.

"Now, I was thinking it would be nice to host a tea rather than an actual bachelorette party. Too bad the Square's tea-room won't be open until after the wedding—at least that's the rumor that's going around. I'm sure we could hold it at Del's Diner, but it's not very . . . oh, I don't know . . . girlie, is it."

Gilda was nearly sixty and she wanted a girlie party? Katie would've thought a "Red Hat" gathering might have suited better, considering the average age of the wedding guests qualified them as baby boomers.

"What's your budget?" Katie asked.

"*My* budget?" Gilda echoed, sounding surprised. She shook her head. "Oh, no, no. This is the matron of honor's *obligation*. Look here." She turned back for the sales counter, fished among the scattered documents, and came up with a piece of paper she handed to Katie, whose eyes nearly popped when she read the centered headline: OFFICIAL DUTIES OF A BRIDESMAID. A long list of dos and don'ts followed. A *very* long list.

"Now, there's not much time," Gilda said, and gently pushed Katie toward the door. "Give me a call when things are set up so I'll know where to arrive. And don't forget to mention the registry on the invitations. I've added that information to the end of the list."

"But—"

"I've got tons of work to get done before next Saturday. Keep me posted," Gilda said, and closed the door on Katie. She turned and watched as Gilda went back to her sales desk, climbed back on her stool, and replaced her glasses on her nose.

Katie's fist closed around the list, wrinkling the paper. At that moment, she wanted nothing more than to wad it into a very tiny ball and throw it away.

You agreed to be her matron of honor, a little voice inside her taunted.

She just hadn't known that Gilda—now forever known to Katie as the over-the-hill bridezilla—meant to work her to death in the process.

Ten

~~~~~~

By the time Katie returned home, the cheese on her pizza had congealed into a new form of rubber. However, a few minutes in the oven revived it to an edible state and gave her time to search through the boxes marked "Living Room/ Desk Drawers" for the phone book she'd packed the week before. As she munched her dinner, batting away the attentions of two cheese-loving cats, she made a list of numbers and started calling around. No one wanted to talk about booking a party on such short notice—and especially not at eight thirty at night. "Call in the morning when the catering manager is here," seemed to be the mantra of every restaurant hostess she spoke with that evening. She couldn't say she blamed them.

"It's not my fault," she told Mason, who nudged his head against her knee, looking for another handout. She peeled a piece of cheese from the slice and gave it to him. Della demanded the same, and soon all she had left were bald patches of hardening crust.

She read through the list of maid/matron of honor duties

again. Some of them made sense: witness and sign the marriage license, make a toast—wasn't that the duty of the best man?—and assist the bride with her dress and makeup on the big day. Even that last was pushing it a bit. Well, maybe if the bride was in her early twenties—but Gilda was near sixty.

Why, oh why had she ever agreed to do this? Then she remembered—she hadn't. Gilda had asked and assumed she'd say yes, plowing on ahead.

And that's just what Katie needed to do: plow on ahead and start making plans for the bachelorette party. Tossing the pizza box in the recycle bin, she found a pad and piece of paper, sat down on the couch—and immediately became a cat magnet—and started jotting down notes for the party. First up, invitations—or could she skip that part and just e-mail everyone on Gilda's guest list? Considering the time crunch, that might be the best idea. And maybe she could find a pretty e-invitation online.

Were they going to have to play stupid games—like Bridal Bingo? Katie rolled her eyes, jostling Della, who sat on her lap. The cat retorted with an indignant, *"Brrrrpt!"*

"My sentiments exactly."

~~~~~~

Although details of setting up the party were still heavy on her mind, Katie welcomed another bright spring morning. No rain—or snow—made it that much easier to load the back of her Focus with more boxes, before taking off for her appointment.

Arriving at her destination, she glanced at her dashboard clock. Right on time. She double-checked the address on the pad before her. This was definitely the place. A look around the unkempt yard and the piles of trash at the end of the drive did not fill her with confidence. The apartment was empty—ready for immediate occupancy—as the man who'd answered her phone call had said. Judging by the garbage they'd left behind, it looked like the former tenants had left in a hurry.

Katie got out of the car and walked up the cracked concrete path, taking note of the broken downspout and missing roof shingles, her feelings of misgiving growing exponentially. But she'd promised the landlord she would definitely consider the place. He'd been adamant that she agree before he would schedule the appointment.

She rang the bell and the door was eased open almost immediately. A gray-haired, haggard-looking man in his late fifties or early sixties stood before her, a four-toed cane clutched in one hand, the newspaper tucked under his arm. "Ms. Bonner?"

"Yes. And you must be Mr. Hartsfield."

"Come in," he beckoned.

The dark entryway wasn't at all welcoming. Would this weird-looking guy bop her on the head with his cane, and—

Get a grip, Katie scolded herself when the man lagged behind, his cane making a crackling sound on the sticky hardwood floor.

"I'm offering the first month free," Hartsfield said from behind her.

Katie broke through the gloom into a bright but filthy kitchen. She walked to the center of the nearly empty room. The only furniture was a paint-spackled, wooden hard-backed chair, which Hartsfield promptly took. He straightened his right leg, massaging his knee.

"I know it's a pit." His tone conveyed more than just weariness—desperation.

"Did you have to evict your last tenants?" Katie asked.

He nodded. "It took me nine months—and the courts—to get rid of those pigs. My sister rented it out while I was in rehab at the VA center in Batavia. Unfortunately, she didn't bother asking for references."

Spray-painted epithets did not complement the wallpaper's columns of dainty roses. A cupboard door hung from its hinge. Holes had been punched through the drywall at irregular intervals. Bare wires dangled from the ceiling where a light fixture had once been.

"I figured if I offered a month's free rent"—he caught her gaze and backpedaled—"maybe two—it might be incentive enough for the next tenant to do a little pre-move-in cleanup. Since my accident, I don't have the stamina to do that kind of work, and I can't really afford to have it done."

Katie sighed. "I'm sorry to hear that."

Hartsfield squinted at her. "Bonner. I used to work with a Chad Bonner. He was an English teacher at McKinlay Mill High School."

"He was my husband."

"A fine man. I was in the hospital when he had his accident. I'm so sorry."

"So am I. What did you teach?"

"Math. I spent my whole career at McKinlay Mill High."

Heather raised an eyebrow. "By any chance did you know Heather Winston?"

He eyed her for what seemed like an eternity before answering. "She was a student of mine. So was Barbie Jackson. It's hard to believe they're both now dead."

"And that the same person probably killed them," Katie said.

Hartsfield frowned. "I heard Barbie fell."

"As far as I know, it hasn't been ruled a homicide—yet. But I wouldn't be surprised if it was. What do you remember about Heather?" Katie asked, recalling Barbie's gibe of days before.

Hartsfield shrugged. "She was a good student, but she was out sick a lot. She wanted to be a model or something."

"Was she a popular student?"

He shook his head. "Not like Barbie. The boys used to fight over that little cheerleader. I wasn't surprised when Barbie had a baby not long after graduation. Her parents threw her out of the house."

"Do you know where she lived after high school?"

He shook his head. "Sorry."

Katie thought about it. Back then there would've been fewer apartment complexes in and around the village. Could Barbie have been living in one of the Webster mansion's apartments? If so, it was no wonder she hadn't volunteered information that might have implicated her in Heather's death. She had definitely been frightened on Tuesday night. Less than twelve hours later, she was dead.

Hartsfield cleared his throat and looked around the kitchen. "What do you think?"

Katie sighed. "Is the rest of the apartment in the same shape?"

He nodded. "You aren't going to rent it, are you?"

"To be honest, it's farther than I wanted to drive to my job. I've got to be out of my apartment in nine days. And I don't have the time or the skills to make the kind of repairs this place needs." She glanced around the kitchen. "It's a shame. It looks like this was once a pretty place."

"That it was," Hartsfield agreed. "My late wife decorated the apartment. It broke my heart to see what those people had done to it." His gaze drooped to the scarred and dirty floor.

Katie looked around the room. Why did she have to disappoint the old man? Then again, maybe she could help.

"Mr. Hartsfield, I have a friend, one of the businessmen in McKinlay Mill, who hires teenagers to work in his pizza parlor. He mentioned that the high school shop class often takes on repair projects for people in need. If you paid for the supplies you might be able to negotiate with the school for student labor. I've heard the kids do a great job."

Hartsfield's dour expression lightened. "I'd forgotten all about that. Thank you for reminding me, Mrs. Bonner. But that doesn't solve your problem."

"No. I have just over a week to find a home, or else inconvenience one—or a succession—of my friends."

Hartsfield squinted at her. "Mrs. Bonner, I have a feeling that you can accomplish anything you set your mind to. No doubt you'll be in your new home and settled in before your deadline."

She squinted at the older man. "Are you psychic, Mr. Hartsfield?"

A smile cracked the older man's lips. "Just a good judge of character."

~~~~~

The drive to Hartsfield's duplex really was longer than Katie wanted to drive on a daily basis. She was already ten minutes late for dealer setup by the time she arrived at Artisans Alley. Polly Bremerton stood outside the employee entrance, with several piles of stacked boxes flanking her. A pale, thin little girl, no more than four, dressed in a pretty red and white polka-dot dress with red stockings and patent leather Mary Janes, stood beside her, clasping the older woman's hand.

Katie grabbed her morning newspaper and sorted through her keys before she got out of her car. She wasn't about to delay Polly any longer. She locked her car door and headed for a tongue-lashing.

"You certainly took your time," Polly said in lieu of a greeting.

"Good morning. And who are you?" Katie asked the girl, as she opened the door.

"Hannah," the child said with a shy smile.

"Haven't I told you never to talk to strangers," Polly growled at the girl.

Hannah's bottom lip trembled, her gaze dipping to the ground. "I'm sorry, Grandmama."

Polly grabbed the first box from the stack and handed it to the child. "Carry this one."

"Polly," Katie chided, "surely that's too heavy."

"It's only got a few items packed in bubble wrap. Hannah won't drop it, will you, girl?"

"No, Grandmama."

"Could you give me a hand?" Polly asked, shoving a box at Katie.

"I really need to get the lights on, and—"

"Well, then as soon as you can," Polly said, and headed off into the darkened Alley, with little Hannah struggling to keep up.

Katie stared after the woman. What gall! Yet she found herself moving the stack of boxes into the building. If anything was stolen, Katie was sure Polly would want her to file a police report and an insurance claim. It wasn't worth the hassle.

By the time Katie had the lights on and the coffee going, Rose and Edie had arrived. They hung up their coats and Rose poured the coffee for the three of them. Edie dropped the familiar favor box on the desk before plunking herself down in Katie's visitor's chair. "All done."

Katie peeked inside the box to see the bundles of lilac tulle encircling five or six of the deep purple Jordan almonds. But Edie hadn't just tied them with the ribbon. Each sachet sported a small label that had been die-cut with a scroll motif, along with the centered words "Gilda ♥ Conrad" in purple and the wedding date.

"Oh, they're darling," Katie said with pleasure, but Edie just waved a hand in dismissal.

"I told you I could make them in my sleep. It only took me a couple of hours, too."

That long?

"Seeing all that tulle reminds me that the matron of honor dress still needs hemming. Do you think we could do that sometime today—just to get it out of the way?" Katie asked.

"How about this afternoon?" Edie suggested.

"Wonderful." She sighed. "I need to tap your brains about a place for Gilda's bridal shower."

"What does she need that for?" Rose asked. "Haven't she and Conrad been living together for something like thirty years? Surely she doesn't need any china or linens."

"Is the woman delusional?" Edie seconded.

"I admit, I was a little surprised myself, but she wants a dream wedding, and a bridal shower. She suggested a tea-room, but except for Tea and Tasties, which is closed, I don't know where there are any. And how can I book a party on such short notice?"

"Have it right in the lobby after hours," Edie suggested. "We can help you decorate. And you should get it catered. That'll save you time, effort, and money."

"Great idea. I can call Blueberry Catering in Parma. They did a great job providing food, chairs, and tables for the gathering after Ezra's funeral, and they pulled it off with only a day's notice."

Katie realized she needed to do something special to repay Edie for all she'd done and her good advice on Gilda's behalf, but before she could say so, Edie spoke first. "I saw Polly's car in the lot and I'm not going upstairs to straighten my booth until she leaves."

"I don't blame you one bit." Rose folded her arms across her chest and propped up the file cabinet. The ladies were definitely here for the duration.

Katie settled at her desk and unfolded her newspaper. "Polly brought in her granddaughter, Hannah," Katie said.

"Oh, she's a cutie-pie," Edie said. "And so well behaved."

"Nice manners, too," Rose chimed in. "But Polly treats that child so badly."

"Just like she treats everyone else," Edie said.

"Does Polly bring Hannah in often?" Katie asked, idly turning to the local section of the paper. Had Hartsfield read about Barbie there?

"Almost every day," Edie said, and sipped her coffee.

Katie frowned. "I've never seen her before today."

"Polly makes her sit in a little rocker in Joan MacDonald's booth," Edie said. "She's as good as gold. I've seen her sit still for close to an hour. Sometimes Hannah pretends to read, but often she has to sit there with nothing to do. It's almost like a punishment."

Katie leaned back in her own chair. "I haven't seen any myself, but Polly must have some good qualities."

"I heard she used to be very active in her church," Rose said. "But so many of the parishioners complained about her bossy ways that they had to ask her to stop volunteering."

"She buys a lot of old clothes at yard sales, repairs them, and gives them to Goodwill and other charities," Edie said.

"That's nice," Katie said.

"I'll bet she only does it so she can take a tax deduction," Edie muttered.

"Come on. Nobody is as bad as we all think Polly is. You've known her the longest, Rose. What do you know about her?"

Rose picked up her cup and took a sip. "She's only ever been an acquaintance." Her brow furrowed as she concentrated. "Polly's garden is the nicest one in all of McKinlay Mill. She must have twenty or thirty varieties of roses."

Katie barely heard her as she scanned the paper's side columns looking for mention of Barbie Gordon's death, but there was none. However, a boxed advertisement on page 4B drew her attention. "Hey, Burt Donahue's weekly auction is tonight in Parma. He's the guy who owned the Webster mansion when Heather disappeared," she said, for Edie's benefit. "Do you want to go, Rose?"

"I'd love to. But don't you need to pack for your move?"

Katie shook her head. "I'm practically finished. I've just got this wedding stuff hanging over me—and there's not much I can do about it in the evening. And since Andy works every night—I'm always free."

"Oh, goody," Rose said.

"Would you like to come?" Katie asked Edie.

The woman shook her head. "I always get suckered in and buy something dumb, like an old moth-eaten antelope head. Nope, you girls can have all the fun."

"We're not going for fun," Katie assured her. "If Donahue can tell us who rented that front apartment, we might be able to trace him or her down and find out who killed Heather."

"Won't the cops already have that information?" Edie asked.

"Maybe," Katie said. "But Detective Davenport isn't likely to tell us what he knows. Although he may have stepped up his investigation since Barbie Gordon turned up dead yesterday. It's likely Barbie knew a lot more than she told either of us."

"Do you really think she was murdered?" Rose asked, anxiety tingeing her voice.

"She knew Heather. And she seemed anxious to tell me what she knew. If only she hadn't been spooked at the diner the other night."

"You spoke to Barbie again?" Rose asked.

"Just for a few minutes. Unforunately, she didn't tell me anything that helped."

Edie polished off the last of her coffee. "You girls have fun playing Sherlock Holmes and Watson. I'll stick with retail."

With her cup in hand, Edie headed out the office door and into the vendors' lounge.

Katie glanced back down at the newsprint ad. Would Donahue have kept records for a business he no longer operated? And if not, would he remember his tenants from two decades past? What if Barbie had been one of them?

Rose cleared her throat, reminding Katie she was still in the office. "Are you thinking about Barbie?"

Katie nodded. "She might have known what happened to Heather and was afraid to tell anyone."

Rose's lips pursed, her expression hardening. "And took that information with her to her grave."

"If she'd told what she knew, she might still be alive. She left behind a daughter and a granddaughter."

"I feel bad for them—but I feel worse for my sister and brother-in-law. They died not knowing what happened to their child. Barbie could've eased their pain." Rose moved toward the door, her eyes filling with tears. "And mine."

Eleven

Katie closed her computer file and sat back, staring at the screen. Checking Artisans Alley's financial spreadsheets had become a daily obsession. At least for the month to date, they were in the black. But paying off the previous owner's debts . . . well, she had a five-year plan. And it might not take that long . . . *if* she won the lottery.

"Penny for your thoughts," came a voice from the doorway. A smiling Seth Landers stood poised at her office threshold.

"I can use the money." Katie glanced at her watch. "What are you doing here at this time of day? Playing hooky?"

"My client settled before the judge could even bang his gavel, so I'm sprung for an hour or so. How would you like to go for an early lunch?"

"I'd love to, but we're shorthanded today, and I have to cover the register when Rose goes to lunch."

"Too bad the pizza place doesn't open until four."

"Don't tell Andy, but I'm about pizza'd out," Katie admitted.

Seth's smile always made her feel better. He sat down on her visitor's chair and grabbed a wrapped candy from the jar on her desk. "Per my promise, this morning I finally got ahold of a friend of mine in the Sheriff's Office."

Katie sat up straighter. "And?"

"Twenty-two years ago, a rookie deputy by the name of Raymond Davenport took a missing persons report on a young woman here in McKinlay Mill. It was the deputy's opinion that she voluntarily left the area to pursue her career dreams." He popped the peppermint into his mouth.

"And that woman just happened to be"—Katie patted her leg in a poor imitation of a drumroll—"Heather Winston."

Seth winked, sketching an imaginary stroke in the air. "Got it in one."

"No wonder the detective's so testy about anyone encroaching on his territory. He blew off Heather's disappearance and now she's come back to haunt him."

"Literally," Seth said. "Have you found out anything new since yesterday?"

"Yesterday?" she asked.

"Didn't you read the newspaper this morning?" Seth grabbed the stack on the corner of her desk.

"Just the local section. Why?" Katie asked.

Seth unfolded the front page and pointed to a picture of Rose and Katie taken at the press conference the day before.

"Oh no," Katie groaned. "Look at my hair!"

"Even worse, I'll bet Heather's ex is really pissed at you for ruining his big homecoming."

"Pissed enough to come after me?" she asked.

"It was stupid of Jeremy to lie about knowing Heather. And if he killed her . . ." Seth's voice trailed off. "And I'll bet you annoyed Detective Davenport—again—by showing him up and asking the right questions of the right person."

"Swell. But at least he now has a suspect in Heather's disappearance and murder. I doubt he would've put two and two together if Rose and I hadn't pointed him in the right direction."

Seth reached out to touch Katie's arm, his expression sobering. "Katie, please don't poke into this anymore. I know you want to help, but I don't want you—or Rose—to get hurt."

"Oh, Seth, don't be silly. We're just asking questions."

"Yes—and probably disturbing a snake's nest."

Katie frowned. "You'll have to come up with something better than that to deter me."

"Okay, Barbie Gordon died under suspicious circumstances. You were seen talking to her at the diner the night before she died."

"How do you know?"

"Because I saw you there. And if I could see you, so could—and probably did—others."

"But you left the restaurant before she arrived."

"Rose forgot her purse. I retrieved it for her just as Barbie sat down. I was almost out the door when you returned."

Katie frowned. "Did you happen to see a stranger, a tall man with a ponytail and a bushy mustache?"

Seth frowned. "I don't think so. Why?"

"One of Rick Jeremy's entourage looked very familiar to me. I thought he might be the one who frightened Barbie at Del's the other night. She flew out the back door in a panic. This was after she'd told me someone had threatened her—and her little granddaughter."

Seth shook his head.

"Did you recognize anyone at the diner?" Katie asked.

Seth frowned. "A couple of my clients. Some of your vendors. Nobody out of the ordinary."

Katie chewed at her bottom lip. "I know I've seen that guy with the ponytail. His face was so familiar."

Seth patted her hand. "It'll come to you. In the meantime, will you at least consider what I said?"

Katie blinked, all wide-eyed innocence.

Seth sighed in defeat. "All right. In the meantime, how about I get a quart of soup and a couple of egg rolls from the Chinese takeout? Then we can still have lunch together."

Katie tried without success to stifle a smile. "Make it hot and sour, and you've got a deal."

~~~~~~~

The cash drawer popped open and Katie scooped up a five, two ones, three quarters, and a penny. "Your change is seven dollars and seventy-six cents. And thank you for shopping at Artisans Alley."

The elderly woman gave her a faint smile, collected her bag of tissue-swaddled stained glass sun catchers, and headed for the exit. Crissy Hunter, McKinlay Mill's buff, forty-something letter carrier, passed her. She held a stack of envelopes and a small brown-paper-wrapped box. "Mail call," she said, and paused to lean against the counter.

"Is it my imagination, or are you wearing shorts?" Katie asked.

Like a diva, Crissy stood back, raised her arms, and turned in a circle to model her uniform. "It's regulation standard. But isn't the red piping down the seam just darling?"

"Yes, but it's still only April—and it's cold out! Aren't you jumping the gun?"

"Summer can't come soon enough for me. I've already started tanning. I'll be a goddess by June."

Katie rolled her eyes but refrained from commenting, let alone giving Crissy a lecture on the increased cancer risk of using tanning booths.

"It looks like mostly bills today," Crissy said, handing Katie the mail. "Not that I pay attention to such things."

Katie shuffled through the envelopes before turning her attention to the small box.

"No return address—hand-canceled in Rochester," Crissy said.

Katie looked up at her. "Not that you noticed."

Crissy smiled and turned on her heel. "See you tomorrow," she called as she headed for the exit, already sorting through her leather mail pouch for the next address's mail.

Katie worked at the tape sealing one end of the box. Peeling it back, she unwrapped the package—a videotape. She slipped it from its cardboard case, but there was no note inside. She examined the wrapping. Block letters, addressed to her personally, with no hint of who the sender might have been. She set it aside to study the old beta-formatted videotape. It did not appear to be professionally recorded, and had no label—although a gummy residue stuck to where one had been until recently.

She was still turning the tape over in her hands when Rose and Edie returned from their lunch break. "Hey, I haven't seen one of those in years," Edie said.

"My first video machine was a Betamax," Rose chimed in, motioning Katie aside and resuming her post at the cash register. "A much better picture than VHS, if you ask me— almost DVD quality. Where'd you get it?"

"It came in today's mail. Do you still have your old beta machine?"

"Oh, no. It died years ago. They didn't make them anymore so I had to replace all my tapes. And now they have DVD players. Before we know it, Blu-ray will eclipse DVD and I'll have to replace everything once again. I never seem to catch up."

"Who do you think sent it?" Edie asked.

"I have no idea," Katie said. She stared at the tape. "I wonder . . ."

"Wonder what?" Rose asked.

"Beta machines weren't as popular, but were still being

used when Jeremy Richards was a film student at the university."

"So?" Edie asked.

"So what if his early work was done on video—not film? It's a lot cheaper."

"Do you think this could be one of his student films?" Rose asked.

"Who knows. We'd have to watch it to see."

Rose didn't look convinced. "Why would someone send it to you?"

"Maybe somebody in Jeremy's entourage sent it," Katie suggested, thinking about the man with the ponytail. "But why?"

"That press conference was only yesterday. Somebody sent that tape out awful quick," Edie said.

"Katie's name was in the paper on Tuesday," Rose said. "In the story about finding Heather's—" She paused, her voice catching. "About finding Heather."

Katie felt a pang of sadness for her friend as Rose pulled a handkerchief from the sleeve of her blouse, blew her nose, and dabbed at her damp eyes. "I'm sorry. Heather's been dead for twenty-two years. I shouldn't fall apart every time I say her name."

Katie stepped closer and touched her friend's hand. "There's no time limit on grief, Rose. If you want to cry, you go right ahead."

Instead, a wan, grateful smile crept across Rose's pale lips.

"Maybe you can find a place to rent a machine," Edie said, which seemed to distract Rose from her grief.

"I can sure try."

"But first, we'd better pin that dress up. Are you doing anything now?" Edie asked.

Katie shook her head.

"I'll meet you in the vendors' lounge," Edie said, and paused to pat Rose's shoulder before she trotted off.

"Are you okay, Rose?"

She nodded. "You go ahead. I'll be fine."

Katie, too, patted Rose's shoulder and headed for her office. She found Edie standing over her desk, perusing the list of official duties of a bridesmaid. "Are they kidding? 'Take care of the emotional needs of the bride. Help her in any way you can to avoid the pre-wedding jitters'?" She shook her head in disgust. "I say slap Gilda upside the head and tell her to get on with it."

Katie refrained from saying so, but she felt exactly the same way. Or in retrospect, did she just feel cheated that she'd let Chad talk her out of some kind of celebration after their own wedding. After their marriage at city hall, they'd gone out to lunch. Their honeymoon was a weekend at their apartment, drinking champagne and eating cheese and grapes while making more plans for the English Ivy Inn on Victoria Square. They'd been so focused on that one aspect of their married lives that when Chad had impulsively taken their savings and invested it in Artisans Alley, their marriage had foundered.

Katie didn't like to dwell on that. But if she was honest with herself, a day didn't go by that she didn't think about her dream, and despite the reality of her situation, she still one day hoped to own that crumbling piece of property and bring it back to life.

Edie placed the list back on the top of the desk. "Glad it's you and not me who's got all that work to do."

"You've already done so much. And now we've got to deal with this." Katie indicated the dress still hanging from her file cabinet's drawer pull. "This"—she shuddered— "dress seems to have been made for a basketball player. It comes down to my ankles, and I don't think it's even supposed to be a tea-length dress.

"Why don't you go into the ladies' room and change into it. I'll get my sewing box and meet you in the vendors' lounge in five minutes," Edie said, and scooted out the door.

Katie looked at the purple horror and sighed.

Five minutes later she met Edie, removed her shoes, and first climbed onto a chair. Edie lent a hand and she moved to stand in the center of the vendors' lounge table.

"Turn around," Edie ordered, and Katie made a three-hundred-and-sixty-degree turn. Edie shook her head. "That is the most repulsive dress I have ever seen. And sleeveless at this time of year?"

"I can't imagine what Gilda was thinking when she picked it out," Katie said, grateful there was no full-length mirror in the lounge. Worse, she was going to have to wear this monstrosity out in public.

"Maybe the original owner has hot flashes. She'd keep cool in this number," Edie said.

"Well, I'm stuck with it. I'm just glad I'll only have to wear it for a few hours and hope that Gilda doesn't plaster her wedding pictures on any social networking websites."

Edie opened her sewing basket, withdrawing a little strawberry-shaped pincushion. "Let's get started," she said, and lifted the hem of the dress. "How short do you want this?"

Katie shrugged. "Just under the knee, I guess."

Edie nodded. "Maybe I can fashion some kind of shawl for you out of what we cut off. You're going to need something to keep warm."

Edie worked at a steady pace, using a measuring tape and leaving a trail of silver pins to mark the new hemline in the folds of fluffy chiffon.

They'd been at it for about ten minutes, and Katie's back was beginning to ache when she saw Polly standing in the doorway. The older woman straightened indignantly. Did she think she was the only vendor in Artisans Alley who could wield a needle and thread?

"I hope you're going to disinfect that table," she huffed. "Your feet are probably full of germs, and many of us eat our lunches there."

"Of course we're going to wash the table, Polly," Katie said, quelling the urge to leap down and strangle the woman.

Polly moved closer to inspect Edie's work, walking around the table as though a nasty smell filled the air. She sniffed. "It's crooked," she said of the pins holding up the dress's new hemline.

With a mouth full of pins, Edie didn't bother to reply and concentrated on her work as Polly stalked over to the counter to pour herself a cup of coffee before leaving the lounge.

"That woman," Edie mumbled.

"Ignore her. I'm sure she just said that to be spiteful," Katie said.

Edie took the pins from her mouth, stabbing them into her pincushion. "All done." She offered her hand and steadied Katie as she made her way down from the table via the chair to the floor.

"I hate to push, Edie, but when do you think you can have this ready for me?"

Edie shrugged. "A couple of days. By the end of the weekend, at least."

"You're a lifesaver."

"Eh, it keeps me busy," she said, and seemed to deflate once again. Polly's presence always had that effect on her. It had the same effect on Katie, too.

"I'd better get out of this dress and back into my real clothes. I'll leave it hanging on my file cabinet and you can pick it up before you leave for the day, if that's okay."

Edie kept looking at the open doorway leading to Artisans Alley's main showroom.

"Edie?" Katie prompted.

"Oh, yeah. Sure."

A wave of pity coursed through Katie. Edie had lost a lot of her confidence these last few weeks, while Polly had morphed into the sourest, most disagreeable woman Katie had ever met.

She frowned. Perhaps her pity was misdirected. She ought to pity Polly more than Edie. What had Clarence the angel told George Bailey at the end of *It's a Wonderful Life*? No man—or woman—was a failure who has friends.

Right about then, Katie felt quite successful.

~~~~~~

Katie hit the enter key on her computer, e-mailing Gilda the prototype bridal shower invitation for her approval. She'd chosen Monday night for the event, as it seemed more of the participants could be free on that day and at that time. And what a nightmare it had been calling and asking for input. After that, she'd hit the phone book and started calling video stores, looking to rent a Betamax machine.

It was slow going. She'd decided against calling the big national chains, instead concentrating on mom-and-pop stores. Most of them seemed to specialize in "adult" features, and none of them had beta video machines to rent. Although some stores still rented out the tapes, none would give out their clients' names—not that she wanted to contact anyone with that kind of taste in entertainment; she just wanted to rent or borrow a machine.

Katie glanced at the tape sitting on her desk. Obviously someone had meant for her to watch it, but why hadn't they transferred the images to a more common format? A stall tactic perhaps? Maybe whoever sent it wanted Heather's killer exposed—but not too quickly. Could it be the same person who left the pillbox necklace draped around Heather's neck when she'd been sealed behind the plasterboard wall?

Katie considered calling Detective Davenport about the tape. He could probably find a beta machine in no time flat—but then she'd never get to see what was on it. And who said this had anything to do with Heather's death anyway?

That decided, she turned her attention to the wall clock. It was time to give the twenty-minute warning that Artisans

Alley was about to close. She pushed the legal pad aside, got up, and headed for the cash registers at the front of the store.

Rose was handling a sale, with Edie wrapping and bagging the customer's purchases. The other cash desk was empty.

"Where are Anne and Joan?" Katie asked.

"They had to leave about a half hour ago," Edie said, pulling a length of tape from the dispenser and sticking it down on a piece of buff-colored wrapping paper.

Katie stepped closer, bending so only Edie could hear her. "If you're here, who's been walking security?"

Edie frowned guiltily. "Nobody. I guess we should've called you to come up and help. But there's hardly anybody here. It's been quiet as the grave."

Rose, who evidently *could* hear them, shot Edie a sharp glance over her shoulder. Edie blushed, and focused her attention on the blown-glass ornaments before her.

Katie crossed to the telephone, punched the public address button, and gave her canned speech. "Thank you for shopping with us at Artisans Alley. We'll be closing in"— she glanced at her watch—"eighteen minutes. Please bring your purchases to the front desk. Thank you."

As anticipated, several customers sidled up to the cash register. Katie reopened register two, handling a few of them herself, taking the money and wrapping the items. In no time at all it was four fifty-five and the lines of customers had thinned. Katie looked up to see Polly Bremerton enter through Artisans Alley's main door as several customers exited. Polly glared at Edie before she headed up the stairs toward her booth.

Rose leaned over the counter, looking down the aisle. "I don't see anyone else. I guess we're done for today."

Katie opened the cash drawer and withdrew the stack of bills from the rightmost partition, thumbing through the stack of ones, making sure they were all going the same direction. "Why does Polly come in so often? Surely she doesn't sell enough that her booth needs attending twice a day."

Rose had already started emptying her till and was separating checks from credit card receipts. "She likes to make sure it's tidy at the end of the day, and says it gives her an idea of what she needs to bring in to restock the next morning."

"If you ask me, it seems more like she hasn't got enough to do to fill her days," Edie said.

Katie smiled. Edie was another vendor who came in daily and often worked four or five days more than the required two days per month, whereas it was difficult to get Polly to walk her scheduled security detail. She seemed to hover around her own booth, which couldn't have been good for her sales. And she'd railed against learning how to use the register, saying it was menial work.

"Well, let's get her out of here," Rose said, stacking the cash and rubber banding it. "The auction preview starts in an hour, and I want to have a good look at everything before the bidding starts."

"Don't we even get time to eat?" Katie asked.

"They have all kinds of food there," Rose said. "That is, if you don't mind pizza and greasy hamburgers."

"Oh, swell," Katie said, cringing at the thought of yet more cheese and pepperoni.

Katie emptied the rest of her own cash drawer. A hoarse scream cut the air. She looked up toward the stairs. "What the heck was that?"

A flushed Polly suddenly appeared at the top. "It's horrible," she cried, her voice rising. "It's just horrible."

Katie scooted from behind the cash desk and handed Rose the wad of cash, checks, and other receipts. "Please finish cashing out. I'll go see what this is all about. Edie, could you lock up?"

Both women nodded as Katie jogged to the staircase, then took the steps two at a time.

Frightened and pale, Polly stood there, wringing her hands, not looking at all like the woman in charge that Katie was used to seeing. "How could someone do this? Why would someone do this to me?"

"Do what?" Katie asked.

"Come and see!" Polly waited and led the way, and Katie, with shorter legs, had a hard time keeping up. Polly abruptly halted, turned her face away, and pointed toward her booth.

Katie gasped. Five of Polly's handcrafted dolls, looking vulnerable with their clothes removed, hung from the ceiling on lengths of cord with tiny nooses around their little wooden necks.

Twelve

Katie stared at the incongruous sight. The once-charming painted smiles on the dolls' carved faces now looked macabre. She did a quick recon of Polly's booth. The locked cabinet's glass door had been smashed.

"I've taken all the harassment I intend to," Polly said, her nostrils flaring with each snorting exhalation.

"You don't know it was Edie," Katie stated.

"Who else could it be?"

"Edie's been working on the cash desk with Rose for the last hour."

"She could have done this earlier. Wasn't she supposed to be walking security today?"

Katie blinked but then remembered the worksheet she placed on cash desk one every day before opening, so that everyone who worked would know their assigned task. "Yes, but—"

"I insist you do something about that woman—*now!*"

Katie didn't know how to respond. Instead, she turned

and walked back to the stairs. She was met by Rose and Edie at the bottom.

"What is it?" Rose asked, her eyes shadowed with worry.

Katie spoke to Edie. "Would you take the day's receipts and wait for me in my office?"

Edie hesitated, then bobbed her head, taking flight like a frightened sparrow.

"Rose, there's broken glass in Polly's booth. Would you get the vacuum cleaner and help her clean up? I'll explain everything later. And don't pay attention to a word she says."

Rose looked panicked. "Is she trying to get Edie in trouble again?"

"I'm afraid so."

Rose nodded and hurried up the stairs.

Katie swung around the banister and threaded through the warren of booths, aiming for the back of the first floor. She paused to survey booth fifty-six, taking note of its size, the placement of electrical outlets, and the lighting, before she turned to start back for her office.

Edie still clutched the wad of cash and checks from the cash desks. She stopped pacing as Katie entered the confined room.

"I don't know what happened upstairs, but please believe me, I didn't do it!" Edie cried.

Katie studied Edie's taut face and her gray eyes, dark with fear. "Please sit," she said, motioning Edie into her shabby guest chair.

With trembling hands, Edie handed Katie the money and perched on the edge of her seat.

Katie stuffed the day's receipts into the top-right desk drawer before turning to Edie. "This nonsense between you and Polly has gone on long enough. I have to put a stop to it."

"But, Katie—"

"I've decided for the sake of peace and harmony that one of you has to—"

"Not leave," Edie protested, her voice breaking into a sob.

"No, move. Debbie Weston will be vacating her booth on Monday. Do you think you could move right in?"

Edie gaped, her eyes widening with surprise. "Me? Move downstairs? But, other people have been on the list much longer. If I move to another booth, won't you get a lot of flack from the vendors who've been waiting longer than me?"

"I'll explain the situation to anyone who objects. If I have to, I'll placate them with a week of free rent." She softened her voice, leaning closer. "But let's not spread word of that around."

With an awkward lurch, Edie captured Katie in a hug. Katie patted her back, catching the scent of cologne— violets? "I'll help you move your stock whenever you're ready," she said.

Edie pulled back. "But Monday's your only day off— and you've got that bridal shower to take care of."

"I'm always here anyway." *And will have to move more of my own boxes to Artisans Alley for storage,* she mentally amended. "And since the shower will be held here, too, it's a win-win situation."

Edie cleared her throat and straightened. "It seems like all you do lately is take care of Rose and me. I'm sorry to be such a burden."

Katie stood. "You're not a burden. You and Rose are my friends. Now, why don't you go look at Debbie's booth to give yourself an idea of how you want to set it up."

"But Rose is eager to go to the auction," Edie said, sounding anxious once again.

"Another five or ten minutes won't matter that much. Meanwhile, I'll go back upstairs and try to pacify Polly."

Edie frowned. "That's a fate worse than death."

She trotted off, but Katie hung back, locking the day's receipts in the safe. She'd deal with it in the morning.

By the time she made it back to Polly's booth, the dolls had been removed and the glass had been cleaned up. A tight-lipped Rose grabbed the vacuum cleaner and made a hasty retreat.

Polly brandished a doll in one hand and shook it under Katie's nose. "My property's been defaced. All the dolls' clothes are missing. I demand restitution."

Much as she knew she had to play diplomat, Katie was tempted to just toss the woman out on her ear. "As far as we know," she began, choosing her words carefully, "the clothes were stolen by whoever . . . whoever did this. You're free to file a report with the Sheriff's Office and your insurance company."

"I'm not insured," Polly snapped.

Neither were most of the other vendors, Katie knew, as the yearly premiums were likely to exceed their total profits. "I'm very sorry this happened, Polly, but I don't believe anyone here at Artisans Alley is to blame."

"You're just saying that to protect Edie Silver because she's your *friend*." She made that final word sound like an insult.

"Is there a possibility someone outside Artisans Alley is angry at you?" Katie asked.

Polly froze. Her eyes bulged and a blush colored her cheeks. For a moment Katie was sure Polly would explode, but then she looked away.

"No. There's no one I can think of who'd—" But her voice faltered. Polly abruptly turned, stuffing the doll into a canvas bag. She slammed the cabinet door shut. Without the weight of the glass, it bounced open again. Without another word, she stalked off in the direction of the stairs.

Katie lagged behind, glancing up at the timbered joists. The cord nooses had been hung from nails pounded into the low ceiling at irregular intervals. Edie was much too short to do it without a ladder. Six-foot Polly, on the other hand . . .

It would be just like Polly to set Edie up for a fall.

Katie had meant to tell Polly that Edie would vacate her booth within days, but instead she'd chickened out. She'd had enough of the woman for one day.

By the time she'd returned to the main showroom, Polly was gone, and the door to the vendor entrance was wide open to the cold April breeze.

~~~~~~

Rose was in a talkative mood as Katie drove them to Donahue's auction house. "She reamed me, as the kids would say."

Katie tore her gaze from the road to throw a surprised look at Rose for her choice of words. "When was this?"

"Right after you spoke to her. I guess you were talking to Edie in your office. According to Polly, there's no fouler demon on earth than Edie Silver. I had to bite my tongue to keep from giving her a piece of my mind. I was so glad when you showed up and I didn't have to listen to her vicious ranting another second."

"I'm sorry you had to take that abuse. Hopefully the tension will lessen once Edie takes Debbie Weston's booth."

"Debbie's leaving?" Rose asked, surprised.

"She's just not earning enough money to make staying at Artisans Alley worthwhile."

Rose sighed. "I feel bad for Debbie—I always liked her—but I'm glad Edie will get to move. What with everything else, Edie's been having problems with her knees. Climbing all those steps doesn't help."

Katie's stomach growled, and she tightened her grip on the steering wheel. "You did say pizza and burgers would be available at the auction house, right?"

"Oh, sure. Coffee, doughnuts, cookies, and sometimes

ice cream, too. It's not healthy food, but it'll take the edge off. Oh, it's just up ahead on the right."

Donahue's Auction Barn wasn't the haystack-shaped wooden structure Katie had imagined. Instead, the squat, concrete-block building looked like it might have started out as a gas station half a century before. Multiple extensions had been added on in every direction in the decades since. The parking lot was clogged with U-Hauls, minivans, and pickups, and Katie ended up leaving her Focus parked on the roadside just north of the building.

Rose practically jumped from the car, the spring in her step conveying her excitement. Katie wasn't sure if it was the thought of speaking to Donahue or the auction itself that had Rose all riled up. Katie's immediate concern was finding something halfway palatable to eat.

Rose held the heavy glass door for Katie. A whoosh of warm air, laden with the stench of stale cooking oil, swamped Katie, making her stomach roil. Maybe she wasn't so anxious to eat from the bill of fare after all.

The hubbub of scores of people talking lent the vast space a carnival atmosphere, and Katie's own spirit of adventure kicked into high gear. Hundreds of cardboard boxes littered tables and the floor. Furniture in every style imaginable crowded the area in front of parallel rows of scuffed wooden folding chairs.

Rose clasped her hands together, reminding Katie of a child in a toy shop. "I love the thrill of the hunt. You never know what treasures you'll find."

Katie frowned. "We're here to uncover clues about Heather's murder, remember?"

Rose seemed to shrink. "I've been trying not to think about it. Burt may not remember anything about those days. Or he might *choose* not to remember. He can be ornery when he wants to be—like a big bully." She gazed around the room. "Burt isn't the auctioneer, so it might be best to wait until the auction starts before we try to talk to him. He usually stays on the floor, but sometimes you can find him in his office making arrangements to take on new merchandise for future sales." Her gaze darted around the room. "I think I'll take a peek at what's on offer tonight. Do you mind?"

"Not at all."

Rose glanced around before she homed in on a table covered in rhinestone jewelry. Katie watched as Rose examined a sparkling piece or two. Looking small and stooped, with her shoulders rounded, Rose looked every bit her seventy-five years.

Katie spied a battered, rust-speckled sign hanging from the ceiling over in the corner—Joe's Java.

The coffee was strong and hot—French roast? She settled for a stale fried cake, as the sight of the grill's greasy buildup made her shudder. A trip to McDonald's—where the kitchen conditions weren't as visible—was definitely on the agenda for later that evening.

Katie wandered the aisles, sipping coffee and nibbling her napkin-wrapped doughnut as she took in the box lots of miscellaneous odds and ends. It seemed like half of Artisans Alley's vendors had turned up, and she was pleased to find she could greet them all by name.

"Did you sign in?" asked a voice from behind her.

Katie turned to find Vance Ingram. "What for?"

"You can't bid if you don't have a card," Vance said, waving his own placard with the number one hundred seventy-four stamped in red ink.

Minutes later, Katie had given her tax-exempt number and business information to a gray-haired woman with saggy jowls, and had received her own bidding card. Not that she planned to use it. Katie's gaze lingered for a moment on the woman's name tag: Sylvia Donahue. She looked far too old to be the owner's wife. Could she perhaps be his mother?

"So this is your first auction, huh?" Vance asked.

Katie nodded. "I always had night classes, so my husband, Chad, would go to auctions alone. He was a regular at these things."

"I remember seeing him here," Vance said.

"He had a good eye. We'd discuss what we wanted to buy for the English Ivy Inn, and he would get it." She sighed. "I suppose I should arrange with the owner to sell it all for me—it's not doing me any good in storage. But there's no way I'll ever be able to afford to open my own B and B."

"Don't be so sure," Vance said and winked at her. "You have a way of making good things happen."

Katie blushed, too embarrassed to acknowledge the compliment. "Have you already looked at everything?" she asked, changing the subject.

Vance nodded. "I got here right at five o'clock. I just hope the pieces I want come up early. There's a movie I want to see on TV later tonight. Although Janey will record it for me if I'm late."

That was just the opening Katie had been hoping for. "You wouldn't happen to have an old Betamax video player, would you?"

Vance frowned. "Maybe down in the basement. What a dinosaur. It weighed a ton—not like the DVD players of today."

"Do you think it still works?"

"I dunno. Maybe. Why?"

Katie brightened and briefly explained about the videotape that had arrived in the afternoon mail.

Vance shrugged. "I'll haul it up and bring it into Artisans Alley in the morning."

"Thanks."

Rose strode toward them like a woman on a mission. "Hi, Vance. They're just about to start."

He nodded a hello, but his attention was focused on the front of the room where a crowd had begun to gather.

"Do you want to get a seat up front?" Katie asked Rose.

"The lots I'm interested in won't come up for at least an hour."

"I'm going to bid on that Victorian bedroom set. See you later, ladies." Vance gave them a quick salute before leaving.

The first item for sale was a marble-topped chestnut commode. Katie watched the bidders raise their cards, amused at the auctioneer's rolling babble as he pitched for higher prices. It sold for ninety-five dollars. "A bargain," Rose declared.

A tall, heavyset man in a dark Old Navy sweatshirt, whose jeans hung low under a beer gut, watched from the edge of the crowd. Rose gave Katie a nudge. "That's Burt Donahue."

"Do you think it's too soon to try to talk to him?"

Rose shrugged. "It can't hurt to try."

They edged their way down the side aisle, waiting until an intricately carved sideboard sold for fifteen hundred. Before they could speak, the auctioneer had already gone on to the next item. "Does it always go this fast?" Katie asked.

"They have over four hundred items to sell tonight. It's better if your stuff goes on the block early. Come the finish, they practically have to give it away."

Katie and Rose watched another three or four items sell before Rose edged close enough to tap Donahue on the shoulder.

"Hey, Rose," he said, barely tearing his gaze from the action up front.

"Burt, I'd like you to meet Katie Bonner. She owns and manages Artisans Alley in McKinlay Mill."

Donahue gave them a sideways glance, his eyebrows rising as a smile lit his face. "Some of your vendors are my best customers," he said, shoving a calloused hand in her direction.

Katie clasped it but noted that Donahue's attention was divided between her and the iron bedstead up on the block.

"Mr. Donahue, do you have a few minutes? We'd like to talk to you about—"

"Heather Winston," he finished for her, his expression going grim.

"Why, yes," Katie said, surprised.

Donahue held up a hand, indicating the back of the room. "It's too noisy here. We'd better go to my office." He led the way.

"He must've spoken to Detective Davenport," Katie told Rose, as they struggled to keep up with Donahue's longer strides. She noticed Sylvia staring at them as they entered the office.

Donahue's headquarters was even more cluttered than Katie's office had been the day she took over Artisans Alley. Stacks of files teetered and spilled around the edges of the cramped room where three army surplus file cabinets could no longer contain them. A large, dry-wipe board held a calendar filled with notations in various colored inks. Newspaper clippings, flyers, and a large map of the area covered the other walls, almost obliterating a framed photo of a gown-clad graduate. Donahue's son? The room's lack of windows made Katie feel claustrophobic once Donahue had shut the door. He ushered them into metal folding chairs before taking his own.

"I already talked to the police," Donahue began. "I don't remember who I rented the place to, and I didn't keep the records past seven years, which is all that the IRS demands. I really don't know what else I can tell you."

Then why had Donahue brought them to his office to talk? Was he worried about bad publicity for the auction house? That didn't seem likely.

Katie shot a look in Rose's direction. "Were you aware that Heather was Rose's niece?"

"Not until the detective told me. Sorry, Rose."

He didn't sound it.

"Thank you. We were hoping you might know something. Heather was murdered. I *have* to find out who killed her."

"Is there anything you remember about that time? There were renovations going on at the mansion," Katie prompted.

Donahue tipped back in his office chair, lacing his fingers and leaning his head back against them, then blew out a breath through puffed cheeks. "I hired a couple of college kids to do the work. One of 'em had a father in the construction business. I figured he probably knew more about drywall than me, but they did a lousy job. I had to call in professionals to finish the work. That old house was nothing but a money pit."

Katie had been bluffing her knowledge of the renovations, but it had seemed a reasonable conclusion and she'd hit pay dirt. "Do you remember the names of the boys?"

Donahue shook his head. His belly jiggled, as did the NRA buckle strapped around it.

"Could one of them have been Rick Jeremy?"

"The famous movie director?" Donahue asked. "I heard on the news that he was in town."

"He was known as Jeremy Richards back then. He was also Heather's boyfriend at the time of her death."

"I don't remember the names of the kids I hired, but I'm pretty sure Jeremy wasn't one of them."

"Do you remember the name of the boy's father's construction company?" Rose asked.

Donahue picked at his bottom front teeth with a thumbnail. "We're talking over twenty years ago, ladies. It wasn't important then—why would I remember it now?"

"Anything you might come up with could help us bring Heather's killer to justice," Rose insisted. "Please, Burt, please try and remember."

"I'm sorry, Rose, I just *don't*." Donahue got up from his seat, as abrupt a dismissal as Katie had ever received.

Katie stood, rummaged in her purse, and located one of her business cards. "If you remember anything, please give me a call."

Donahue took it from her and placed it on top of the messy desk. "Sure thing."

Katie gazed down at the cluttered work space, knowing it would soon swallow the card. "Thank you for talking with us. C'mon, Rose."

Rose muttered a thank-you and followed Katie back to the main auction hall. The auctioneer was looking for another ten dollars for an oak rolltop desk but was disappointed when no other bids came through. "Sold, for one hundred and fifty dollars."

"Do you want to stay?" Katie asked Rose.

"My box lot of rhinestones hasn't come up yet. Not that I really want to give Burt another nickel of my money. But I *am* in business, and he only gets a cut of the profits."

"That's the spirit," Katie said, and patted her friend's shoulder.

"Do you think he was lying about Heather?" Rose asked.

"The fact that he wanted to get rid of us so fast says a lot. But we can't make him talk. We'll just have to find another way to get the information we need."

"Such as?"

"I don't know. I'll have to think about it." Katie watched the auctioneer stroll over to a walnut armoire. "The woman up front who took my tax number—"

"Sylvia?" Rose prompted.

"Yeah. Is she Donahue's mother?"

Rose shook her head. "She's his wife. But I think she's at least five or six years older than him. And she looks it, too."

"She's not the most cheerful woman I've ever met."

"She had a career before Burt made her quit to help run the auction house. That made her kind of bitter."

"What kind of career?"

Rose nodded. "She was an RN. They say she started as an army nurse, assigned to a MASH unit—just like on the old TV show, only she was in Vietnam. I guess she loved it."

"Being a nurse or being in the army?"

"Both. Come on, let's go sit up front," Rose said, and grasped Katie's elbow.

They wormed their way up to a couple of empty seats in the third row as the last of the furniture up front was being hauled away.

"Let's pick up the pace—we've got two hundred box lots to get rid of," the auctioneer said. "This first is a bunch of old toys—must be six or seven." He grabbed something at random, holding it over his head. "Lookin' for a dollar, now-a-dollar, now-a-dollar—who'll gimme two, gimme two, gimme two?"

The auctioneer waved the doll around by its cloth body.

Katie gasped and clutched Rose's arm. "Hey, that's one of Polly's dolls!"

Thirteen

The hypnotic sound of the auctioneer's voice was all that registered in Katie's startled brain. "Four-gimme-four—gimme-four—" he called.

"Four!" Katie blurted, and stood to wave.

Heads turned in her direction.

"You're supposed to raise your card," Rose said.

Katie looked around her in panic. "I don't know what I did with it!"

Rose raised her own card, giving the auctioneer a nod.

"Five-gimme-five-gimme-five—"

Katie looked for the other bidders, but it was hard to see with so many bodies jammed into the sales area.

"Ten-gimme-ten-gimme-ten—"

"Who's bidding against us?" Katie asked anxiously, glancing around them.

"Fifteen—fifteen—fifteen—"

"Do you want it?" Rose asked.

"Yes!"

Rose calmly raised her card.

Within a minute, the bids skyrocketed from fifteen to fifty dollars. Frantic, Katie perched on the edge of her seat, her stomach doing flip-flops until the auctioneer yelled, "Sold!" She sagged on the hard wooden chair. "Did we get it?"

But Rose was already on her feet, handing her card to one of the attendants. She waited for him to sign it, then she returned to her seat, carrying the box of dirty toys and plunking it onto Katie's lap.

Rose shook her head in disgust, lip curling. "You were robbed."

Katie pawed through the contents. A filthy, naked Cabbage Patch baby, whose sparse hair had been chopped close to its vinyl head, two vintage, naked Barbie dolls, one with molded plastic hair, and another with a dirty bubble cut, a Raggedy Ann whose left arm was missing, and the cloth-bodied doll with the carved wooden head, which looked like it had been chewed. On its right hip seam, a machine-embroidered blue tag read "Handmade by"—but the name beneath had been snipped off.

"Poor Polly," Rose said, her voice hushed.

"I don't understand."

"Well, obviously she—"

"Do you mind," said an annoyed voice behind them. "I'm trying to bid!"

Rose glared at the woman but clasped Katie's arm, pulling her up. "Come on."

They headed for the Joe's Java sign. A number of people had taken a break from the auction and sat on the black paint-chipped chairs at tiny metal ice cream tables, but they had no trouble finding a couple of empty seats. "You were saying, about Polly?" Katie reminded Rose.

"It's obvious to me that her supplier has been ripping her off."

"What do you mean?" Katie asked, puzzled.

"While I was picking up the glass in her booth, she went on and on about the missing doll clothes and how much they were worth, that they were antiques—and that you had said they were all fakes. I had a look at one of her dolls. I'm no expert, but it looked real to me."

"That's the problem. The woman from the Folk Doll Confederation said the doll clothes were made from antique cloth. So were the bodies of the dolls. Even the stuffing in the one Polly showed me was old."

"I'll bet that's why Polly was taken in. She knows all about antique fabrics, but she's not the expert she thinks she is when it comes to folk dolls. This tag proves the dolls really are fakes."

"Where would someone get this kind of label?" Katie asked.

"Most of the fabric stores sell them—at least, they stock the more popular names. It might've even said, 'Handmade by Mother.'"

Katie looked back toward the action at the front of the cavernous room. "Did you see who was bidding against us?"

"No, why?"

Before Katie could answer, she saw Vance hurrying toward them. His voice cut through the buzz of conversation. "Rose, your jewelry lot's about to come up."

"Gotta scoot!" Rose said, and dashed back for the auction area.

Katie turned her attention back to her purchase and examined the doll's wooden neck and shoulders. They'd probably been gnawed by a puppy. She ran her thumbs over the indentations. How could someone let an object made with such craftsmanship be destroyed? And yet, as she studied the doll, she could see that the detailing wasn't as refined as on the dolls Polly sold. The fabric looked old, but that could be achieved by tea-dying. No doubt about it, this doll was an earlier incarnation of the ones Polly Bremerton sold as antiques. As much as Katie disliked Polly, she'd have to let her know about the deception.

She shook her head. "Poor, poor Polly."

~~~~~~~

Despite her best efforts to persuade him, Burt Donahue wouldn't disclose the name of the person who had previously owned the box lot of dolls.

"This isn't doctor-patient confidentiality," Katie argued.

"No, but I have an obligation to my clients. I *know* her. I just met *you*."

Swell.

Rose bought three box lots of jewelry, a Delft vase, three Doulton figurines, and a vintage glass coffeepot, all of which looked like a lot more value for the money than Katie's box of sorry-looking dolls. Still, as the evening wore on, Katie found herself growing more and more attached to the pathetic group, determined to fix them up and find them a good home . . . or . . . maybe keep them.

It was then she realized she'd contracted the same disease her late husband had acquired some years before: collectoritis. Well, there were worse things for someone in the retail business to suffer from. And she had to admit how right Rose had been about the thrill of the hunt. This would not be her last auction.

The next morning, Katie loaded her car with as many boxes of her belongings as she could squeeze in before heading for Artisans Alley. The box of dolls had the honor of riding shotgun in the passenger seat.

With all the added weight, the Focus rode low to the ground. At this rate, it would take another seven days to empty the apartment of its stash of cartons. And she still had to deal with the furniture. *One thing at a time,* she told herself, *one thing at a time.*

Katie pulled into Artisans Alley's lot ten minutes late. Vance Ingram's pickup was already parked in its usual spot.

It wasn't uncommon for him to arrive before her and open the building for vendor setup, although it looked as though no one else had shown up so far. Katie grabbed the furniture dolly that stood inside the door, loaded it with boxes, and trucked them in until she had three piles, four boxes high, plus the dolls. She took the first load back to her office and found Vance in the vendors' lounge.

"Morning, Vance. Sorry you didn't get the bedroom suite last night," she said in greeting. "It looked really nice."

"It was too rich for my blood," he muttered.

The twelve-inch analog color TV from Katie's office sat on the table beside a behemoth of a video recorder.

"Wow, those old VCRs were big," Katie said, easing the dolly to a halt.

"Nearly ruptured myself bringing it in," Vance admitted.

"You should've waited for me." Katie watched as he hooked coaxial cable from the player to the TV. "Let me get my tape."

"Hold on, we don't even know if it works yet. I brought an old tape I found in my basement. We'll test it with that." Vance hit the power switch and a red light glowed on the front panel. "So far, so good." He pressed the eject button and a metal cage popped up. He placed a tape into its maw and pushed the apparatus back down, then reached over to turn on the TV and change the channel to three.

"Would you like to do the honors?" he asked.

Katie stepped forward, pressing the play button. Immediately, the TV screen went from snow to black. They watched expectantly, but nothing appeared on the screen. The old machine began to whine. They peered through the plastic window on top of the machine to see the tape winding onto the spool in jerky movements.

"Ah, hell." Vance stabbed the stop button.

"You tried," Katie said, but her tone didn't hide her disappointment.

"I haven't given up yet." Vance stared at the machine for

long seconds. "This is gonna take some thought—and maybe a pot of coffee."

"I'll make it," Katie offered.

Vance waved her off. "No. You finish with your boxes. I think better when I'm doing something mundane." He grabbed the empty pot and headed for the tap in the washroom.

The coffeepot was gurgling as Katie finished piling the boxes in her office, which was beginning to look like a warehouse, and a very cramped one at that.

"First things first," she told herself. She put the box of grubby dolls on her guest chair, pulled them into sitting positions, and thought about covering their nakedness.

Katie sighed. Now she was just getting silly.

She opened the safe, counted out money for the cash drawers, and thought about vacuuming the front entry before opening. She found she actually liked doing that task. Like Vance, occupying herself with something mundane helped her clarify her thoughts. She had a lot to think about: her fruitless apartment hunt, Heather, Polly's dolls. And something Donahue had said the night before was niggling at her brain. But what?

After filling the cash drawers, Katie dragged out one of the Hoovers. As she pushed the vacuum back and forth across the carpet, she reviewed her short conversation with the auctioneer. Donahue had hired college boys to do the renovations at the Webster mansion. Jeremy had been a college student. Was it possible he had helped with those renovations? He wouldn't even admit to knowing Heather, so it wasn't likely he'd own up to being on the premises where, years later, her bones were found.

No, it wasn't that. Whatever Donahue had said had been about Heather herself. But what was it?

Then it hit her. She'd asked him if he'd known that Heather was Rose's niece. "Not until the detective told me." That meant they'd identified the bones as being Heather's.

Yet she couldn't remember Rose saying she'd been officially notified.

That aggravating Davenport.

Katie unplugged the vacuum and wound up the cord. It was time to get some answers.

Before she made it to her office, however, Rose intercepted her at the side entrance. Her face looked bleached of color, every line etched deeply. Katie reached for Rose's elbow to steady her. "What's wrong?"

Rose dabbed her eye with a tissue. "Detective Davenport paid me a visit at home this morning to tell me—"

"They've identified the bones as belonging to Heather."

Rose looked up. "Yes. He told me . . ." She hiccuped on the word. "He said I could start planning her funeral."

"Oh, Rose." Katie hugged her. "I'll be glad to help you. Come back to my office and sit down, have a cup of coffee, and we'll talk."

Katie led the older woman to the back of the building, where Vance was now seated at the vendors' lounge table. The cover was off the old video machine, and its guts were exposed. A variety of tools were spread across the table, and Vance wore a head loupe like a crown, its twin magnifying lenses giving him owl eyes. "Hi, Rose," he said offhandedly, picking up a screwdriver. "You ever think of installing more light in here, Katie?"

"We'll talk about it later," she said and directed Rose to her office.

The box of dolls was soon relegated to the top of the file cabinet. A sniffling Rose sat in Katie's own desk chair. Katie hightailed it back to the lounge to pour a cup of coffee, then closed her office door for privacy. She sat down in the other chair. "What else did Detective Davenport say?" she asked gently.

"Not much. I asked him if he'd spoken to Jeremy Richards, and he said he couldn't talk about the case. I'm Heather's only living relative and he won't tell me anything."

Katie sighed. "Well, if he won't tell us, there's no reason we can't ask ourselves." She rolled her chair over to the file cabinet, opened a drawer, and took out the phone book. She thumbed through the yellow pages until she came to the hotels section. Grabbing her phone, Katie punched in a number. It rang.

"Hyatt Regency, this is Margot. How can I help you?"

"Mr. Jeremy's room."

"I'm sorry. He isn't taking calls."

"I'm a family member and I must speak to him. Is anyone taking calls for him?"

"Please hold."

Unlike Katie's experience days before, this operator hadn't immediately cut her off. The phone rang three, four times. Why hadn't she thought of that ploy days before? Voice mail picked up. "You have reached Mark Bastian. Leave your name, number, and a short message. I may or may not return your call." *Beep!*

My, that was blunt.

"This is Katie Bonner; you might remember me from the press conference the other day. I'd like to speak to Mr. Jeremy. It concerns Heather Winston. I'd really rather not talk to the press about this. I'm sure Mr. Jeremy would rather I didn't, too." She left her number and hung up.

Rose clutched her damp tissue. "Do you really think he'll call?"

"No, but at least we've tried."

Rose nodded, resigned.

"Would you like me to call Mr. Collier at the funeral parlor?" Katie asked.

Rose shook her head. "That's my duty as Heather's aunt. What kind of funeral do you plan when there's no body—just bones?"

"I'm sure Mr. Collier will have all the answers. I'll let you have some privacy," Katie said, rising and giving Rose's shoulder a pat. She stepped toward the door but paused. On impulse, she grabbed the box of dolls before she closed the office door behind her.

Vance had swiped a fire-glazed ceramic lamp from booth eighty-eight—its price tag dangled from under the shade—and more of the video recorder's insides were now lying across a newspaper he'd spread across the table.

"Will it live?" Katie asked.

Vance peered at her from under the head loupe, his blue eyes magnified and menacing.

"I think I'll just leave you two alone for a while," she whispered, hefted her box, and headed for the cash desks.

Booth twenty-two featured reference books on just about every craft or aspect of collecting. Katie borrowed two volumes, one on doll values, one on repairs, and took them to the cash desk. According to the first book, the Barbie dolls might actually be worth some money. She patted bubble blonde Barbie's hair and remembered Barbie Gordon from days before at the diner—wide-eyed and frightened for her little granddaughter. And now very much dead.

Katie picked up amputee Raggedy Ann. The clothes were in good shape, albeit in need of a wash and iron. Maybe she could sell them on eBay. The thought of throwing away the armless doll brought an unexpected gush of anguish, so she set it aside. It was the handmade wooden-and-cloth doll that really drew her attention. The poor thing had probably suffered terribly, locked in the jaws of a West Highland terrier or a poodle.

Okay, so she was a sucker for the quaint painted face, but did any little girl really outgrow her love for dolls? This one she'd dress and name. This one she'd keep.

"Where did you get that?" asked a menacing voice

Katie looked up. Eyes bulging, head lowered like an angry bull, stood a red-faced Polly Bremerton.

Fourteen

"Polly, you're here early." That was a dumb thing to say. Polly *always* arrived at Artisans Alley before opening.

"I said, where did you get that?" Polly demanded.

Katie handed Polly the doll, only then noticing that little Hannah stood beside her grandmother. "I bought this last night at the Auction Barn."

Polly's mouth dropped open, her face going ashen as she thumbed the snipped label hanging from the seam. "I-I don't know what to say."

"I'm so sorry, but it looks like your supplier has cheated you."

Polly's gaze darted from the doll to Katie's face.

"If it's any consolation, the woman from the Folk Doll Confederation did say the dolls were worth the price you're asking for them."

Polly's face contorted, and for a moment Katie thought she might cry. But when she spoke, her voice was steady. "Thank you, Katie. I only wish I could offer them for sale. Without their clothes, they're simply not worth as much."

"Jean Selkirk sews doll clothes. She may be able to help you out."

Polly scowled. "I could make them myself. I was a seamstress for over thirty years. It's just that . . ." Her words trailed off, and she swallowed whatever else she'd meant to say, and instead managed, "Thank you for the suggestion."

She was taking this much better than Katie had anticipated.

Hannah tugged on Polly's jacket. "Mine, mine, Grandmama."

"No, dear, this belongs to Mrs. Bonner." She handed the doll back to Katie. "Your dolls are at home. You can play with them later."

Hannah's lower lip trembled and she bowed her head.

Suddenly Katie wanted to stuff the doll under the counter to get it out of sight. Instead, she replaced it in the box and moved it aside. Since Polly seemed to be in a better mood than usual, it looked like the best time to broach a more difficult subject.

"I've had a talk with Edie Silver. You two just aren't compatible neighbors. So, in the interest of vendor harmony, I've decided to move her to another location."

"Where?" Polly demanded.

"Downstairs."

Polly's eyes flashed. "That's not fair. I've been here longer than she has. I should be the one who gets the better booth."

"I realize that. That's why I've decided to give you two weeks free rent as compensation. And I'll also move you to the top of the list. The next time there's an opening, you'll be the first I offer it to."

"It's still not fair," Polly muttered, but her anger wasn't as intense as Katie had anticipated. "When? When does she move?"

"Monday."

Katie could almost see the wheels turning in Polly's brain as she mulled over that piece of information. "Very well," she said at last, and turned her attention to the little girl. "Come along, Hannah. Grandmama has to straighten her booth." She clasped the girl's hand and strode toward the stairs, small Hannah struggling to keep pace with Polly's brisk gait.

The phone rang twice before stopping. Rose must have finished her conversation with the funeral director and answered the call. Katie dove back into the book on doll values.

"Katie, pick up line two," said Rose over the public address system.

Closing the book, Katie stepped over to the wall phone. "Katie Bonner."

"Ms. Bonner—it's Mark Bastian."

"Oh. I wasn't expecting to hear from you so soon."

"Well, your message did sound rather like a threat," he grated.

One point for Bastian. "Mr. Jeremy doesn't pick up his award until tomorrow evening. I'm sure you—and he—would like the day to go smoothly. Another story in the paper wouldn't help."

"No, it wouldn't. What do you want?"

"Just an opportunity to talk. To refresh Mr. Jeremy's memory about Heather Winston."

"You said you had pictures of them together."

"Yes, and we've shared them with the police."

A long silence followed. "Rick doesn't deny he knew Ms. Winston. He just didn't remember her at first. There's nothing sinister about that."

"It *was* a long time ago," Katie admitted, "but he's had two days to remember. Would he be willing to talk about Heather with her family?"

Another long silence. "Mr. Jeremy's already spoken to

the police about it." At least Heather was now an "it" instead of a nobody to Jeremy. "What's to be gained by talking with the dead girl's relatives?"

"Closure. Mr. Bastian, Heather was murdered. As one of the world's great directors, Rick Jeremy coaxes believable emotion from all his actors. I'm sure if he tried he could muster a little show of sympathy for Heather—his former girlfriend."

Silence. Then, "Touché." Was there a hint of amusement in Bastian's voice?

"Then he'd be willing to speak to Heather's aunt?" Katie pressed.

"I don't know."

"If not Mrs. Nash, then how about me?"

"I'll ask. Will you be at this number later today?"

"Yes."

"Okay, I'll let you know."

"Thank you."

Katie heard a click, and then the line went dead.

She hung up the phone. Two surprises in one morning: Polly's lack of anger, and perhaps an audience with the world-renowned Mr. Rick Jeremy.

The day was looking up.

~~~~~~

"He's dead, Jim."

Katie blinked at Vance, who hovered over the vendors' lounge table like a surgeon in an operating room. "I beg your pardon."

"Doctor McCoy on *Star Trek* always said that to Captain Kirk when one of the red-shirted security guys got nailed by a Klingon or some other alien." Vance looked down at scattered parts of the video recorder. "It might not have been quite dead before, but now I've killed it."

Katie let out a disappointed breath.

"I'm not giving up," Vance assured her. "It's just time to call in an expert."

"Oh, no. How much is that going to cost?" she asked. She didn't even know if the tape had anything worth watching on it. Maybe whoever sent it to her just wanted to taunt her.

"Cost?" he mused. "Maybe a pizza."

"How's that?"

"Vance Junior's a wiz at fixing just about anything electronic and is more than willing to work for food. Tomorrow's Saturday—no school. He can probably look at it then. I'll ask him about it when he gets home this afternoon."

Katie smiled. She'd met Vance's son on a number of occasions and liked the bright-eyed teenager. "A pizza I can handle. And I know just where to get it."

~~~~~~

Angelo's Pizzeria was closed at this early hour, but Andy liked to make his own dough—he often said he liked the feel of working with it. It was likely he'd be in back, watching in rapt attention as his heavy-duty mixing machine pulled on the elastic mix of flour, water, and yeast.

Since his car was parked out front, Katie figured he'd come into work early on that bright sunny morning. She pressed the bell, letting it ring for a full twenty seconds before Andy appeared in the darkened shop.

"All right, all right, all right already." He unlocked the door, letting Katie in.

"Have you ever thought of making cinnamon buns with your beloved dough?" She gave him a kiss. "I'm starved."

Andy stood, openmouthed, looking blank. Katie gave him another kiss, softer this time, but he stood stiffly in her arms. She leaned back. "Earth to Andy."

He gazed into her eyes. "What did you just say?"

"Take me out to breakfast. I've used up or packed all the food in my house, and I'm hungry."

"No, no—about cinnamon buns."

Katie shrugged. "Make me one?"

His smile broke into a devastating grin. "Oh, the benefits of having a girlfriend with a marketing degree. Do you think I could handle it?"

"What are you talking about?" she asked, confused.

"Cinnamon buns—making and selling them."

Katie threw her arms into the air in defeat. "Why not—you're here almost twenty-four hours a day anyway."

Andy looked thoughtful. Was it a trick of the light, or were dollar signs actually dancing in his eyes?

"Hey, I was joking."

"Not me. I wonder . . ." he murmured, and he was off, heading for his back room, which contained his dough-making equipment and resting racks.

Katie followed. Sure enough, Andy was thumbing through a recipe book he'd taken from a shelf. "All I'd need is sugar, cinnamon, butter—"

Katie's felt the weight of the world suddenly upon her. "Does this mean I'll get to see you even less?"

Andy waved a hand to shush her while he continued to read. His face went slack for at least ten seconds. Was he having some kind of seizure?

"Andy?" Katie whispered.

He shook himself back to awareness. "Before you arrived, I was standing here making the dough and think-ing about how much I still owe on all this equipment—wondering how the hell I could pay it off sooner." He nodded toward the king-sized mixer with its evil-looking bread hook. "If I could bring out another product . . . I don't even have to bake it myself . . . I could premiere it with local grocery stores, starting right here in McKinlay Mill, and build a following—"

"Whoa, whoa! How about making one batch before you build an empire?"

He looked up at her, as though disoriented. "Huh?"

"You don't even have a bulk recipe," she reminded him.

"So, I could find one—or adapt one."

"It'll take a lot of experimentation," she pointed out.

"You could be my guinea pig."

"Oh, thanks."

"No, I'm serious." He dropped the book on the work table and grabbed her in a joyful hug, kissing her hard.

"You're welcome," she breathed, coming up for air.

"What a team we'd make. If only—"

"Yeah, if only I liked to make pizza and you liked running an artisans arcade."

"I can dream, can't I?"

"So can I. And right now I'm dreaming about breakfast at Del's Diner. Toast and home fries."

"What about a cinnamon bun?"

"I'll need my palate clear when I sample one of Angelo's world-famous buns." She pinched his left buttock.

Andy straightened proudly, jerking a thumb at his chest. "No way. I'm naming them after *me*, not the shop." He grabbed her hand, leading her through said shop. "Come on, I'll buy you that breakfast. And we can make plans for the future."

She smiled. The day was indeed looking up.

~~~~~~

Toast, eggs, and home fries never tasted so good, but best of all, Andy's expansion plans meant one more thing. "I'm going to have to hire help," he said, shaking his head and looking down at the scribbled notes on his napkin.

"Like an assistant manager who'll free you up in the evenings," Katie hinted, pushing away her empty plate.

"Definitely. I'll need to devote all my time to developing and marketing my new product. I'm putting a help-wanted ad in the paper as soon as I get back to the shop."

Katie sank into her booth seat. Maybe they *wouldn't* get to spend more time with each other.

Ten minutes later, Andy dropped her off at Artisans Alley's front entrance. The parking lot was beginning to fill—always a good sign.

Rose was at cash desk one, taking care of a customer, and Katie slipped behind the counter to help her wrap the order. "Can you go with me to the funeral parlor this evening?" Rose asked as she rang up a collection of ceramic butter stamps.

"Of course. What time?"

"About six?"

"Sure."

"Oh, and some guy called. Mark somebody or other—started with a B."

"When?" Katie asked, her eyes growing wide.

"About an hour ago. But he left a number."

Katie wrapped the rest of the order with more speed than skill and hurried to her office to return the call. The video recorder was still spread across the vendors' lounge table, but Vance had covered the deceased with a cloth, no doubt to keep out the dust. On it was a folded piece of paper with a drawing of a tombstone. Some smart aleck had written "RIP" on it.

Katie closed her door, found the message, and dialed. Bastian answered on the first ring.

"Mr. Jeremy will see you, but not here in Rochester," he said, his voice cool.

"McKinlay Mill?" she suggested.

"Considering what happened there, that wouldn't be a good idea either. How about somewhere in between. Someplace quiet, but public. A restaurant perhaps?"

They settled on The Golden Fleece in the town of Greece, at eight.

"Come alone," Bastian said, and hung up.

Come alone? Fat chance. Not that Katie expected any trouble. All she wanted to do was talk. What were they expecting, blackmail?

She realized with a start that they probably were.

Katie picked up a pencil and doodled boxes on the message pad next to her phone. Andy would be working, and Jeremy didn't want to see Rose. Besides, whatever Jeremy had to say might upset the old woman.

On impulse, Katie grabbed the receiver and dialed Seth Landers's office number. The secretary put her right through. "Any chance you'll be hungry around eight o'clock tonight?"

"No date on a Friday night, huh?" Seth asked and laughed.

"I won't dignify that question with an answer."

"What did you have in mind?"

"Delicious Greek food. Roasted rack of lamb smothered in . . . something. Feta? Yogurt?"

"And what do you get out of this?" he asked suspiciously.

"A supper other than pizza." It was the truth!

"And?" he prompted.

"Okay, I'm meeting Rick Jeremy. We're going to talk about Heather Winston. His bodyguard slash secretary said to come alone. I don't want to."

"So, you want me to act as your bodyguard?"

"You did once offer to be my big brother when I needed one," she reminded him.

"Yes, I did. Okay. Toss in a bottle of wine and you've got a deal."

"Thanks, Seth. You're a peach. And, uh, from your quick acceptance, it looks like you don't have a date tonight either."

~~~~~~

The sun was still high in the sky, with another two hours until it set, when Katie followed Rose's little red car into Collier's Funeral Home's parking lot. Katie got out, locked her car, and waited for Rose. There were no tears tonight. Rose was composed and resigned.

The panel of stained glass lilies on the ornate oak door

flashed as Luther Collier held it open for them. He'd apparently been waiting for them. The pudgy, elderly man was somber in a dark suit, crisp white shirt, and muted tie. "I'm so sorry we have to meet again under these circumstances, Mrs. Nash. It must be six years now since your husband passed."

"You have a phenomenal memory, Mr. Collier," Rose said, sounding touched.

Collier shrugged, looking pleased. More likely he had a halfway decent database filled with the names of all his past customers. "Please step this way to my office."

Katie glanced into the various rooms, breathing a sigh of relief that there wasn't a coffin in sight.

They took seats before Collier's polished cherry desk. "After we spoke this morning I called the medical examiner's office. I'm afraid your niece's remains have not yet been released. It's possible that may not happen for several more days, perhaps even weeks."

"Detective Davenport did mention that. And although Heather lived her whole life here in McKinlay Mill, I think her parents would want her to be buried where they were, in Florida. And as she died such a long time ago, I thought a memorial service would be more appropriate than a funeral."

Collier's gaze dipped to his folded hands on top of the desk blotter. No sale. "Very well."

"But I would like to hold the memorial service here. It's such a lovely place."

That cheered the funeral director.

Katie found her thoughts wandering as Collier gave his pitch for the services he could provide. Foremost on her mind was her meeting with Rick Jeremy. What was she going to say to him anyway? "Did you kill Heather?" Like he would admit to it. Would he be angry to see her arrive with Seth in tow? Maybe she could convince Seth to sit in the bar while she had her meeting.

Today was Friday. That meant she had only three days to buy a gift for Gilda Ringwald's bridal shower. Or could the trouble and expense she'd incur to pull off the affair be considered a gift in itself?

Had she been out of her mind when she suggested Andy bake cinnamon buns? Would the heady odors of cheese, sauce, anchovies, and garlic that permeated his ovens contaminate the sinfully delicious cinnamon buns he hoped to make a killing on?

She winced at that last thought—remembering why she was here at the funeral parlor—and surfaced from her reverie to hear Collier sum up the arrangements for Heather's memorial service. "When I receive Ms. Winston's remains, they'll be placed in a plain but dignified wooden box. I'll make arrangements for their shipment to the Florida cemetery. The death notice will appear in tomorrow's paper, and the service will be Sunday afternoon."

Rose nodded. "I'd like you to officiate, Mr. Collier. You did such a nice job at Ezra Hilton's service last fall."

"Thank you, Mrs. Nash. Is there anything else I can do to ease your pain at this difficult time?"

Rose shook her head and stood. "No, thank you."

Katie and Collier rose to their feet, and Collier walked them to the door. He offered Rose his hand. "I'll see you on Sunday. Good evening."

Rose nodded and turned to leave.

"I have a few more questions for Mr. Collier," Katie said. "I'll see you tomorrow at Artisans Alley, Rose." She waited until Rose got safely in her car and waved as the car pulled out of the lot, then turned back to Collier, who waited patiently by the door.

"How can I help you, Mrs. Bonner?" Collier asked at last.

"I didn't see any notice in the newspaper of the arrangements for Barbie Gordon. Do you know when the service will be?"

He shook his head, his gaze downcast. "I don't expect there will be one."

"No funeral? But what will happen to her—her . . ." She couldn't bring herself to finish the sentence.

"I got a call from Mrs. Gordon's daughter inquiring about my . . . er, rates. I'm afraid we weren't able to come to an agreement on price and the services she requested."

"But that seems so . . . so callous to not even acknowledge that she once walked this earth."

"Poverty often precludes observing all the amenities of life . . . and death."

Katie sighed. "Yes, I suppose it does."

"I did suggest a competitor from Rochester." He pursed his lips. "Cheap and Cheerful Funerals, although I'm not even sure Miss Gordon can afford them either."

"Oh, dear."

"Will there be anything else, Mrs. Bonner?"

"No, thank you, Mr. Collier."

Katie headed for her car. She'd expected to meet Barbie's daughter at a wake of some sort. Katie had been one of the last people to see Barbie alive. She owed it to Barbie's survivors to tell them what she knew. And the sooner the better.

Fifteen

Instead of heading straight home, Katie steered her car in the direction of Route 8. Some ten minutes later, she knocked on the single-wide trailer's aluminum storm door and waited. Maybe no one was at home, yet if she concentrated, she was sure she could hear a television. She glanced at her watch: It was time for *Wheel of Fortune*.

She knocked again and the front door was wrenched open by a purple-haired, sullen-looking young woman in her early twenties. "Yeah, wha'ddya want?"

"My name is Katie Bonner. I knew your mother."

The woman lowered her head. Her lower lip trembled and she swallowed. "Yeah, well . . . she's dead."

"I know. I'm so sorry. I came to pay my respects."

The woman sighed and held the door open, beckoning Katie to enter.

The dim interior smelled like stale grease. The heat was set to stifling. Katie navigated a narrow path through stacked boxes to what resembled a living room. The woman moved a sewing basket from a chair so she could sit, then resumed her place on the couch and went back to folding a stack of laundry.

Katie tried not to stare, but her gaze was drawn to the gold studs on each side of the woman's pierced nose. Whatever did she do when she caught a cold?

Oh, swell, Katie thought. *I'm now officially an old fart.*

She cleared her throat. "I didn't know your mother well. She never told me your name."

"Donna." She blushed. "Madonna, actually. And yeah, I was named after the singer. I can't stand it."

"And your daughter?" Katie asked.

"Fawn."

As if on cue, the little girl came racing in from another room, her little bottom hanging out of a pull-up diaper. "I go potty by myself, I go potty!"

"Good girl," Donna said, and pulled up her daughter's drawers. She reached behind her on the couch, grabbed a box of cheap cookies, and handed one to the child. "Go play."

Fawn snatched the treat and stuffed it into her mouth, then raced for the TV stand and the box of toys underneath. She dumped it, tossing dolls and stuffed animals over her shoulder until she'd found the one she wanted—an obviously much-loved homemade sock monkey. She clutched the toy under her chin and plunked herself into a little wooden rocker. "Big money, big money," she cheered.

Katie turned her attention back to Donna. "I wanted to offer my condolences and ask if there was anything you needed."

Donna looked around the trailer and pushed up the sleeves on an oversized brown sweater, revealing a rainbow tattoo on her left upper arm. "How about a million dollars? Fawn's father's in jail, so I get nothing from him. I work at McDonald's in the village. That's not enough to pay the monthly electric bill in this dump. I can't move. I'd never pull together first and last month's rents. I already had two years on welfare, so I can't go back on it. My ma didn't own this dump. I figure Fawn and I have got a couple of months before we're evicted. Then I don't know what we'll do."

The bitterness in Donna's voice made Katie wince. And she thought she had housing problems. "You really depended on your mother."

"Yeah, for everything. I don't even have the money to give her a decent burial. I can't go back to work unless I can find someone to watch Fawn. And yet, if I don't work, I can't support us." She sighed. "Everything's turned to shit."

Fawn's small head snapped around. "Mommy, don't swear. Gramma will be mad," she scolded.

"I know, sweetie. I'm sorry. You watch TV," she encouraged, and the girl happily turned back to the set. Donna studied her child and lowered her voice to speak to Katie. "I didn't tell her Ma's dead. She's too little to understand. She thinks her grandma's at all-day bingo." Donna sniffed, rubbed the back of her hand under her nose, and resumed folding tiny T-shirts.

"What about your father? Is there a chance he could help you?" Katie asked.

"Joe Gordon wasn't my father. When he and Ma broke up five years ago, he made it clear he wanted nothing to do with either of us. Ma wouldn't ask my sperm donor for help. She said she didn't want to ruin his reputation." Donna's snort of laughter held no mirth. "He ruined *her* reputation when he got her knocked up and walked away from his responsibilities. He never lifted a finger to help her when her parents disowned her."

Donna sniffed again. "Ma would still be alive if she hadn't gone to the damned Webster mansion the other night."

"What was she doing there anyway?"

"Probably visiting the scene of the crime."

"Because of Heather Winston?" Katie surmised.

Donna nodded. "Ma figured it was only a matter of time before the cops figured out the whole mess, but she didn't want to volunteer any information and implicate herself. Now it's too late."

A rivulet of sweat dripped down Katie's neck. "What did she know?"

"Nothin' about who killed Heather. Least, that's what Ma said. It was *where* they found her."

"In the wall?" Katie asked.

"Yeah. In what used to be Ma's studio apartment."

~~~~~

"Barbie Gordon lived at the Webster mansion?" Seth repeated. He looked devastatingly handsome behind the wheel of his sleek Mercedes.

Katie nodded. "At the time when Heather disappeared. Barbie told her daughter she had to move—right after some workmen had done some renovations in her apartment. There was a terrible smell that wouldn't go away."

"Well, we know what—or who—caused that."

Katie leaned back against the cool leather seat. She'd just had time to change into her one cocktail dress—basic black, with matching leather pumps and a string of pearls around her neck—and rake a comb through her hair before Seth arrived to pick her up. The shadows were lengthening as they crossed the town line into Greece. The dash clock said seven fifty-two. Knowing German engineering, it was probably correct. They might still make it on time.

"And Donna isn't about to volunteer the information to Detective Davenport, so that leaves—"

"You to do the dirty work," Seth finished. "And right about now, you're at the top of his shit list."

"You got it."

Seth flexed his fingers on the steering wheel. "When are you going to tell him?"

"Tomorrow, although he may already know. He doesn't share that kind of information with me. And maybe after speaking to Rick Jeremy, I'll have even more to tell him."

"I thought you promised me you weren't going to poke around in this murder investigation."

"As I recall, I didn't exactly promise anything. And I'm not really poking into anything. I visited Donna to pay my respects."

"And this conversation with Jeremy?" he prompted.

Katie squirmed. "Okay, but I'm not going to poke too hard. This conversation is more for Rose's peace of mind."

"Does she know about it?"

"I may have forgotten to tell her," Katie admitted. "But only because I didn't want to upset her. And Jeremy isn't likely to tell me much more than Heather was a sweet young thing, they held hands, and that he kissed her maybe once or twice. Yada, yada, yada."

"With no mention made of raging hormones and how a young man's fancy turns to . . . What does it turn to? Spring or love or something, right?"

"I wouldn't know. I was never a young man."

Seth tried not to smile but didn't succeed. He pulled the Mercedes into the last available parking space outside The Golden Fleece at precisely seven fifty-nine. He killed the engine and removed the keys. Katie waited for him to open her door and help her out. If only Andy were as gallant. But then Andy appreciated her in ways that Seth never could.

Seth held the restaurant door, letting Katie enter first. Standing in the entryway, dressed in what could only be an Armani suit, was the ponytailed man from the press conference.

"You're not Rick Jeremy," Katie said.

The stranger eyed Seth. "And you didn't come alone."

"Looks like we're both disappointed."

"Does this mean I don't get dinner?" Seth asked.

"I sure hope not. I'm starved." The stranger thrust his hand at Seth. "Mark Bastian."

"Seth Landers. And this is Katie Bonner."

"We've spoken." Bastian eyed Katie's neckline. "And I recognize you from your picture in the paper."

His words caused her memory to flash. Now she realized where she'd seen this man before—in Heather's snapshots. His hair had been lighter, bushy and unkempt in those days, and the ever-present sunglasses hadn't yet become a fashion statement.

"You knew Heather, too," Katie said. It wasn't a question.

Bastian nodded toward the hostess standing before them. "Let's go sit down."

A waiflike being—with no womanly attributes like breasts or a derriere—led them to a linen-clad table set with sparkling crystal, silver, and candlelight. Upon opening the menu, Katie realized the hostess probably couldn't afford to eat here. Maybe that's what accounted for her lack of body weight. Katie put the thought out of her mind as the older, more ample waitress appeared to recite the restaurant's specials and take their drink order.

Seth was the first to initiate conversation. "Are you originally from the Rochester area, Mark?"

Bastian sipped his water. "Yes. Grew up in Pittsford. Led the Pittsford-Sutherland baseball team to victory in my senior year."

"And college?"

"The university."

"No ivy league school for you?" Katie prodded.

At last, Bastian removed his sunglasses, pocketed them, and met Katie's gaze. "My mother had stomach cancer. Dad didn't want me to leave the area. She died during my junior year."

Katie swallowed. "I'm so sorry."

"What was your major?" Seth asked.

"Theater, of course. That's how I met Rick. We were both in the Film Studies program, although with different focuses. Rick always knew he wanted to be a director."

"Why isn't he here instead of you?" Katie asked.

Bastian leveled his stony gaze at her. "You really didn't think he'd show, did you?"

"Yes, I did. Why are *you* here?"

He shrugged. "I want to hear what you have to say."

"You mean whether I intend to try and blackmail Jeremy?"

Bastian's gaze didn't waver. "Yes."

Katie shook her head. "I only want information on Heather's last days."

"Unfortunately, very few of Heather's friends remain in the area," Seth said. "In fact, her best friend was found dead only two days ago."

Bastian's eyes flashed. "Barbie's dead?"

Katie shot Seth a quick look. "Yes. Did you know her well?"

Bastian shook his head, but the news had obviously unsettled him. "We were . . . acquainted . . . for a very short period of time. She had a baby. That complicated things."

Could Bastian and Barbie have been lovers? How crass was it to just ask?

"What was Heather's relationship like with Mr. Jeremy?" Seth asked. Katie was grateful for his nonthreatening demeanor and his reassuring tone. He would've made a great doctor with a comforting bedside manner.

"Heather wasn't anything special," Bastian said. "Barbie introduced them. Heather helped Rick with a school project, and when it was over, she dumped him."

"What kind of school project?"

Bastian exhaled loudly and fidgeted in his chair as though trying to decide how to answer. "She acted in a short he did. She was pretty. Didn't she want to be a model or something?"

Katie absently nodded, thinking about the Betamax tape back at Artisans Alley. "Where did you meet Barbie?"

Bastian shrugged. "Around."

The waitress arrived with their drinks, setting them down on cocktail napkins embossed with the restaurant's golden sheep logo. "Are you ready to order?"

"We need a few more minutes," Seth said, and gave her one of his dazzling smiles. The young woman winked and turned away. She couldn't know Seth would rather date the mustachioed bartender than her.

"Did you ever visit Barbie at her apartment in McKinlay Mill?" Katie asked. "More to the point, did Jeremy?"

"What are you getting at?" Bastian asked.

"Barbie Gordon lived in the building where Heather's remains were found. As a matter of fact, they were found in what had *been* Barbie's apartment."

Though the lights were low, it was evident that Bastian had paled. "No, I—" But he didn't finish whatever it was he had to say—instead, he gulped his martini.

"What is it that you do for Mr. Jeremy?" Seth asked, diverting the conversational flow.

"I'm his personal assistant. I handle all his arrangements."

"Will you be in town long?"

"Until Sunday." Bastian took another sip of his drink. "If I didn't know better, I'd say this was turning into an interrogation. Is that your specialty, Seth?"

Seth shrugged. "I am a lawyer."

Bastian's eyes widened in what might have been panic.

"As a matter of fact, I not only represent Katie, but Heather's aunt, Mrs. Nash, as well."

Bastian reached for the napkin on his lap, carefully folded it, and set it on his place mat. "I think I've been set up."

"I'm not here in an official capacity," Seth said. "I just happen to be friends with both Katie and Rose."

"I asked him to come, because I didn't want to be here

alone. You're suspicious of me—I'm suspicious of you. Why did you tell me to come alone?"

"I meant no press."

"I thought that was understood," Katie said.

The waitress hovered uncertainly behind Bastian. "Are we ready to order?" she asked hopefully.

For a moment, Katie thought Bastian might bolt, but Seth quickly answered that he'd have the rack of lamb. Bastian ordered a Greek salad, and Katie did likewise.

"How does one get to be a personal assistant to a world-famous movie director?" Seth asked, once they'd handed off their menus.

Bastian captured the toothpick-skewered queen olive from his drink and ate it. "Years of fetch and carry. Rick and I drove out to California together after graduation. We were roommates for a while. Movie and TV jobs were few and far between, and we were competing with UCLA grads."

"Did you ever accept any acting jobs?" Katie asked.

Bastian hesitated. "I've always been behind the camera in some capacity." Not exactly a lie, but he hadn't answered her question either.

"But didn't you ever work as an extra? I hear they're well fed at least."

"Usually," he said. He signaled the waitress and pointed to his empty glass. "Another round?"

Katie had barely touched her glass of chardonnay but Seth accepted the invitation.

"Did the four of you hang out together?" Katie pressed, eager to get the conversation back on track.

"For a couple of months."

"What did you do?"

"Got drunk, mostly. In Barbie's tiny apartment."

"Did you have recent contact with Barbie?" Seth asked.

Bastian shook his head. "No. I haven't seen or talked to her in what—twenty-two years?"

"Did she tell you who fathered her baby?" Katie asked.

Bastian shook his head once again.

Katie dug into her purse, unearthing the envelope of Rose's pictures. She offered them to Bastian. He took them from her, shuffling through them, pausing on one of Barbie in her cheerleader's outfit. The lines around his eyes relaxed a bit. "I'd forgotten how pretty she was."

The waitress arrived with a big tray that not only contained the second round of drinks, but also their dinners. Bastian pursed his lips, shoved the pictures back in the envelope, and handed it to Katie as the waitress distributed their plates.

Seth tucked right into his entrée, but Katie pushed a grape tomato around her heaping plate of greens. "What do you remember about Barbie and Heather's friendship?" she asked.

Bastian shrugged. "There seemed to be a kind of rivalry between them." He laughed. "For a while, Rick thought Barbie might be hot for him."

"Was that what caused Heather to break up with Rick?"

"They had a nasty argument about another guy. It sounded like Heather had had a thing for this guy since high school."

"Did she tell Jeremy the man's name?"

"Not that I know of."

Barbie must have known. Could the best friends have been interested in the same man—someone other than Richards? "When did Heather break it off with Jeremy?"

Bastian stabbed his fork at a piece of bell pepper. "A couple of days before she disappeared. It was already over between me and Barbie. I didn't care."

They ate in silence for a few moments, but Katie had one other loose end for Bastian to tie up.

"Did you and Jeremy work on the renovations at the old Webster mansion?"

Bastian abandoned his fork for his martini glass. "Yeah.

The owner hired me because of my father's reputation. We did a pretty good job. Certainly worth what he paid us—which was jack shit."

"What kind of repairs?" Seth asked.

"A drop ceiling, some woodwork, and a little drywall."

"Was this before or after Heather disappeared?" Katie asked.

"Before. And no, we didn't wall her up."

Katie frowned. "Did you tell Detective Davenport any of this?"

"I haven't been questioned," Bastian said.

"Did Jeremy volunteer that information?"

"I don't know. We don't talk much."

"But you work for him. I thought you said you're his personal assistant," Katie said.

Bastian didn't blink. "Yeah, but when we talk, it's just business."

Seth cleared his throat, interrupting the uncomfortable moment. "Did you ever meet any of Heather's other friends?"

Bastian shook his head. "I don't think so. McKinlay Mill was a backwater. Its only redeeming quality was Barbie's apartment and the availability of cheap beer."

The waitress reappeared. "Is everything all right here?"

Seth smiled. "Just fine."

The conversation turned to other subjects, with Seth taking the lead. As Katie listened to Bastian talk about his work and career, she got the impression he led a pretty empty life. How sad he never found anyone to share it with.

She found her thoughts wandering. Was the whole Jeremy Richards/Rick Jeremy angle a bust? There were other sources of information she could tap, and she'd make sure she found time to look into it in the morning.

Katie had intended to pay for the dinner, but Seth, the dear, picked up the check. "You've got moving expenses coming up," he whispered and gave her a wink as, true gentleman that he was, Seth pulled out Katie's chair for her.

Bastian followed them from the restaurant. He gazed over the parking lot before turning to offer Seth his hand. "This evening ended differently than I thought it would. Thanks for the conversation."

He turned to Katie. "It's a pity we'll never meet again."

"Who says we won't?"

Bastian's answering smile was sly. "Then again, maybe we will." He reached for her hand and kissed it. "Until then." With a final curt nod, he stepped off the sidewalk and into the gloom.

Katie watched his silhouette until it merged with the shadows and was gone.

"What do you think of him?" Seth asked.

Katie still stared into the darkness. "He missed his calling. He should've been an actor."

"You think he was lying?" Seth asked, and started for his car.

Katie kept pace. "You don't have to lie to not tell the whole truth."

~~~~~~

Katie was up before dawn on Saturday morning and baked the last of the peanut butter cookie dough in her freezer, filling the apartment with a heavenly aroma—and she ate only two of them for her makeshift breakfast.

After piling them onto one of her two unpacked dinner plates, she filled the back of her Focus with boxes and lamented that her life had fallen into a rut. She should've spent more time looking for somewhere to live rather than chasing the shadows surrounding Heather's death.

She was down to just six days, with still no replacement apartment in sight. Her own apartment had been grabbed the moment she'd informed the complex manager of her intention to vacate, so staying another month was out of the question. She could land somewhere for a week or two, but it was the cats' fate that worried her. If worse came to worst, she could always board them with her vet. Expensive, inconvenient, and certainly nothing the cats would enjoy, but it was a viable alternative.

"First things first" was beginning to be her motto. Once she opened Artisans Alley for morning setup, she'd surf the Internet for background info on Rick Jeremy. Perhaps she'd find the key to his relationship with Heather in the body of his work. And she'd see what she could find on Mark Bastian, too. She'd spend an hour on the project—no more, because if she had to, she'd call every apartment complex in a twenty-mile radius to find an opening.

That decided, Katie headed off to work.

She pulled into Artisans Alley's parking lot, eased the gear shift into park, and shut off the engine. With a brief glance to her rearview mirror, she saw a flash of red behind her, breaking the gray morning monotony. "What the—"

Katie grabbed her purse and keys, hopped out of the car, and slammed the driver's door. The sign in front of the Webster mansion was larger than last time. Big red letters proclaiming FOR SALE.

Katie jogged the hundred yards or so, her purse thumping against her side. The sign must have gone up the night before, after she'd left Artisans Alley. She'd have seen it otherwise.

She topped the mansion's stairs and pounded the door, not that she expected anyone to answer this early in the morning. There wasn't a light on in the place. She shaded her eyes to look inside the mansion's foyer. Nothing but the demolition detritus, although the floor looked freshly swept. She didn't know Janice and Toby's home phone number—didn't even know where they lived so she could go over to talk to them.

Katie turned away, feeling dejected as she walked down the wooden steps. She didn't pause to write down the real estate agency's phone number—she had it committed to memory from all the times she'd called Fred Cunningham about the property during the years she'd hoped to buy and renovate it.

"You can't afford it," she said out loud, her cheeks hot with—what, anger? That wasn't right. Frustration, more likely. "You can't buy it," she said more firmly. *Ahh, but what if you could,* said an insidious little voice inside her. *What if some bank manager somewhere had a creative plan that would allow you to—*

That would sink her deeper into hock than she already was. Buying was one thing. Renovating was another. And without Chad, how could she hope to run an inn on her own?

You could get a partner, the little voice taunted. *Someone with the capital to get the project moving, someone to—*

No! Then it wouldn't be *hers*.

Katie approached Artisans Alley, noting that the downspout on the southeast corner had come loose again. She fumbled with her key, stabbed it into the lock, and fought the urge to kick something.

Sixteen

~~~~~~~~~~

"I wouldn't go in there, if I were you," Katie heard Vance warn someone. "She's in a bit of a snit."

That was an understatement. Katie leaned back in her office chair. From there she could just see the vendors' lounge coffeemaker, where Vance was pouring himself a cup. Still Katie's curiosity had been piqued. It had better not be Polly Bremerton outside her door, or else she just might—

"Katie?" Andy's cheerful face appeared in the doorway. The delight in his eyes dimmed when she turned a glower on him.

"Nobody should look so happy this early in the morning," she growled.

"I've got something wonderful for you," he taunted, his body half hidden from view by the door frame.

"It had better be," she said, unable to keep the edge from her voice.

Andy popped into the office, holding a towel-draped

tray. With the skill of a magician, he whipped it off and
proclaimed, "Voilà—breakfast."

The heavenly scent of cinnamon buns enveloped the office. Stacked pyramid style, each squared-off spiral of
dough and spices was thickly coated with a shiny white
glaze, looking good enough for a spread in *Martha Stewart
Living*.

Vance moved to stand behind him. "Whoa-hoe. Food."

"They're—they're gorgeous," Katie stammered, her bad
mood almost forgotten. Almost.

"It's my third batch, and I think it's the best." Andy
breathed almost reverently. "I've been playing with the mix
of spices. See if you can guess my secret ingredient."

"I'll get napkins," Vance volunteered. He disappeared
for a moment, reappearing with a handful.

With exaggerated care, Andy transferred rolls onto separate napkins and presented one to Katie and Vance as
though bestowing the sacrament.

Katie took a bite of the still-warm concoction, letting it
lie on her tongue to better savor the flavors. "Mmmm," she
groaned, mouth still full, reluctant to swallow, yet eventually she had to. "These are to *die* for."

Vance swallowed. "I've never tasted a cinnamon bun
quite like this. What's the difference?"

"A hint of cardamom. It's a delicate balance," Andy explained.

Vance licked icing from the fringe of his moustache.
"You've got a winner here, Andy. When can I buy a dozen?"

"Not quite yet. But why don't you share the rest of these
with the other vendors. It might spark interest for future
orders."

Katie made a grab for the plate, snatching another sticky
roll, glad she'd eaten only two of the peanut butter cookies
before leaving the apartment. "Not until I get my fair share."

Vance also took an extra roll, placed it on a napkin, and
set it on the vendors' lounge table. "For Vance Junior. He'll

be here in a while to look at that old video recorder, Katie.
If he ever gets out of bed." Vance disappeared around the
corner with the plate and a fist full of napkins.

"They're even better with a cup of joe. Buy you one?"
Andy offered.

"I get mine for free," Katie said.

"Then how can you miss?" Andy grabbed her cup from
the desk, returning in seconds with steaming coffee, doctored just the way she liked it.

"Thanks." Katie took a sip and nibbled on her cinnamon
roll, feeling the tension within her ebb.

Andy perched on the edge of her desk. Speckles of flour
dotted the rolled-up sleeves of his sweatshirt. His muscled
forearms seemed rigid with anxiety. Not what Katie expected after his culinary presentation.

"I saw them put up the for-sale sign on the mansion late
yesterday," he said quietly. "I thought about calling you but
knew it would just upset you. I figured you deserved a good
night's sleep."

"I didn't get that either, but what else is new?"

"Katie, why do you torture yourself over that wreck of a
place?" Andy asked.

"Because it was supposed to be *mine*. We almost had
enough to close the deal when Chad invested in this—
this"—she held off from swearing—"money pit," she finally
spat. "It'll take me five years just to get out of debt. I'll never
get to open the English Ivy Inn. Never." She covered her
eyes to hide stinging tears.

Andy's warm hand settled on her shoulder. "Life handed
you a pile a crap in this place, but look what you've done in
only six months. It's a going concern again. You've got
happy vendors . . . well, most of them. No creditors are
breathing down your neck, and you've got the world's best
neighbor in Angelo's Pizzeria."

Katie uncovered her eyes, turning her head to look at
him. Andy's eyes were red-rimmed from lack of sleep. His

jaw bristled with unshaved whiskers. How long had it taken him to make three batches of cinnamon rolls?

"My ad for the assistant manager's job will be in tomorrow's paper," he said in what sounded like a peace offering.

Katie had to clear her throat before she could speak. "That's great, Andy. And it looks like you'll get to fulfill your dream of Cinnamon Bun King."

"And if you're *real* lucky, you can be my queen."

Katie eyed him speculatively. "The job better come with one hell of a tiara."

Andy bowed, took her hand, and gently kissed her knuckles, just like Mark Bastian had done the night before. Katie didn't feel up to telling him about that right now. "What are you doing for lunch today?" she asked.

Andy released her hand and straightened. "I've got a vendor coming in to give me a dog and pony show. I might need some different equipment if I'm going ahead with a new product."

Katie sighed. "Tomorrow, then?"

"I'll pencil you in my Day-Timer." His goofy smile made Katie laugh. "By the way, which of your old lady friends does the crafts? Rose or Edie? I can never keep 'em straight."

"Edie, why?"

He shrugged. "Just curious. Maybe she can tell me who could make me some fake cinnamon rolls to put in my front window. For marketing purposes," he clarified.

"Oh, right."

Andy nodded at the roll growing cool on her desk. "Eat up. They're at their peak right now, not unlike their creator."

Katie shook her head. "Oh, the power of the inflated male ego."

Andy pulled her from her seat, folding his arms around her. "Let's go out on a real date sometime next week. A movie, dinner, anything you want."

Katie pulled back, their gazes locking. "It's a deal, but with one proviso."

"What's that?"

"We eat anything but pizza."

~~~~~~~

"Debbie's gone," said a cheerful voice in a singsong cadence.

Katie looked up from her computer screen to find Edie Silver standing in the doorway of her office looking flushed. "So soon?"

"Today was the only day her daughter had free to help her move out. Is it okay if I start taking my stuff to her booth?"

Katie glanced at the wall clock. Artisans Alley had opened its doors half an hour before. "I'd rather you didn't. It doesn't look good if customers see us restocking during business hours."

Edie's mouth drooped, making her look like a sad, tired bulldog. "I know, but I *really* want to get away from Polly as soon as I can."

Katie stared into Edie's gray eyes, her willpower draining away. She was a sucker when it came to old people—especially Rose and Edie. She saved her document and stood. "Okay. I don't have a lot of time this morning, but I could give you a few minutes to help pack."

"I've already started. I was here when Vance opened this morning. I stacked all my merchandise in shopping hand baskets and have been bringing them down two at a time."

"What about your display pieces?"

"Vance and Billy are going to move those. We should be done before lunch."

Katie waved a hand in submission. "Okay, finish up. I'll be up to help in a few minutes. I need to make a few calls first."

Edie beamed. "Thanks, Katie."

Katie searched her desk for the list of prospective vendors. Several calls later, she had set up appointments with two crafters and a sculptor to inspect Edie's old booth. With luck, she'd rent the space within a day.

By the time Katie made it upstairs, Edie had placed the last of her crafts into a basket. All that remained were five or six display pieces, including a long table covered with a cloth of cheerful Easter bunnies rolling eggs across a pale green background.

"What do you want me to do?" Katie asked.

"If you could fold the cloth and knock down the table, I'll tell Vance we're ready to move these display pieces."

"Will do," Katie said as Edie picked up the last plastic shopping basket and headed for the stairs.

Katie grabbed the cloth, which was actually two pieces of carefully matched fabric with a seam down the middle. Edie had hemmed the edges, adding a pretty white ruffle. Katie folded it neatly and bent down to look at the table's legs. Underneath were a scattering of boxes that Edie had obviously forgotten she'd stashed. Katie nested the smaller boxes into the larger ones. Most were empty, but one was nearly stuffed with handcrafted doll accessories—clothes, shoes, wigs—a darning egg, and a couple of bisque doll arms and legs: most of the missing items from Polly Bremerton's booth. She dug deeper into the box and found other bits and pieces, most from booth eighty-seven, which was kitty-corner to Polly's booth. Katie sat back on her heels, the cinnamon bun turning to lead in her stomach.

Okay, there were two possibilities to consider. Either Polly herself had taken the items, planting them in Edie's booth to incriminate her or—and this was something Katie did not want to believe—Edie *had* been stealing.

Then again, someone else might have done it just to see sparks fly from afar. She gazed at the other booths nearby. This back section of Artisans Alley wasn't exactly Siberia, but it wasn't as well traveled as other sections of the upper floor. Was one of the newer vendors vying for a better location, hoping to incite insurrection as a diabolical plot to move up Artisans Alley's pecking order by eliminating the competition?

Nah, very few vendors with upstairs booths made much more than their rent on a weekly basis. It wasn't money but the love of what they were doing that kept them here week after week.

Katie folded in the carton's flaps and took the box back to her office. Next she pulled out her list of vendors and traced down to number eighty-seven. This vendor made primitive-looking animal sculptures out of clay. She punched the phone number onto the phone's keypad.

"Hi, Joan. It's Katie Bonner from Artisans Alley. Have you noticed any missing items from your booth?"

"Off and on. Mostly little things."

Katie picked up a horse decked out in a saddle and reins, rocking it back and forth until it appeared to be walking across her desk. "How come you haven't reported it?"

"I figured shoplifting was just a consequence of being in business."

"Well, I'm happy to tell you that I may have found a bunch of them. I'll keep them in my office until you can get in to pick them up."

"Oh, don't bother. Just put them in the basket for reshelves." She laughed. "Who knows, the quicker they're back in my booth, the quicker they might sell."

"Will do," Katie said.

"I'll see you on Monday. Bye."

Katie replaced the receiver. Could Polly have put some of Joan's items into the box so it wouldn't look so terribly suspicious? Maybe. But then Katie remembered something Rose had said days before. Edie had been confused some months before when her medication had been changed.

Could kleptomania be another symptom of a prescription drug interaction, or was Katie just looking for excuses to explain away the truth?

She replaced the items in the box and put it under her desk and out of sight.

Talk about an act of denial.

"Miz Bonner?"

Vance Junior stood poised to knock on the doorjamb. Dressed in dark baggy pants and shirt, with a pink do-rag tied around his cropped fair hair, the boy looked like every other McKinlay Mill High School slouch. Only his keen blue eyes betrayed the intelligence he tried to hide. "My dad says you want that old VCR fixed."

"Yes, thank you, Vance Junior."

The boy cringed. "Aw, please don't call me that. It makes me feel like some dorky old country singer. I like VJ better."

"Thanks, VJ," she amended. She grabbed her mug and followed him back into the vendors' lounge.

Within a minute, she'd poured herself yet another cup of coffee as VJ stuffed a cinnamon roll into his mouth with one hand and inspected the VCR's innards with the other.

"Oh, there you are, Katie," Edie said upon entering the vendors' lounge. "Can you give me a hand putting my stuff out? Hi, Vance Junior."

VJ winced again and swallowed. "Hi."

"Edie there's something we need to talk ab—"

"I can see your problem," VJ said, interrupting her as he bent over the VCR. "The motor's seized up. You also need some new drive belts—these are shot. Might cost five or six bucks. Is that okay?" He looked up at her.

"Hurry up, will you, Katie? The customers can't buy my merchandise if it's sitting in baskets," Edie said tartly, and marched off again.

Katie stared after her, startled by Edie's sudden brusque demeanor—or rather the return of her usual demeanor. She turned back to the boy who was still awaiting an answer. "Do whatever you need to do."

"Uh, my dad said something about pizza later," VJ hinted.

"Whatever you want. Do you need the money now?"

"Nope. You can pay me later."

Katie nodded. "I better go help Edie."

VJ settled into a chair and started tinkering with the motor.

Katie started for Edie's new booth. On second thought, she changed direction. Before she confronted Edie, she needed more information. She'd talk to Rose first. Either way, she was going to have to deal with what she'd found up in Edie's old booth.

Swell. Just swell.

Seventeen

Artisans Alley had been open for almost an hour when Katie sidled up to cash desk one. A few customers ambled among the aisles, but it looked to be a slow sales day. Rose had her nose buried in a romance novel, its cover showing two scantily clad figures clinging to one another.

Katie leaned against the counter. "Have you noticed anything different about Edie lately?"

Rose looked up from her book. "Different?"

"When Edie first came to Artisans Alley she was . . ." Katie faltered. She had to get this right. "A very dynamic individual. Yet lately she's been . . ." Her voice trailed off.

"Kind of frail?" Rose offered.

"Yes." Katie waited, but Rose made no other comment. "She seems to have—" Had Edie been a man, Katie might've said that she'd grown some balls. Vulgar—but an accurate assessment. "Overcome that in the past half hour," Katie finished tactfully.

"What are you saying?" Rose asked.

Katie thought about it. How had she felt just minutes

ago? Like a fool? Like she'd been taken in? Manipulated? Or had she just imagined Edie's sudden transformation back to her old forceful self?

"Nothing." As Rose and Edie were friends, she decided it would be better not to discuss the situation with Rose. "I'm going back to my office to make some calls. Holler if it gets busy and you need help."

"Sure thing," Rose said, her gaze dipping back to her book.

VJ had disappeared from the vendors' lounge, probably off to buy the parts the old VCR needed, Katie thought as she cut through to get to her office. She sank into her chair and eyed the phone book. She didn't want to call every apartment complex within a ten- or twenty-mile radius of Artisans Alley. She was tired of living in one of those boring, cookie-cutter rabbit warrens. That's why she'd targeted her home search at finding a duplex.

No, if she was really honest with herself, she wanted to live in the old Webster mansion, and that was never going to happen.

The box of wedding favors still sat on her desk. It was time to declutter—which would also delay her phone book search. Getting up from her chair, she grabbed the box and headed for the cash desk again. "Rose, I'm going to drop these off to Gilda and take a walk around the Square. I'll be back in a few minutes."

Rose waved a hand in acknowledgment, not shifting her gaze away from her book.

Katie left the building and started across the parking lot, navigating past parked cars lined up in front of the Square's shops. The cool gray morning hinted at rain showers to come—always good for perking up afternoon sales.

Katie made a beeline for Gilda's Gourmet Baskets. The quicker she relinquished custody of the wedding favors, the happier she'd be.

The bell over the door tinkled cheerfully as Katie

stepped inside Gilda's shop. There seemed to be a lull in business, which was the perfect time to talk—about a number of subjects.

Gilda was busy putting together yet another one of her wonderful gift baskets. She held a stemmed wineglass with a piece of iridescent curly ribbon tied on. She took a small pair of scissors and pulled the ribbon until it curled artistically. Katie took in the rest of the basket's contents. "Someone else getting married?"

Gilda looked up and smiled. "Yes. Lots of brides. The bridal shower package is one of my bestselling baskets, along with my themed baby shower and birthday creations. Somehow, I never get tired of putting these gift baskets together."

Which again reminded Katie that she needed to get a shower gift for Monday. And where was she going to find the time to do that? She'd have to shop Artisans Alley, because it wasn't likely she'd find time to go anywhere else in the next few days.

She set the box on the counter. "Here are the favors. There are fifty of them. I hope that's all right."

"Oh, it's perfect. Thanks." Gilda peeked inside the box. "You did a lovely job. Thank you."

"I can't take credit for another woman's work. Edie Silver, one of my vendors, did them for me."

Gilda's smile faded just a little. "Oh. I thought you might have had some fun putting them together."

"I'm afraid I'm not very crafty. Edie said she's made a lot of these over the years."

Gilda sighed, her unspoken disappointment obvious. Katie pretended not to notice.

"Everything's set for the bridal shower on Monday," Katie said. "I couldn't book a place on such short notice, so we're having it in the lobby of Artisans Alley. I've already sent out the invitations."

Gilda lips pursed. "I had my heart set on a tearoom."

"I'm sorry, but there just wasn't time to find one and set it up."

She sighed. "I'll just have to make the best of it, I suppose."

Yes, you will, Katie thought sourly, and had to bite her tongue not to say it. "We'll decorate it nicely, and Blueberry Catering will do a great job with the food."

Gilda perked up. "They do nice work," she allowed, and went back to curling ribbon.

Katie had expected just a little bit more gratitude for her efforts, but when it wasn't forthcoming, she decided to forge on to other subjects. "Have you had to field many calls from the press since the . . . remains . . . were found at the Webster mansion?"

Gilda shook her head. "As Ezra Hilton's death last fall proved, there's no such thing as bad publicity. In between wedding arrangements, I managed to poll most of the other merchants; we all agreed that we saw a spike in business the day after the young woman's bones were found." She brandished a thumbs-up.

As long as they were talking Merchants Association business, Katie went on. "I'm still concerned about the unrented spaces on Victoria Square. I've spoken to Fred Cunningham from Cunningham Realty. It looks like the old Tea and Tasties location *will* once again open as a tea shop. The new owners take possession at the end of the month and hope to be up and running within three weeks of occupying the space."

"That's terrific," Gilda said. "I'll get Ann Tanner to send them the Merchants Association welcome information."

"Thanks."

The phone rang, which gave Katie the perfect excuse to exit. She gave a quick wave as Gilda picked up the phone. As she left the shop, two customers entered, which pleased her. What was good for one merchant was good for all of Victoria Square.

Katie gazed around the parking lot. She could just head

back to Artisans Alley, but she'd meant it when she'd told Rose she wanted to walk around the Square. She passed Wood U and waved at Dennis Wheeler, who seemed to be polishing a handcrafted wooden bowl. He waggled his cloth in return as Katie quickened her pace and headed east. As she'd hoped, the Webster mansion's front door was open. Katie headed up the steps. "Janice? Toby?" she called.

"C'mon in," Janice yelled.

Katie stepped over the threshold. The crime tape was gone. The mansion's dark interior felt more chilled and damp than the outside air. Katie hugged herself for warmth as she took in the work tools stacked in neat piles. The boxes from the attic had been brought downstairs. Janice appeared from the hall with a broom in hand. She seemed older than she'd been five days before when Katie had first met her.

"I'm glad you're here, Katie. Toby had to work and I don't like being here on my own anymore."

"I saw the sign outside. I'm so sorry you had to put the place back up for sale. What happened?"

Janice sighed and her face seemed to collapse. Her distress was obvious. "Losing nearly a week to the police investigation really hit us hard in the pocketbook. When the contractor canceled, it meant we'd have to put off the construction for up to two months. That set a domino effect in motion. The electrical work can't be done until the walls are moved. The plumber can't come in until the floor joists are reinforced. All of a sudden we're drowning in debt, with no hope of opening until late summer—if then."

"But you'll still be paying your mortgage, even if you don't work toward opening."

Janice frowned. "To tell you the truth, I just don't think we could go through with it now. It was bad enough when you found that skeleton in the wall. But this last death . . ." She shook her head. "Just being here upsets me. I'd never get a good night's sleep in this house knowing what happened to those women."

"But a lot of old houses have a scandalous history. If you market it right—"

Janice shook her head. "I *don't* want to do this anymore."

And I'd sell my soul for the opportunity to try, Katie thought bitterly.

"I was going to come over to Artisans Alley today to try to sell some of this old junk. Do you think any of the vendors would buy it?"

"It's possible. I'll spread the word," Katie promised.

"Thanks. Can you give me a hand loading these tools into the car?" Janice asked.

Katie mustered her most reassuring smile. "Sure."

Twenty minutes later, and with her minivan loaded, Janice gave Katie a halfhearted wave as she pulled out of the Victoria Square parking lot.

It began to drizzle as Katie started back for Artisans Alley. She let her gaze swivel toward the pizza shop and the apartment above it. If only Andy would let her rent it, part of her dream of living on Victoria Square would've come true, but even that seemed impossible right now.

Damp and disheartened, Katie entered Artisans Alley via the main entrance, as the side entrance was locked during business hours. The lobby was huge and empty—a vast wasted space during the times when no special sales event was planned. She paused, remembering something the real estate agent who'd represented the Webster mansion had once said. If she could get a small cafe going on-site, she'd be able to keep customers in-house to buy the vendors' wares—and she'd make more money, too.

Katie knew next to nothing about food service, but she supposed she could learn. No doubt Andy would be a font of useful information on the subject—*if* he wished to share it. Or maybe she should try to rent the space for special events after hours. Perhaps for bridal and/or baby showers and other such gatherings. Having extended hours—and a captive buying audience—would please her vendors . . . if she could get enough of them to commit to working during those times.

She filed the thoughts away for future contemplation and entered Artisans Alley's main showroom.

Arms crossed and sporting a sour expression, Edie Silver stood at cash desk one. Katie winced as she realized more than an hour had passed since she'd promised to help Edie arrange her new booth. "Edie, I—"

"Where have you been?" Edie demanded. "You said you'd help me!"

"I did what you asked. As I told you before, I have other things I have to get done today. Honestly, I expected you to move your merchandise on Monday, not today."

"And I told you why I needed to do it today."

"I'm sorry, I—"

Edie didn't bother to listen. Instead, she turned on her heel and stalked off.

Katie flushed, suddenly transported back to first grade. Mean Mrs. Memmitt had chastised her just as harshly when she'd found Katie had fibbed about having a pony in her backyard.

"Edie," Katie called, but the older woman didn't turn or slow down. Katie looked to Rose, who merely shrugged.

Katie swallowed the lump in her throat, noticing several customers staring at her in judgment, as though she'd just blasphemed the Pope.

"I didn't—" she started but let the words trail off. She did too have other things to do, but in all honesty she hadn't wanted to help Edie with her booth because she felt used.

"Can you help me with this order?" Rose asked with just the hint of a clipped tone, and Katie stepped up to the counter to bag a customer's handmade paper note cards.

The busywork soothed Katie's frayed nerves. Edie's expectations reminded her of another obligation she hadn't fulfilled—telling Rose about her meeting with Bastian. Rose would no doubt want to know what Katie had learned but would be hurt that she hadn't been invited to attend the dinner meeting. She seemed to be disappointing everyone she spoke to that day.

Katie waited until the customers had departed to speak. "Remember that call you took yesterday from Mark Bastian?"

"Vaguely," Rose said, already flipping through her paperback and withdrawing her makeshift bookmark.

"He's Rick Jeremy's personal assistant."

Rose slammed her book shut, her eyes going wide with interest. "Great! What have you found out?"

Katie gave a recap of her conversation with Bastian—leaving out where it had taken place—including what he'd said about having a place to get drunk.

"Why didn't you tell me this yesterday?" Rose asked, sounding hurt.

Katie gave a guilty sigh. "Because I only spoke to him last night." *And please don't ask me where.*

Rose didn't. Instead she said, "You suspected it might be him and Jeremy who did the renovations at the mansion."

Katie nodded.

"Why were they replacing the walls in Barbie's apartment?"

Katie opened her mouth to speak, realized she had no answer, and then shut it. Bastian had said he'd done some drywall, but he didn't specify where. Instead she asked, "What do you mean?"

"If they were in the habit of going over there to hang out, presumably the apartment was intact. What happened to the walls that they needed to be replaced?" Rose asked.

Katie felt even more uncomfortable. "I don't know. It never occurred to me to ask."

Rose raised a wispy eyebrow. "Maybe you should call him back and do just that."

~~~~~

Katie punched the phone number into the keypad and waited. "You have reached Mark Bastian. Leave your name, number, and a short message. I may or may not return your call."

Beep!

Katie slammed the phone's receiver back into its cradle. She'd left a message more than an hour before but kept trying the hotel every fifteen minutes in hopes Bastian might have returned. Jeremy would pick up his lifetime achievement award later that evening. No doubt they were taking advantage of any possible PR opportunities they could get, of which there seemed to be many. In between calls, Katie had retrieved the newspapers from the recycling box and cut out every article that mentioned Rick Jeremy. A sidebar gave his filmography. That might help with her Internet search.

She spread the cuttings out before her, still pondering why Bastian and Richards had been hired to fix Barbie's apartment. Why hadn't she thought to look more closely at the area that had encompassed Barbie's apartment when she'd been there hours earlier?

On impulse, Katie dialed another number.

"Cunningham Realty," answered a male voice.

"Fred? It's Katie Bonner." She waited impatiently as they exchanged pleasantries. "Any chance I can get a walkthrough at the old Webster mansion today?"

"Katie." He said her name with an air of pity and subtle irritation. He'd been only too willing to take her through the mansion during those years when he thought she might buy the place. But now he knew her financial situation—how much she owed and exactly how long it would take her to get out of debt. "You know you can't afford it," he said, reasonably.

"Please, Fred, it's important to me."

Fred sighed deeply. "I don't have the time today. Maybe Monday or Tuesday—"

"I wouldn't ask, except . . ." Her words died off. Jeremy would be gone by tomorrow—back to Los Angeles. If Bastian didn't give her another audience, she might lose the opportunity to confront him with . . . what? What evidence could she possibly find at this late date? But she knew she had to try.

"How about if I stop by Artisans Alley and drop off the key?" Fred suggested.

Katie's hope soared. "Fred, I could kiss you."

"Don't tell my wife about that. And you've got to promise not to tell anyone else that I'm letting you into the place. And for heaven's sake, *not* the owners."

"I promise, I promise."

Fred sighed, sounding weary. "Okay, I'll be there a little after four. See you then."

Katie hung up the phone, jubilation coursing through her. Her feet did a jig under her desk until someone cleared his throat to her right. VJ stood in her doorway, trying hard not to laugh—but not entirely succeeding.

"Miz Bonner, I got the video recorder going. Ya wanna see an old episode of *Dragnet* my dad taped years ago? I've already tested it and it's working fine."

"Wow, that was quick. But *Dragnet* doesn't interest me. Let me get my own tape." In seconds she'd retrieved the beta tape from her desk drawer and was standing next to VJ at the venders' lounge table. The TV was on but showing only electronic snow. A harsh hiss issued from its speaker. Vance ambled up as VJ shoved Katie's tape into the machine.

"Ya wanna push the 'play' button?" VJ offered.

"Sure." Katie hit the switch with perverse delight. A loud hum replaced the static as the TV screen went a murky green. Was the tape a duplicate of a duplicate? Tinny music began before a picture formed. Fuzzy titles appeared and Katie's mouth dropped open as she read them:

JER-MARK PRODUCTIONS PRESENTS
STAR WHORES—Episode 3
Starring Sleazy Galore
Once upon a time, in a suburb far, far away . . .

"A porn flick?" Vance asked, aghast.

"Yeah!" VJ said with obvious relish.

A tall, thin woman decked out in a cheap-looking, silver lame catsuit strutted across the screen. Her short, Clara Bow wig might have been purple—it was hard to tell through the distortion. The audio was so lousy Katie couldn't make out what the woman was saying to a stringy-looking guy in a Luke Skywalker karate suit. There was something familiar about the man's stance, but his appearance was all wrong. The hair should've been darker. He, too, was wearing a bad wig. The flesh tones bled into the predominantly green background.

The woman spoke again, and the camera angle changed to give her a close-up. She simpered, her pouting lips a garish green.

"Holy smoke," Katie breathed, "it's Heather Winston."

Eighteen

VJ hit the video recorder's stop button. The TV let out a blast of white noise and the screen went back to snow. "Let's fast-forward it. Maybe it gets better."

He pressed the appropriate button and the bulky machine's innards whirred with renewed vigor as the analog counter spun forward.

Katie's only knowledge of movie production had been gleaned from magazine articles, but even she could tell the difference between video and film, and Heather's movie debut had been made on film. The movie's opening scene had been staged at the McKinlay Mill town park. Could the rest of it have been shot in town as well? It took hot white light to properly film indoor scenes. And if so . . .

VJ hit the play button and the TV glowed green once again. A large, creased, rounded object bounced up and down on the screen, and Katie squinted to make sense of the image. The camera pulled back and she goggled at a man's bare backside as a woman's exaggerated groans of pleasure issued from the TV's speaker.

Vance whipped a hand in front of his son's eyes. "You shouldn't watch this. Your mother would kill me if she knew."

VJ pulled the hand away. "This is tame compared to HBO. Let's fast-forward it some more to see—"

Vance hit the stop button. "No!"

"Dad, I'm sixteen. In another three months, I can go see any NC-17–rated movie I want."

"Yeah, well, until that day—"

"Your father's right, VJ," Katie piped up, but she, too, wanted to watch—not the movie, but the end credits. "I don't want to be responsible for—" For what? Corrupting the boy? At sixteen, VJ was probably a lot more worldly than she'd been at the same age—her great-aunt Lizzie had seen to that. Thanks to TV, violent video games, and rap music, kids were exposed to more of the seamier side of life than Katie had ever been—or probably ever would be.

"Anyway, thanks for fixing this old video recorder. What do I owe you for the parts?" she said.

"Seven dollars and four cents. Uh . . . and a large pizza with double cheese, pepperoni, onions, peppers, mushrooms, sausage, bacon, and ham."

Cholesterol city! Katie bit back a smile. "That, too. Hang on, let me get the money." As she stepped into her office, the phone rang. She answered it. "Artisans Alley. How can I help you?"

"Mrs. Bonner. It's Kevin Hartsfield."

The man with the wrecked apartment. What could he possibly want?

"Oh, hello."

"I wanted to thank you for putting me onto the high school's work-for-credit program. The senior boys' Industrial Arts class will start repairing my house on Monday."

"Oh, that's terrific. I'm so glad I could help."

An awkward silence fell until Hartsfield cleared his

throat. "I . . . uh . . . saw in the morning paper that Heather Winston's memorial service is tomorrow afternoon."

"Yes. I hope you'll be able to make it. It would mean a lot to Heather's aunt."

"Have the police had any luck finding out what happened to her?"

"Detective Davenport never tells me anything," Katie almost blurted but stopped herself in time. "Not that I know of. It happened such a long time ago."

"That's too bad." Hartsfield's voice had an odd inflection. Did he actually sound relieved?

Keep him talking—keep him talking.

"I know Heather's aunt would love to hear anything you remember about Heather from her high school days." Especially once she found out about Heather's post–high school antics.

"I don't know what I could say except that she was a good student."

Stall, stall!

"Was she involved in any after-school activities? Perhaps the Drama Club?"

"Not that I recall. As you said, it was a long time ago. We all moved on."

Only, thanks to whoever placed her body between sheets of drywall, Heather hadn't.

That wasn't entirely true. Heather had lived another eighteen months after high school graduation. Long enough to get involved with Jeremy Richards and make at least one porn film—maybe more.

Stall, stall! something inside Katie implored

"I met Barbie Gordon's daughter the other day."

"Oh?" Now Hartsfield sounded interested.

"Without her mother to help out, Donna is in desperate need of financial as well as emotional support."

"What's that got to do with me?" he asked.

"I was thinking . . . you're probably the only person around who knew Barbie back then. Do you have any idea who Donna's father might be?"

"It's been over twenty years," he said, mildly reproachful.

"Yes, but circumstances change. Perhaps her biological father might welcome contact from his daughter."

"I'm sorry, Mrs. Bonner, but I was Barbie's math teacher, not her guidance counselor. As I recall, she was very independent—not the type to confide in just anyone."

Katie sighed. "I suppose you're right."

Just then, VJ poked his head into her office, looking hopeful. Katie held up her right index finger, signaling him to wait a moment.

"I do hope you'll be at the service tomorrow, Mr. Hartsfield," she pressed.

"I can't promise—but I'll try. Good-bye, Mrs. Bonner."

Katie hung up the phone. She stepped back to open the safe, doled out money from petty cash, and handed it to a smiling VJ.

"Is it okay if I order the pizza tonight, Miz Bonner? Some friends are coming over and we're going to play Xbox."

"Sure. I'll let the owner over at Angelo's know to expect your order."

He pocketed the money. "Thanks, ma'am. See ya."

Ma'am! No way could Katie ever get used to being called *that*!

She followed the boy out and watched as he disappeared into Artisans Alley's main showroom. Vance was packing up the tools his son had left behind.

"VJ's a good kid," Katie said.

"Yeah. He gets good grades, helps around the house, and never gets in trouble. He's just about the perfect son." Vance closed his toolbox. "Now if we could just teach him to pick up wet towels and take out the garbage on a regular basis, life *would* be grand."

Katie smiled. "Oh, I almost forgot. Can you close for me tomorrow night? I need to be at the funeral parlor for Rose's niece's service."

"No problem. It'll give you a break from dealing with Polly."

"Isn't it a sad commentary to prefer to attend a funeral than dealing with that woman. But she does have some good ideas for placating the artisans here at the Alley."

Vance's eyes crinkled. "I'm an artisan. Why don't you try to placate me?"

Katie smiled and told Vance of her conversation with Polly several days before.

Vance nodded. "We could ask Burt Donahue to come in and give appraisals. He specializes in antiques, but he's knowledgeable about a lot of specialty items, too. I think he charges by the piece, but that's pretty standard."

"Damn, I could've asked him the other night at the auction house. I'll have to give him a call."

Vance glanced down at the recorder. "What are you going to do about the videotape? Will you tell Rose what's on it?"

"If it ends up helping to solve Heather's murder, she'll have to know. I want to watch the credits at the end before I do anything else."

"I thought you might. I fast-forwarded it for you and reset the counter in case you want to see them again." Vance hit the play button.

Tinny music issued from the TV's speaker as a long list of blurry names scrolled past, none of them familiar. Katie watched the credits two more times before she noticed a pattern. She jotted down a few of the names and the copyright year.

"All the names have similar initials. MB, BJ, JR, and a couple of HWs."

"Is that supposed to be significant?" Vance asked, closing his toolbox.

"Probably not to anybody but me."

"What do you mean?"

Katie doodled boxes on the edge of her pad. "Well, you could see the production values were shoestring at best. I'll bet only four people worked on the film, taking on phony names in the credits."

"You think you know who those people are?"

"Betty Jasper the costumer had to be Barbie Jackson. Hilda Wentworth could've been Heather Winston." She frowned. "I guess I should share my suspicions with Detective Davenport."

Vance's laugh was mirthless. "Better you than me."

Katie removed the tape from the machine and hit the power button to switch it off. Then she grabbed her pad and went back to her office and dug out the creased business card Detective Davenport had given her months before.

His voice mail picked up on the first ring. She waited for the beep and spoke. "Detective, it's Katie Bonner. I have a piece of—" She couldn't call it evidence—it wasn't part of Heather's crime scene. But it did represent a Pandora's box of questions pertinent to the case. The great Academy Award–winning director Rick Jeremy would not want the world to know how he'd started his now-illustrious career. Katie studied the Roman numerals on the paper before her. The film's copyright had been for the year of Heather's death. She'd been the film's star, while Barbie and Bastian had apparently done most of the grunt work.

Barbie said she had evidence for Katie, but she'd also indicated she was holding on to it for leverage. She'd been killed that night. The tape had been mailed the day before her death. Count Barbie out.

Bastian had to be the one who'd sent it to Katie. By his own admission, his relationship with Jeremy was strained. Did he always travel with a bad copy of *Star Whores*, just waiting for an opportunity to let someone know of its existence?

Yet why kill the cash cow? He hadn't seemed the vengeful type. Or despite his claims to the contrary, he was more of an actor than he professed to be. The bad wig hadn't changed his appearance enough to hide his identity as Heather's co-star. And why send the tape to her, not Rose or the police?

Too many things didn't add up.

Davenport's voice mail beeped and disconnected.

Damn!

Katie dialed again, left another message and her phone number. Eventually Davenport would get back to her. If he didn't call before Jeremy's award ceremony that evening, she'd make more of an effort to track him down tomorrow.

"I understand you found my property," said a voice from the open doorway. Polly Bremerton's fierce blue-eyed gaze bored into Katie.

She put the phone down. "I beg your pardon."

"I saw Joan MacDonald at the grocery store a few minutes ago. She said you'd found a number of her missing items. I assume you found mine as well."

Katie's gaze darted to the floor and the box under her desk. "Yes, but—"

"Where did you find them?"

"Inside Artisans Alley."

"Where, specifically?" Polly demanded.

Katie bent down to retrieve the box and mumbled a reply.

"I didn't hear you."

"Upstairs." Katie set the carton on her desk and opened the flaps.

Polly stepped forward to rummage through the contents. "Nearly all of this is *my* property." She faced Katie. "Did you find this in Edie Silver's booth?"

"Yes, but—"

"I told you that woman was stealing from me, but you wouldn't listen. I want her arrested, and I expect you to call the police right now."

"Now, Polly, be reasonable. I don't know that Edie hid these items in her booth. They were behind a lot of other empty boxes. For all I know, you may have put them there to implicate her."

Polly's cheeks glowed pink. "How dare you accuse me!"

Katie stood her ground. "Since the day Edie arrived, you've done nothing but snipe at her."

"You're just sticking up for her because she's your friend—and she does you lots of little favors. I saw her working on those wedding favors, and then pinning up that dress."

Katie couldn't argue with that.

"I've been taken advantage of one time too many," Polly continued. "I'm not going to stand for this kind of treatment any longer. I just can't take any more!"

Katie shied back from her. "If you feel strongly about it, feel free to call the Sheriff's Office and make a complaint."

"*Me*, call them?" Polly looked absolutely horror stricken.

"It's doubtful they'd even write up a complaint, as you've already recovered your missing property, but you can give it a try."

Polly's breaths were coming in snorts once again. "Well, I-I . . . I'll think it over," she said at last. She hefted the carton into her arms and stormed from the office.

"Please put Joan's items back in her booth," Katie called after her, but Polly continued on without a backward glance.

Katie frowned after her. Polly's overreaction to the whole situation was puzzling. There had to be more on her mind than just Edie and the trinkets missing from her booth. And why did she balk at the thought of calling the Sheriff's Office?

What did she have to hide?

Nineteen

"I didn't do it," Edie said, her eyes bulging in indignation.

"I don't think you did either, but Polly does, and we may have to deal with the repercussions," Katie said reasonably.

Edie turned back to a table display of floral arrangements in her new booth, tweaking a bit of silk greenery. The muscles in her face did odd gyrations before she spoke again.

"I'm sorry I was so short with you earlier, Katie. It was unfair of me to expect you to drop everything to help me this morning."

"Edie, I—"

"No, no," she continued, her voice growing softer as she plumped up a basket of artificial peach-colored tulips. "I know you don't like us setting up while Artisans Alley is open, but I just bulldozed through the rules to get down here today." She turned back to Katie. "Dealing with Polly these past few weeks as been unbearable. No one's ever pushed my buttons the way she has, and I'm ashamed of how I reacted." Her gaze was hopeful. "No hard feelings?"

The corners of Katie's mouth twitched. "Not from me."

Edie picked up the basket of cheerful tulips. "Then I hope you'll accept this arrangement as an apology."

Katie held out a hand to rebuff the offer. "Oh, Edie, you don't have to—"

"They'd sure cheer up your office."

That was asking a lot, as despite all Katie's efforts to redecorate the place, it still looked terribly shabby. Still, she accepted the offered gift. "Thank you."

Pounding footsteps caused both women to turn as Vance charged up the aisle, pausing at the edge of Edie's booth. "Burt Donahue's out front. Now might be a good time to ask him about coming in to appraise customers' treasures," he puffed, slightly out of breath.

"Good idea," Katie said. "Where is he?"

"The main showroom." Vance beckoned her with his hand. "Come on."

"Thanks again, Edie," Katie said and, still clasping the basket of silk flowers, hurried off in Vance's wake.

Burt Donahue stood near Rose's downstairs booth, examining a glass display case filled with gleaming gemstone pins and necklaces. A number of people seemed to be clustered around him, reminding Katie of Rick Jeremy's entourage. Unlike Jeremy's minions, the two men and one woman brandished the same almost-sneer as their esteemed leader.

Katie marched up to the auction house owner, extending her hand. "It's good to see you again, Mr. Donahue."

Donahue shook her hand, rather too firmly, and glanced around the cavernous showroom, his flinty gaze landing on a pyramid of handcrafted teddy bears dressed in Easter bunny outfits in the next booth.

"I haven't been here in years. It was just after Ezra opened the place." He glanced down at the basket of silk tulips in Katie's hand, a smirk creeping onto his lips. "Looks a lot different. Your influence, no doubt."

Katie flexed her fingers and figured the gibe referred to the crafters who now shared space in what had once been a fine-arts-only arcade. "What brings you to Victoria Square, Mr. Donahue?" she asked in her most cheerful voice.

"The Webster mansion. I heard it was back up for sale. I may want to purchase it again."

"Oh?" Only days before he'd declared the mansion to be a money pit.

"I've been following the progress the Square's Merchants Association has made these last few months. The time may have come for an upscale B and B to join the mix. I've been looking for a good investment opportunity," Donahue explained.

Katie's stomach took a tumble. Not that she could ever hope to buy the place, but Donahue, with his brusque personality, was all wrong for the role of innkeeper. "Would you run it yourself?"

"My son has a degree in hotel management from Cornell. He and his wife would take charge." That explained the framed photo of the graduate in his office.

"Which means our grandchildren would be much closer to us," said the older woman at his side. Katie recognized the nondescript, wrinkled, and saggy-jowled woman as having taken her tax information at the auction house days before. She still looked more like Donahue's mother than his wife.

"Will you put in an offer today?" Katie asked.

Donahue shook his head. "Sylvia and I just did a walk around the outside. We'll wait until Paul gets here. Our decision will be based on the degree of renovation the place needs."

Katie frowned. The mansion had stood empty for at least five years. Why would Donahue suddenly want to own a property he'd dumped nearly twenty years before?

"Have you spoken with Detective Davenport again concerning Heather Winston's murder investigation?" Katie asked.

Donahue frowned. "No, and I don't expect to. That's ancient history. Besides, I never even met the young woman."

"We'd better go, dear," said Donahue's wife, already pulling on his arm.

"Wait!" Katie pivoted to block the auctioneer. "I have a business proposition for you."

Donahue raised an eyebrow. "Oh?"

"We'd like to schedule a time for you to come and appraise our customers' treasures. I understand you do this as a sideline."

"Yes, yes," he said, waving a dismissive hand. "Give Sylvia a call at the auction house on Monday and we'll set something up." With that, he walked away, followed by his wife and entourage.

Vance cleared his throat and for some reason looked embarrassed. "Uh . . . he's a busy man."

Katie glared at him. "Nobody's that busy."

Vance shrugged and glanced at his watch. "We're closing in another twenty minutes."

"Yeah. Would you make the announcement? I need to get back to my office."

"Sure."

Katie headed toward the back of the building, but when a voice hailed her, she stopped.

"Katie!" Rose's eyes were bright as she hurried through the mazelike aisles to join Katie. She clutched a business-sized envelope in one hand. "Fred Cunningham just dropped this off."

Katie stuffed the basket of silk tulips under her left arm and tore open the envelope. "I've got a theory about the need for the renovations in Barbie's apartment over at the old Webster mansion." She brandished the three-inch skeleton key. "Want to help me check it out?"

~~~~~~

The puddled parking lot and low-hanging clouds framing the decrepit old house did little to dispel the sinister aura that seemed to radiate from it, making it look like the set of a bad horror movie. In all the years Katie had longed to buy it, the mansion had never before affected her that way. Knowing two women had died—no, been killed—there intensified the feeling.

Katie turned the old-fashioned key in the lock, opened the heavy oak door, and allowed Rose to precede her into the gloomy entryway, wondering if anyone on the Square had noticed them enter. She eased the door shut, but the sound seemed to bounce around the dank, empty structure.

She flipped the light switch, but the bare bulb hanging in the naked ceiling fixture shed scant light. Janice and Toby had removed the pressed-foam panels from the suspended ceiling, but the network of white support rods still crisscrossed over their heads.

Katie turned on her flashlight, waving its beam over the ceiling.

"What are you looking for?" Rose asked.

"Evidence."

"Of what?"

"I'll let you know when I find it." Katie glanced around the room. She needed a ladder, but Janice had taken all the tools. She could go back to Artisans Alley and get one, but that would draw too much attention to the fact she was poking around the old place.

"Hang on to this, will you?" Katie handed Rose the flashlight and went off in search of a chair—a crate—anything to boost her higher.

A drawer in the old butler's pantry provided a plastic knife, and one of the upstairs bedrooms provided a rather wobbly paint-specked chair, but together she was sure they'd serve her purpose.

Back in the front parlor, where Barbie's studio apartment had been, Katie stepped onto the chair.

"Be careful," Rose admonished.

Katie could almost reach the metal strips. Damn those nineteenth-century architects and their ten-foot ceilings.

She looked around. In the corner sat a large plastic bucket filled with plaster debris.

She jumped from the chair, jarring every inch of her body from her toes to her teeth.

Rose frowned. "We should leave—before you kill yourself."

"Not yet." Three strides later, Katie was at the bucket. She was tempted to just tip it out, but that would only advertise the fact someone had been in the house. The rented Dumpster was still out back, and she used the rear door to get to it, glad the Ryans hadn't installed a security system.

The bucket was not a good fit on the old chair. "Hang on to and steady me, will you?" she asked Rose.

Worry darkened the old woman's creased face, but Rose held Katie's hand as she climbed the rickety stair. "Be careful. We'll be in so much trouble if you get hurt," Rose admonished.

"I'm not going to get hurt," Katie grated. She took the flashlight back from Rose and panned the beam across the knobby original ceiling above the support rods. The plaster should have been smooth, but the paint had flaked away in a number of places. Clutching the plastic knife in her right hand, she reached up to scrape the ceiling. Old paint chips fluttered down on her face and she had to blink them away. When had the original ceiling last been painted? If her theory was correct, it was after Heather's death, and therefore the chips would be lead free.

"Do you have an envelope or a piece of paper?" Katie asked Rose.

Rose rummaged in her handbag, coming up with an empty envelope, its backside sporting a grocery list.

Katie handed her the flashlight again, and scraped the knife against the plaster. Again and again Katie repeated the action before Rose helped her down from her perch.

"Why did you do that?" Rose asked.

Katie dumped a few of the white flakes onto her left

palm. Using the plastic knife, she turned a few over. "See this black stuff?"

"Mold?" Rose suggested.

"Soot. I think there was a fire in Barbie's apartment, which is why they had to replace the walls."

"What's that got to do with Heather's death?"

"It's just a hunch—but I think Heather might have witnessed the fire."

"I don't understand."

Katie studied Rose's puzzled expression. What she had to say would forever change Rose's perception of her long-dead niece.

"Katie, please tell me. I have a right to know," Rose implored.

Katie sighed, and with Rose's help, climbed down to the floor. "You know that beta videotape I got in the mail the other day?"

Rose nodded.

Katie chose her words carefully. "Heather was the lead in an early Rick Jeremy movie."

Roses eyes widened, looking pleased—as if being captured on film meant some kind of immortality for the dead girl. "She never mentioned it to her parents or me."

"I'm not surprised. It was a real low-budget film. They filmed outdoor scenes here in McKinlay Mill. And I'll bet they used Barbie's apartment as one of their sets."

Rose glanced at the floor where the walls had recently come down. "But the space was too small for that. Surely there wasn't room for more than just a bed."

"I'm afraid that's about the only prop they needed."

Rose's eyes went wider still as her cheeks flushed. "Are you saying Heather starred in a-a pornographic movie?"

Katie was no critic, but there was nothing stellar about Heather's performance.

"I'm so sorry, Rose."

Shaking her head in denial, Rose turned away. "No. You

must be mistaken." Then she whirled on Katie. "I want to see that tape."

"I don't think that's a good idea."

"I won't believe it until I see it for myself."

Katie rested a hand on Rose's arm. "You haven't seen your niece—or even videos of her—in over twenty years. Do you really want to remember her like that?"

Tears filled Rose's blue eyes and she swallowed back a sob. "I-I don't know. But if her killer forced her into that terrible lifestyle, it'll only make me more determined to see him brought to justice."

Katie placed what she hoped was a comforting hand on Rose's shoulder. "Okay, but I must warn you, you won't like what you see."

"Heather is dead. I've already faced the worst. How can this be more upsetting that that?"

Katie wasn't sure how to reply.

Heather had been dead for more than two decades. But could Rose face the death of her sweet memories of her only niece?

~~~~~~

"Turn it off," Rose moaned, her voice shaking, and buried her face in her hands.

Katie hit the old VCR's stop button and squeezed her friend's thin shoulder. "I'm sorry, Rose. It was stupid of me to mention it to you. I shouldn't have put you through this."

Rose let out a long, shuddering breath. "No, I needed to see this. I needed to know—" But she didn't finish the sentence. Instead, she rubbed at her eyes, still refusing to meet Katie's gaze. "You said you had a theory about Barbie's apartment."

"Half-baked, but—"

"Please tell me," Rose implored.

Katie felt as though she'd already hurt the old woman enough for one day, yet she took a breath to steel herself before answering. "The backdrop behind the bed appeared to be some kind of metallic paper. It wavered during some of the more"—she choose her words carefully—"energetic scenes. The lights they used to film are very hot. I wouldn't be surprised if it caught fire and—"

Rose nodded. "The soot you showed me on the back of the paint chips pretty much explains what happened."

Katie nodded. "The walls had to be replaced. Mark Bastian told me he and Jeremy started the work but didn't finish it. I believe him. Whoever did complete the job must've walled up Heather."

Rose's expression hardened. "Burt Donahue said he couldn't remember who actually did the work. Do you think he's lying?"

"Not necessarily. He could've hired anyone out of the Penny Saver to do the work. It's been so long, I'm not sure we can track down the people or company who actually did the work."

"It's a job for the Sheriff's Office. If we could ever get that tactless Detective Davenport to show a little interest in the case."

"I've got a call in to him, but it's a Saturday night and Heather's case is about as cold as you can get."

"But Heather's best friend died in the same building only days ago. She *knew* something about Heather's death. She had to. You said she was about to tell you something important back at Del's Diner, but that was before someone scared her off."

"Yes. If only she'd trusted me," Katie said and sighed.

"Then again, why should she? Barbie didn't know you any more than she knew me."

"Exactly. Until that last day, I don't think Barbie really believed Heather's killer would come after her. She'd kept silent for twenty-two years."

"But isn't it odd that Jeremy Richards comes back to town and then Barbie's murdered? Someone sent you that tape. Someone wanted you to make the connection between Heather and Jeremy and Barbie. Who could it be?"

Katie was determined not to air her suspicions. Not without more proof. Instead, she shrugged.

Rose pushed back her chair from the table, struggling to get to her feet. Katie lunged forward to help, but the old woman waved her off. "I'm going home. Heather's memorial service tomorrow will make it a difficult day. I need to get some sleep."

Katie watched as Rose gathered her beige raincoat from a peg on the wall, then carefully tied the white plastic rain bonnet under her chin.

"Do you want me to drive you home?" she asked.

Rose's smile was devoid of wattage. "No, dear. But thank you for asking."

Katie walked Rose to the side exit. "You don't have to come in to work tomorrow."

"But I want to. At least for a few hours. It'll help me bide time before Heather's service." Her voice broke on the last word. Rose pursed her lips, struggling to control her ragged emotions. "I'm so glad Iris and Stan never knew about *that*." Her acid glare raked across the ancient Betamax. "It would have killed them." She turned away and shuffled toward the back door. "I'll see you tomorrow, Katie."

Katie made sure Rose got safely into her car and drove away before she went back into her office to retrieve her purse and keys. Showing Rose that videotape had been one of the hardest things Katie had ever done. Despite her claims to the contrary, would Rose ever be able to forgive her for spoiling her image of Heather as a sweet young girl?

Yet, as Katie thought about it, she'd seen no hint of humiliation in Heather's face. Instead, she thought she'd seen . . . triumph. Could Heather have deluded herself into thinking she could be some kind of porn queen? Or perhaps she believed that it might launch a career that would lead to bigger and better things . . . and make her rich.

Twenty-two years after the fact, they'd never know.

Katie donned her jacket and retrieved her purse from her desk drawer. Patting the pockets, she located her key ring. She glanced down at the desk, looking for the envelope and the key to the Webster mansion. Pawing through the papers didn't reveal the envelope either.

Katie turned off the office light and stepped into the vendors' lounge. No key on the old Formica table either.

She'd lost it. Good grief. How was she going to explain that to Fred Cunningham?

"Oh, swell."

Twenty

With his arms crossed, and his face twisted in a scowl, Andy looked more than a little annoyed. "Vance's kid ordered a *sheet* pizza with *double* cheese, *double* pepperoni, *double* sausage, *double* bacon, *double*—"

"Why don't you just say he ordered double everything?" Katie sat atop the wooden counter that separated the customers from the workers at Angelo's Pizzeria. She stared out the window at the darkened Webster mansion across Victoria Square, swinging her feet and smacking them into the wainscoting.

"Because he didn't want pineapple and anchovies. And will you stop banging the counter?" Andy ordered from his pizza-making station.

Duly chastised, Katie stilled her feet. "How much do I owe you?"

He waved a hand in dismissal. "Nothing. I'll charge it to overhead. Do you want a calzone or a slice of pizza?"

It was all Katie could do not to flinch. "Have you got any of those cinnamon buns left?"

"Nope. I'll bring you one for breakfast. I'll make you a small veggie pizza." Andy grabbed a mound of dough from the rack to his right. "How goes the apartment hunt?"

Oh, dear. Another sore subject.

"Lousy. I meant to call every complex in a ten-mile radius, but instead I frittered the whole day away." Andy didn't roll his eyes, but he looked like he wanted to. "And no," she said before he could speak, "I'm not going to beg to rent your apartment upstairs. I've decided it's much too small for my needs."

"Lucky for you it's not available, then."

Did that mean that despite his complaints about tenants he'd already rented it?

Katie sighed, deciding not to give him the satisfaction of asking. She turned to face him. "What's your big news of the day?"

Andy tossed the dough in the air with the skill of a vaudevillian juggler, his grin as wide as Katie had ever seen. "The salesman assured me I really don't need much new equipment to start making cinnamon buns on a large-scale basis. It's more a matter of timing and logistics."

"And?" she prodded.

"I made an appointment for Monday morning to talk to the manager of the McKinlay Mill Big M. I'm going to take samples, too. If he likes them, he promised me a minimum daily order of two dozen a day to start. He'll give me a one-month trial."

"And after that?" Katie asked.

"We'll see. If I could get into the larger chains in Rochester . . . well, then I could buy your English Ivy Inn for you."

Katie's breath caught in her throat. It would never happen. Oh, but what fun it was to dream . . . Could Andy step into the role Chad was supposed to have played? What would that do to their budding relationship?

And why was she even pinning her hopes on a flip remark made in jest.

Still . . .

"Do you think you can cook as well as you bake?" she asked.

"I can follow a recipe. Why?"

"Because you could be the English Ivy Inn's chef."

Andy threw out his plastic-gloved hand, striking a theatrical pose. "Why zen you'd haf to call me Chef Andeeeee," he said with a bad French accent.

Katie giggled. "Ooh la la!"

Andy squinted and looked beyond her. "Hey, what's that?"

"What's what?" Katie asked.

"Either my eyes are going bad, or there's a light on over at the old Webster mansion. I thought you said the Ryans had abandoned it."

Katie's head spun around so fast she was in danger of whiplash. "Ohmigod, you're right." The place had been dark only minutes before. Had Toby and Janice returned? No, Janice had been adamant: She no longer wished to even be inside the old building.

Katie jumped down from the counter, panic churning her insides. "Andy, the real estate agent let me borrow the key today and I lost it. If someone found it and vandalizes the place—"

"Slow down—slow down!" Andy cautioned.

"Oh, please, you have to come with me in case—"

"Okay, okay," Andy said. "Keith—" He turned to the boy manning the pizza oven. "Cover for me, will ya?"

"Sure thing," the kid said, straightening with a sudden air of authority.

Andy pulled the plastic gloves from his hands and hopped over the counter with the grace of a gymnast. He grabbed Katie's hand and pulled her toward the door. "Let's go!"

The brisk April night air stung Katie's cheeks as she and Andy jogged the length of the Victoria Square parking lot to the old Webster mansion. Katie had a stitch in her side by the time they made it up the creaky steps. The old oak door was ajar and Andy plunged ahead, throwing it open and bounding inside. They bolted into the front parlor and Andy stopped dead, throwing out an arm to stop Katie from venturing farther.

"Holy crap," he murmured.

"What, what?" Katie asked, then saw the prone figure stretched out on the Masonite subflooring. No mistaking the beige coat and the white rain bonnet. "Ohmigod! Rose!"

~~~~~~~~

"Is that better, Mrs. Nash?" asked the dew-eyed young nurse in blue scrubs as she adjusted the ice bag against Rose's temple. Katie couldn't help but wince when she saw the gold stud that gleamed on the nurse's pink tongue.

"Yes, thank you." Rose looked ancient and frail propped against the raised emergency room bed.

"As soon as the resident signs the papers, you can go home. I'll go check on it," she said and patted Rose's arm.

Rose glanced askance at Katie, who stood close beside the bed. Her lips pursed. "Go on. You've been dying to say it."

"Say what?" Katie asked in all innocence.

"'I told you so.'"

"But I didn't tell you not to go to the mansion on your own, simply because it never occurred to me that you'd do something so—"

"Stupid? No, but you would have."

"I haven't even asked you what you were doing there."

Rose folded her arms across her chest like a petulant child. "Not yet, but you will."

Katie sighed. "If nothing else, I need a good story for the real estate agent as to why you got hurt—and if you'll be suing. Fred Cunningham gave me that key so I could look the place over. He'll be furious if he finds out you were there on your own."

"But *you* were there."

"Not until after someone conked you on the head. Did you see who did it?"

"That's a good question," came an annoyed rumbling voice from the split in the makeshift curtained wall. Even with his hands shoved deep into the pockets of his shabby raincoat, pudgy, balding Detective Davenport bore absolutely no resemblance to TV's Columbo.

"Detective, what're you doing here?" Katie asked.

"The dispatcher told me about a nine-one-one call from the old Webster mansion. I'm investigating two murders there, remember?"

Katie spoke through clenched teeth. "We're not likely to forget. Did you get my message?"

"Yes, but first things first." He turned his attention to Rose. "What were you doing at the mansion, Mrs. Nash?"

Katie glanced at her friend. Rose looked every day of her seventy-five years.

"This will sound silly to you, Detective, but my niece died in that building. I just needed to be alone there."

Davenport's scowl deepened. "Did someone hit you or did you fall?"

Rose sat up straighter in the bed. "I most certainly did not fall. I was just standing in the middle of the room, lost in thought. I heard a sound behind me but before I could turn, someone hit me."

"And you didn't see who it was?" he asked.

Rose shook her head and winced. Katie gently patted the old woman's shoulder.

"But I got the impression the person was tall," Rose said.

Davenport grunted and turned toward Katie. "What's all this about a porno movie?"

Katie explained about receiving the beta tape, its stars,

and the production people listed in the credits of the early
Rick Jeremy production.

"I want that tape," he growled.

"And you can have it. But you have to give us a ride back
to Artisans Alley. I rode along with Rose in the ambulance
and now we're stranded."

"Don't you have friends you can call on?" Davenport
grumbled.

"Didn't you just say you wanted that tape?" Katie countered.

The detective sighed. "Okay, I'll give you a ride."

"Good, because I have another theory and more evidence
to turn over to your department. That is if you want it."

Davenport's eyes narrowed. "What evidence?"

Katie told him about the hot lights needed for filming
and the reason for the renovations in Barbie's apartment
just prior to Heather's death.

"I'll grant you, it's plausible," Davenport admitted.

"I'll bet whoever killed Heather came after Barbie. My
guess is Mark Bastian and Rick Jeremy will be the next
targets."

"Why do you say that?" he asked.

"Because they were originally hired to do the renovation
work at the mansion."

"How do you know?"

"I had dinner with Bastian last night. He told me."

"Why didn't you tell me this before now?" Davenport
barked.

"I assumed Jeremy would've told you."

"Well, he didn't."

"And I suppose you never bothered to question Bastian?"

"Why should I? No one told me he knew the dead
woman."

Katie shrugged. "You got me there. But I definitely think
it would be in your best interest to look out for Bastian and
Jeremy's welfare while they're here in town."

"It's too bad you waited so long to tell me about all this," Davenport grumbled.

"Why?"

Davenport frowned. "Don't you ever listen to the news?"

"When do I have the opportunity?" Katie asked. As she studied the detective's dour expression, her stomach did an uneasy twist. "Why?"

"Because someone shot and killed Rick Jeremy earlier this evening."

Twenty-one

"He's dead?" Katie cried, panic coursing through her. "Are you sure?"

"I didn't see the body, but Chief O'Brien of the Rochester PD assures me the man was the proverbial doornail." Davenport scowled. "Am I sure? Of course I'm sure! I am in charge of the Winston and Gordon homicide investigations. I've had *some* experience in these matters."

Well, duh!

"Any idea who's responsible?" Rose asked. She didn't sound all that sorry, probably because she was still thinking Jeremy was the villain in this whole mess.

Davenport shook his head. "But O'Brien will keep me informed."

"Where did it happen?" Katie asked, shock still rippling through her.

"Just outside the Dryden Theater. Jeremy was there to rehearse for the awards ceremony. A marksman got him with one shot to the head."

"My God—what about Mark Bastian? If someone is killing off Heather's friends—"

"Calm down, Mrs. Bonner. Chief O'Brien may have already taken measures to protect the man. I'll give him a call to make sure." Davenport pulled a cell phone from his inside breast pocket and exited the cubicle.

"Good Lord. Three down." Rose's already pale face had blanched. "I was so angry at Jeremy for dragging Heather into such a sordid lifestyle, but I'd never have wished him dead."

Katie remembered her last sight of Bastian only a day before—his shoulders slumped with an air of defeat. He hadn't been totally open with her, yet what he had revealed seemed to come from the heart. Had he been acting then, too?

"Jeremy and Bastian were supposed to leave town tomorrow. I wonder if Mark is at the hotel or if he'll go stay with relatives?"

"And put them in danger?" Rose asked.

"He may just want to get away from the press."

"I couldn't blame him for that." Rose craned her neck. "Have you seen my shoes?"

Katie retrieved Rose's pumps from under the bed and helped her put them on.

Rick Jeremy was dead, and just hours before he was to receive his lifetime achievement award from his alma mater. The impact of his death—perhaps assassination—made Katie cringe. She considered sorting through the mishmash of emotions washing through her, then reconsidered. Numb about covered it all, which was about all she could handle right now.

The nurse returned with a wheelchair and a file folder. "Just sign this paperwork and you'll be free to go, Mrs. Nash."

Judging by the formidable stack of forms, Rose would have writer's cramp by the time she finished.

Katie's thoughts wandered back to Bastian. Had he ultimately been a friend or foe to Rick Jeremy? They were no longer friends. Bastian has practically said that. And he'd sent Katie the tape knowing she'd suspect Heather's boyfriend of killing the young woman. Had Bastian done it in hopes she'd be the key to Jeremy's downfall? Had he hated Jeremy enough to kill—or arrange to kill—the man?

"It just doesn't wash," she said aloud.

"Sure it will," the nurse said, indicating the smudges on Rose's raincoat. "Just use one of those enzyme detergents. Gets blood and all kinds of gunk out of my scrubs every time."

Rose smiled sweetly as the young woman helped her into the wheelchair.

Detective Davenport showed up at the curtained opening. "A detective from the RPD will have another talk with your buddy Bastian, and I will, too. But first I want that videotape."

"Bring the car around and we'll be right out," Katie said, shrugging into her own jacket.

"I am not your chauffeur," Davenport retorted.

Katie glared at the man. "Stretch your imagination, Detective." At his puzzled look, she clarified. "Pretend."

~~~~~~

The drive back to McKinlay Mill would've been a silent one, at least concerning Davenport, who never uttered a word. Katie used the time to call Edie and arrange for her to stay the night with Rose. Edie agreed without hesitation, as though eager to please Katie after their encounters earlier in the day.

"I don't need a babysitter," Rose bristled.

"Someone came after you tonight. I want to make sure they don't try again."

Edie's ancient blue Ford Escort was sitting in Rose's driveway, its lights off but its motor running. The Sheriff's Office's cruiser stopped and Davenport got out to open the rear passenger door before Edie emerged from her car. She held a small suitcase in one hand and a plastic grocery bag swung from her other wrist. She shoved that at Davenport and, with her now free hand, snagged Rose. "This'll be so much fun! I brought over the kinds of stuff my granddaughter trucks around with when she goes on sleepovers."

Katie led the way to the house. The motion detector light went on. She slipped Rose's house key into the lock and opened the door.

"Microwave popcorn and nail polish—we can do each other's toes. Won't that be fun?"

Katie turned on the kitchen light and the others trooped in behind her. Davenport rolled his eyes but complied with her request that he check out Rose's house to make sure it was secure.

"You've got my home phone number. Give me a call at home if you need anything," Katie said as Davenport practically pushed her out the door.

They listened for the click of the deadbolt lock before heading for the cruiser.

Katie didn't bother to try to initiate conversation with the dour cop until after they arrived at Artisans Alley. She disabled the security system, unlocked Artisans Alley's vendor entrance door, and switched on only enough of the lights so that they could navigate to the back of the building in safety. "This'll only take a moment."

Katie circled the big chrome and red Formica table, stopped in front of the hulking Betamax, hit the power switch, then pressed the eject button. The metal cage popped up, but it was empty.

"Uh-oh."

Davenport, who'd been staring at his shoes, looked up. "I don't like the sound of that."

"It's gone," Katie said.

"The tape? Maybe you put it away." He was being too nice.

"No. It was in the machine when I locked up earlier this evening."

"Who besides you has keys to this place?"

"Vance Ingram. But he had no reason to take the tape. And if he did, he would've at least left me a note."

"Call him." It wasn't a request.

Katie did, and apologized profusely for interrupting Vance's family time. As expected, he hadn't taken the tape or returned to Artisans Alley since he'd left just after closing.

"And now it's my turn to apologize," Vance said contritely. "I had no idea VJ would order the world's most expensive pizza."

"Don't worry about it. I'm just glad he could fix the player."

"Well, tell Andy I'll make up for it in future sales."

"I will. Good night." Katie hung up the phone.

Davenport's glower deepened.

"I don't know what to say, Detective. I don't know where the tape could've gone."

"Nobody tripped the alarm, and nobody else is supposed to have keys to this place. Have you had trouble with any of your vendors lately?"

Only Polly Bremerton. But why would she take the tape?

Davenport squinted at her. "You're hesitating."

"One of the vendors has accused another of stealing things from her booth. But I found the missing items this morning and I've taken steps to remedy the tension."

Davenport stared beyond Katie to the cavernous main showroom behind her, where only sporadic safety lighting broke the gloom. "This is a big building. There are a lot of places a person could hide. Someone could have waited until you locked up, taken the tape, and either left the building—"

She finished his thought. "Or is still here? But why?"

Davenport actually looked concerned. "Mrs. Bonner, you may have a bigger problem on your hands than just petty theft."

~~~~~~

"He walked through Artisans Alley with me—twice—poking around dark corners and everything." It felt surreal to be surrounded by bare walls in what used to feel like home. Katie leaned back against the couch and put her feet on the bare coffee table, then repositioned the phone at her ear. With her other hand, she scratched her cat Mason's large, flat head. He purred contentedly at her side on the couch. Despite her efforts, she was still encircled by boxes. It wouldn't be hard to leave this place. Too bad she had nowhere to go.

"Gee, that doesn't sound much like the cop you've come to despise," Andy said.

"I don't hate the man—he just annoys me," she clarified. "He was almost nice. It was kind of spooky."

A cacophony of voices and the ringing of a telephone filtered over the airwaves.

"Oops—gotta go, babe. The shop phone's ringing off the hook."

"Don't forget you penciled me in for lunch tomorrow," Katie said.

"See you then."

"Love you," she said, but Andy had already clicked off his cell phone. Katie frowned and replaced her phone on its receiver. "Well, the other day he told me he loved me," she told the cat. Mason stretched and rolled onto his back, exposing his furry white tummy. Not to be outdone, Della, the little tabby cat who sat on the back of the couch, swished her tail so that it thumped against Katie's neck. "Don't worry. I love you guys, too."

The phone rang and Katie snatched it up, expecting Andy once again to declare his undying love.

"Katie? It's Mark Bastian."

Oh, well.

"You called?" he asked.

"Yes. I'm so sorry about Rick. More than sorry," she admitted. "Shocked and terribly upset."

"Yeah, it isn't every day you see your employer's head blown apart," Bastian grated.

Hadn't Jeremy's death tempered Bastian's bitterness even a little?

"Did he still have family in the area?"

"His parents. Rick was divorced—three times. Thank God he never had kids. His folks are planning the funeral. It'll look like the Academy Awards when all the actors he worked with over the years come to town for the service."

"Will you be there?"

"I've been Rick's Mr. Logistics since college. It'll be just another Rick Jeremy production. Hey, it's my job." For all his cynicism, Bastian's voice broke on the last words.

Katie traced her fingers along Mason's belly, wishing she had some words of comfort to give the man on the phone. She gave him a few moments to pull himself together.

"Did Rick have any enemies?" she asked.

"No. Like I said, we haven't been friends for years, but he always took care of me. He felt a sense of obligation to all his friends—and former friends."

"Did that include Heather?"

"Honest, Katie, she *did* dump him. Like everybody else, Rick figured she'd bugged off for New York and her modeling career. It was a pretty nasty breakup. When she said she didn't want or need him, he believed her."

Mason nipped at Katie's wandering fingers, warning her to leave his tummy alone. "I know about the fire in Barbie's apartment. And so do the police," Katie said.

"I figured you for a sharp lady."

"You sent me the *Star Whores* tape, didn't you?"

He laughed. "I wondered why you didn't ask me about it last night."

"Because beta machines aren't all that common any-

more. I only got to see it this morning. You look so much
more handsome without the cheesy wig."

"It wasn't one of my more sterling moments," he admitted.

"Why did Heather agree to do it?"

"Agree?" He sounded incredulous. "It was her idea."

Oh, dear. Was that what Barbie meant when she'd said
Heather was no Miss Goody Two-shoes?

"If you think Heather was some innocent young girl cor-
rupted by a couple of film students, you've definitely got
the wrong impression," Bastian said. "*She* convinced Rick
that he could finance the rest of his college education by
making porn films. And damned if she wasn't right."

"How many films did the four of you make?"

"Only two. But that was enough. We distributed them to
mom-and-pop video shops and some adult bookstores in
Western New York. You saw the quality of that tape. We
didn't have the equipment to make professional copies. As
it was, we borrowed the machines at the university, doing
the work in the middle of the night. About ten years ago,
Rick became obsessed that someone would link them to
him. He had me try to locate and destroy them all. The one
I sent you is probably the only one in existence. Make no
mistake, it was a real risk for me to send it to you."

Risk for whom? "Where's it been all these years?"

"In a box, buried in my father's basement in Pittsford."

"Had you always planned to someday make it public, to
humiliate Jeremy?"

"No. But when I heard on the news that they'd found
Heather's remains in that old house, I felt I had to do what
I could to uncover the truth."

"No matter who it hurt?"

Bastian didn't answer.

"What is the truth, Mark? Did you or Jeremy kill
Heather?"

"I can't speak for Rick, but I swear I didn't do it. And we

were all in trouble when Barbie's apartment caught fire. We thought the owner was going to sue us. Either that or have us arrested."

"Did he threaten you?"

"Oh, yeah. He made us not only pay for the repairs—but do them, too. He said he'd go to my father, and I wasn't about to let that happen."

"But you said the owner didn't let you finish the job," Katie insisted.

"That's right. When Heather called Jeremy to end their relationship, she also told him we didn't have to finish the repairs, that she had taken care of it."

"How had she taken care of it?"

"She didn't say, just that she didn't need Rick anymore and good-bye forever."

"Did you or Barbie actually speak to Heather before she disappeared?" Katie asked.

"No. It was Rick who told me what she said."

"Did Heather make any money off those films?"

"No. She was out of the picture by the time we started seeing any cash. Rick wasn't happy about the whole deal, especially as he was behind the camera filming me with his girlfriend. It bothered him—a lot. He never felt good about the money and shared the profits with Barbie and me equally. And I guess he figured it was insurance that we'd keep quiet in the future."

"Did it?"

No answer.

"Did Jeremy keep you in a job because he was afraid you'd one day try to blackmail him?"

More silence.

"Mark?"

"I did throw it in his face once. I was drunk. I guess I was jealous of his success—*and* the beautiful women who threw themselves at him. It was petty and stupid and I wish to God I'd never done it."

"And that's what ruined your friendship?"

"No. Our friendship was never the same after he saw me doing it with Heather," Bastian said bitterly.

"But he didn't abandon you. He made sure you had a job all these years."

"Sometimes I think it might've been better if he had just told me to go to hell and fired me."

It was Katie's turn to be silent.

"Katie, please don't give the cops that tape. Rick's dead. It would be the ultimate betrayal if that film became public now."

"Unfortunately, I don't have it anymore. I was about to turn it over to the detective in charge of Heather's murder investigation, but it's gone missing."

Bastian sounded panicked. "Someone stole it?"

"Yes. And I don't have a clue who could've done it."

Twenty-two

The lights were already on at Angelo's Pizzeria when Katie drove past at seven fifty-eight the next morning. Poor Andy, closing after midnight and back again to make cinnamon buns for her breakfast. Katie felt a little guilty, but only a little if it meant he'd have to hire an assistant manager and they could ultimately spend more time together. His ad for the job was supposed to be in the morning newspaper. She'd check while she drank her first cup of coffee.

Several vendor cars and vans were parked in the back lot, their owners getting out to unload their vehicles when they saw she had pulled in. Among them was Polly with her little granddaughter, Hannah.

Katie gathered her purse and the bulky Sunday newspaper, locked her car, and hurried to open the door to let the vendors in. Next on the agenda was coffee. She probably wasn't the only one who needed a cup. Back at the apartment, her coffeepot was already packed, and Katie hadn't felt like searching for it. Today she'd have to make a point to call all the apartment complexes in and around Rochester. She *had* to find a place to live—or if nothing else, a sublet.

Once inside and settled, Katie measured coffee and dumped it into the filter basket, set it in the coffeemaker, and hit the start button. Too restless to wait for it to brew, she went back to her office. Her cluttered desk did not welcome her. The answering machine blinked hopefully: just one message.

"Hi, Katie, it's Fred Cunningham. I've got a hot prospect for the Webster mansion. They want to see the house ASAP so I'll be by to pick up the key before lunch. See you then."

Katie's shoulders sagged. No doubt Fred would be showing the property to Burt Donahue. Sooner or later it would penetrate her thick skull that she was never destined to own that money pit, but Katie wasn't yet ready to give up all hope.

She turned her attention to a stack of envelopes on the right side of her blotter. Saturday had been so hectic she hadn't even had time to glance at the mail.

She retrieved the letter opener from her desk drawer and opened all the envelopes. Bills, bills, bills. Two solicitations to advertise in local ad rags and . . .

She removed the folded piece of white paper from a nondescript envelope and scanned the brief message.

MIND YOUR OWN BUSINESS

A skull and crossbones leered up at her from under the words.

Katie exhaled a shaky breath. Detective Davenport wasn't going to like this. Seth was sure to say, "I told you so," only maybe not with those exact words. And Rose would be frantic with worry . . .

The coffeemaker had finished its chugging. Katie grabbed her mug, noting that her hand shook as she poured. The note had rattled her more than she wanted to admit.

Katie toyed with a sugar packet. Only two people could've written that note. Rick Jeremy or Burt Donahue.

Jeremy's story was that Heather had dumped him. She'd disappeared without telling another soul she'd broken up with him. According to Bastian, it was Jeremy who'd said Heather told them to stop work on the apartment. Was Jeremy angry enough at his budding acting protégée to wall her up alive because she'd spurned him?

Was Donahue a credible suspect? His apartment had been damaged, but insurance would've paid for the repairs if Jeremy and Bastian hadn't been bullied into making them. Donahue had no apparent reason to kill Heather or Barbie. And yet . . . Katie remembered the man's NRA belt buckle. Was he a member or was it just something he'd picked up at the auction house to keep his pants from falling down?

Then there was Kevin Hartsfield. Something about him bothered Katie. He seemed to have known Barbie was dead before the news hit the papers or other media. He lived outside of town and apparently had no friends or local support system. Nonetheless, could he have been plugged into the local gossip pipeline anyway? And something about the way he spoke about his former students didn't seem right. Had he known something about Heather and Barbie he hadn't told her?

The sound of pounding footsteps caught Katie's attention. Polly hurried through the vendors' lounge and out the back door without even a word of greeting. Preoccupied, Katie turned away and doctored her coffee before heading back for her office. She happened to glance out the window to see Polly jump in her car and pull out of the parking lot.

Polly alone?

Where was Hannah?

Katie set her cup down with a *thunk* on her desk and started for the back stairs at a brisk walk. If Polly had left that little girl all on her own in her own booth . . .

Katie rounded the corner. Sure enough, small Hannah sat in a child's wooden rocking chair across the way from Polly's booth, her wee fingers white where she clenched the armrests. Silent tears trickled down her pale cheeks.

Katie glanced around to see if Polly had left the child in someone else's care, but there were no other vendors in sight. She swallowed her fury and crouched down next to the girl, softening her voice. "Hannah, where's your grandmama?"

"I don't know. She told me to stay here. If I don't she'll, she'll—" Her lower lip trembled and she screwed her eyes shut.

"Why are you crying?"

The girl hiccupped. "My toys—all gone."

Katie reached into her jeans pocket for a clean tissue and dabbed at the girl's face. "What happened to them?"

"I put them away. Until I saved my money. Grandmama says you have to buy the things you want. I have two nickels and three pennies." The teary girl's gaze traveled to the empty booth where Edie's merchandise had sat until the day before.

"Did you put them in a box under the table?" Katie asked gently.

The small head nodded. Hannah pointed to the bare walls, her lower lip trembling. "They're all gone."

"Did you take the things from your grandmama's booth, and the other stuff like the little horse?"

Hannah nodded. "I want to be like Grandmama. She makes pretty things."

Katie looked up at the shelf behind the girl, seeing the clay horse that had been in the box of missing items she'd found the day before. The other things that had been missing from this booth accompanied it. Katie stood and took the horse down, handed it to Hannah. "Is this one of your toys?"

Hannah's mouth opened in a joyful grin. "Mine, mine!" She held it to her chest, her small body twisting back and forth with pure happiness. "I can pay for it." She reached into her jacket pocket and withdrew five coins, holding them out for Katie to see. "Is it enough?"

Katie smiled, her heart about to break. "I think so. Why don't we go buy it, and then we'll see if we can find something good to eat."

But Hannah shook her head. "Grandmama said I'll be in trouble if I don't stay here 'til she comes back."

"It's pretty lonely up here. Why don't you come downstairs and keep me company until she gets back. You won't be in trouble. I promise."

Hannah thought it over. "Well . . . okay."

Katie offered Hannah her hand and gently squeezed the small fingers as they curled around her own. "Do you like cinnamon buns?"

Hannah shrugged her shoulders and laughed. "I don't know what they are."

They started off toward the stairs. "Well, then you're in for a *big* treat."

~~~~~~

Hannah had drawn three pictures of her clay horsey, and Katie had found not only Andy's ad but had circled two possible apartments in the newspaper's "For Rent" section. She was still pondering what—and even if—to tell Detective Davenport about the sort of threatening note she'd received when the McKinlay Mill Cinnamon Bun King arrived with a plate full of heavenly delights.

"Boy, am I glad to see you," Katie said, and gave Andy a quick kiss.

He looked down at the child seated at the table. "I see you have a new friend."

"Yes. Andy, this is Hannah. Hannah, this is Andy."

Hannah looked up. "Grandmama says I'm not allowed to call grown-ups by their first name."

Katie nodded. "Then you may call him Mr. Rust."

Hannah giggled. "Rust is on my daddy's car."

Andy looked down his nose at Katie. "And I went to college for four years for this kind of abuse."

"It could be worse," Katie offered.

"How?" he demanded.

She shrugged, unable to suppress a smile. "I dunno. It could be raining."

Andy glowered at her, set down the plate of cinnamon buns, and moved the hulking Betamax machine from the vendors' lounge table to the floor. Then he and Katie joined Hannah at the table for a leisurely breakfast.

Hannah scraped a finger full of white glaze from her cinnamon bun, sampling it. "Mmm. Good!" she declared, and concentrated her efforts on unraveling the concoction.

"So where's Grandma?" Andy asked Katie, and took a bite of his bun.

"Who knows. She took off in her car, leaving Hannah upstairs all alone in her booth. She's got a lot to answer for."

Andy glanced at the black circles on the newspaper laid flat before Katie. "Looks like you've got a couple of prospects on the home front."

"It's too early to call and ask what their pet policies are. I'll do it later. And I guess I better call a couple of movers for estimates. Man, I really bungled this new-home hunt."

"You're running a business. That takes up all your time."

"You're being kind." She watched as Andy took another huge bite of cinnamon bun. A mischievous imp came to life within her. "By the way, a tall, dark, and handsome man called me last night."

Andy grinned. "Of course. That was me."

"He called *after* I spoke to you."

Andy's grin faltered. "Oh?"

Katie decided not to tease him any further and told him of her conversation with Mark Bastian.

"You aren't attracted to him, I hope," Andy said with reproach.

"If I wasn't so enamored with you, I could be," Katie

admitted. She sighed wistfully. "He comes with a lot of baggage that I just couldn't handle. But I think he's basically a good guy. I hope he can conquer the demons that haunt him. He deserves to be happy."

"Then you don't think he had anything to do with Heather's—" Andy paused and glanced at Hannah, who was coloring the tail on yet another horse picture. "D-E-A-T-H?"

"No." But unease filled Katie. Jeremy was dead. Surely his death was connected to Heather's and Barbie's. But what if it wasn't? She shook her head, dismissing the notion. She didn't want to discuss Heather, the note she'd received, or her other suspicions in front of Hannah. It could wait. She'd tell Andy about it over lunch.

Andy drained his cup and slapped it onto the table. "I've got a ton of dough to make for tonight's pizza." He leaned over and kissed Katie's lips. She pulled his face closer for a slower, more sensuous kiss.

"Oh, lady, if we were only at my place," he breathed, and kissed her again.

"If only I had a place nearby," she answered, and gave him another lingering kiss.

"Yuck!" Hannah squealed and covered her eyes with her hands. "Just like Mommy and Daddy."

Andy pulled back and smiled. "I predict that one day you'll like kissing a boy."

"Not me," Hannah declared. "Boys are icky."

"Only until you're about thirteen," Katie told her, and glanced askance at Andy. "Then they become . . . different."

Andy cocked his head in her direction. "Am I different?"

"The best."

~~~~~~

"And you say it'll be available next week? That sounds . . . wonderful." Katie clenched the phone and grimaced. She couldn't bear the thought of living in yet another cookie-cutter apartment complex, and it was her own fault for not finding suitable accommodations sooner. "Yes, I can be there to inspect it tomorrow morning at nine. Thank you." She hung up the phone.

Katie glanced at the threatening note that poked out of her upper-right desk drawer. She'd procrastinated long enough. It was time to call Detective Davenport.

Hannah appeared at Katie's side, waving yet another crayon drawing of the little clay horse. "Can we hang this with the others?"

Katie smiled. "Sure."

Hannah was such a pretty, well-behaved child. That Polly could have abandoned her so readily nearly broke Katie's heart. And where were the girl's parents? They probably had no clue how Polly treated the child—and would be horrified to learn she'd left Hannah alone at Artisans Alley.

Katie closed her desk drawer. She attached a piece of tape to the top of the drawing and stuck it to the front of her file cabinet.

Hannah folded her thin arms over her chest, studying her artwork with pride. "One day I'm going to have a *real* horse. He'll be just like the Black Stallion and I'll go for rides and win races and make big money."

Big money. Hadn't Barbie Gordon's granddaughter, Fawn, used the same phrase? Poor little Fawn. No daddy, no grandma, and likely a life of poverty before her. Like Katie, Fawn's mother, Donna, faced a housing crisis. She needed a place to live and would lose her minimum wage job if she couldn't find affordable day care. Hannah's parents probably depended on Polly for day care, too. It was with a pang of regret that Katie realized it was probably better that she and Chad had never had to face that hurdle.

Hannah's eyes shone with pride as she studied her drawings. Right now she didn't have a care in the world. No one was sending her threatening notes like the one Katie had received. Mark Bastian had sent her the tape, so it was unlikely to be him trying to intimidate her. For a moment Katie even considered Detective Davenport as a possible suspect. After all, he was always complaining about her constant interference.

Katie thought back to the other night at Del's Diner. Barbie Gordon had said that a lunatic had threatened little Fawn. Had she received a similar threatening note? Would Donna know if she had?

"What are you doing in here?" Polly Bremerton thundered and stepped through the office doorway. She yanked Hannah's arm, turning the girl around and making her cry out. "I told you to stay put upstairs"

"Polly!" Katie scooped up the child. Hannah wrapped her arms around Katie's neck, burying her face in Katie's shoulder.

"Stay out of this, Katie. This is family business," Polly growled.

"I will not stand by while you manhandle this child. There are laws to protect kids."

Polly's eyes blazed, but Katie wasn't sure if it was with anger or terror. She'd had nearly the same reaction the day before when Katie told Polly to make a police report about the missing items from her booth.

Brushing past Polly, Katie set Hannah back down on her feet in the vendors' lounge. "Why don't you go sit at the table and color while I talk to your grandmother."

Hannah seemed to grow smaller as she pulled her arms tightly around her and looked uncertainly from Katie to Polly. Finally, she escaped to the safety of a chair at the big Formica table, farthest away from her grandmother. Had that monstrous woman ever hit the girl?

Katie turned back to Polly. "I brought Hannah down here, Polly. It was irresponsible of you to leave a four-year-old alone in your booth. Anything could have happened. What if she'd pulled a shelf down on her or broken something and gotten cut?"

"Hannah would've stayed put if *you* hadn't interfered."

"What would her parents think if I told them about this?"

Polly straightened defiantly. "You don't even know their names."

"McKinlay Mill is a very small town. If nothing else, I could ask someone from your former church. I'm sure a number of them are Artisans Alley vendors."

Polly's eyes bulged, but she didn't challenge this. "I suppose you'll use this incident to throw me out. You've been looking for an excuse to get rid of me."

"Until this week, I've had no reason to treat you any differently than any of my other vendors. But I am putting you on notice. If you continue to disrupt the harmony here at Artisans Alley, or leave Hannah here unattended, I'm afraid I'll have to ask you to leave."

Polly leaned closer and lowered her voice. "People who cross me are very sorry afterwards. Very sorry indeed."

Katie didn't have time to react to Polly's threat. Donna Gordon suddenly appeared at the office doorway, clutching a bulky black plastic garbage bag.

Noting Katie's diverted attention, Polly turned, her expression souring. "What're *you* doing here?"

"It's a free country," Donna said with a sneer in her voice.

Bitch, Polly mouthed, and stalked past the young woman into the vendors' lounge. Grabbing Hannah's arm, she yanked the child from the chair.

"My horsey!" Hannah wailed as Polly dragged her toward the door.

Katie's heart was thumping as she crossed to her office window that overlooked the parking lot. Polly hauled Hannah to the car and forced her inside. She didn't even belt the girl in before she slammed the door, wrenched open the driver's door, and got in. She revved the car and took off with gravel flying.

"That woman," Katie growled.

"Mrs. Bonner?"

Katie turned back to Donna. "I'm sorry. Polly grates me the wrong way. And the way she treats that poor little girl . . ."

"She always was a mean old witch."

Katie scrutinized the young woman's face. "It sounds like you know her well."

"Years ago she and my ma were in the same sewing circle. She was always a bitch." Donna brandished the bag by her side. "I heard you don't just sell fancy schmancy crap anymore. I'd like to rent a booth. Do you have any openings?"

Katie blinked. "Well, yes, but what would you sell?"

Donna removed the bag's twist tie and scooped out a rectangular red velvet pillow embellished with white cord, tassels, and black-and-white beads. She handed it to Katie.

"Oh, Donna—it's gorgeous."

Donna's smile was hopeful. "Do you think they'd sell?"

Katie turned the pillow over to admire the workmanship. "Definitely."

"So, when can I set up?" Donna asked.

Katie handed the pillow back. "Do you have a valid tax certificate?"

The young woman looked confused. "A what?"

"So you can collect state sales tax," Katie explained.

"Collect it? I pay it every time I go to the store," she said, and laughed nervously.

"That's right. But as a vendor, it's your responsibility to take the tax from each of your items sold and pay it to the state."

Donna looked confused. "How am I supposed to do that?"

Katie explained what a tax certificate entailed and that it could take several weeks to a month to obtain one from the state. She also told Donna the monthly booth rental was expected in advance, and watched the young woman's hopes dwindle further.

"I can't afford that. I need to *make* money, not *spend* it. And I need cash *now*!"

"Unfortunately, I'm in the same boat. But I can ask around to see if any of the vendors would be willing to carry your pillows for a commission. They're very pretty and I'm sure they'd sell well as Victoriana. While you're waiting for your certificate, you could continue working on your product so you can eventually stock your own booth."

Donna glanced down at the pillow in her hand and frowned. "I didn't make these. My ma did before she died. She was a whiz with a needle and thread. She could make just about anything." Her eyes filled with tears and her bottom lip trembled. "God, I miss her."

Katie fought the urge to give Donna—a virtual stranger—a hug, and instead grabbed the tissue box from her desk, offering it to the young woman.

"I'm sorry." Donna wiped her nose. "I didn't mean to—"

"I'll tell you what, I'll let you use my booth number. I'll take care of the taxes, too. Do you have any other things to sell?"

Donna sniffed and looked away. "Sort of. But—"

"Tomorrow's setup day. Why don't you bring them around then?"

"I can't. I found a sitter for Fawn, and I and need to work all the extra hours I can get over at McDonald's."

"Could you bring them over later this afternoon or tonight?"

"Okay." Donna's lip trembled. "You're being real nice to me, Mrs. Bonner. Thanks."

"Call me Katie." This time Katie did gather the tearful young woman into a gentle hug, then pulled away. "There's a restroom right around the corner. Why don't you splash some water on your face and then we'll go talk to some of the vendors about using your pillows as accent pieces in their booths. I'm sure we can work something out and put your pillows out for sale today."

"Thank you." Donna sniffed and bent to pick up the bag of merchandise.

"You can leave them here." She jerked her right thumb toward the door. "The bathroom is just over there."

Donna nodded and left the room.

Alone once more, Katie flopped down in her office chair. Donna and her problems had distracted her from Polly's threat. The second threat of the day—and it wasn't even noon! Added to that, she hadn't had the opportunity to tell Polly it was Hannah who'd done the pilfering in her own and others' booths. That was sure to get that sweet little girl into even more trouble.

And she wasn't content to hope that her threat to contact Hannah's parents would inspire Polly to mend her bad care-taker ways. Maybe Rose or one of the other vendors knew how to contact them. She'd make a point to ask.

Katie opened the desk drawer to study the threatening note once again. She didn't want to call Detective Daven-port. He'd probably only yell at her for messing up poten-tial fingerprints, and she could do without more stress. He said he'd be at Heather's service that afternoon. She'd tell him there. That would also buy her time to figure out who it was who might wish her harm—before they could carry the threat one step further.

Twenty-three

"You're not wearing *that* to Heather's service, are you?" Rose stood in Katie's office doorway, pointing at Katie's well-worn jeans and sweater, her expression stern.

Maybe I should just install a revolving door, Katie thought.

Rose's hair, neatly coiffed, was ensconced in its white plastic rain bonnet. Under her raincoat, which no longer bore the scuffs marks from the night before, she wore a vivid pink floral print dress, hose, and cream-colored pumps. Her scowling gaze was fixed on Katie's sweater and jeans.

"No, my suit is out in the car. I didn't want to take the chance of spilling anything on it," she explained.

"Oh, then that's good."

"How are you feeling today, Rose?"

"Perfectly fine. It takes more than a bump on the head to put me out of commission." Her gaze flitted to the bag Donna had left on the office floor. "Where did you get those gorgeous pillows?"

"Barbie Gordon's daughter wants to sell them." Katie handed one to Rose.

"They'd look perfect next to the beaded necklaces in my booth. Do you think she'd let me display them?"

Katie's lips twitched into a smile. "I bet I could talk her into it. What kind of a commission do you want?"

Rose held out a blue velvet pillow. "Nothing. If those pillows help sell those necklaces, I'll owe her."

"Thanks, Rose. She can really use the money."

Rose took out another pillow, scrutinizing the needle-work.

"I had another unpleasant encounter with Polly this morning." While Rose rummaged through the bag, inspecting each of the pillows, Katie told her how she'd found Hannah alone and that the child had admitted taking the items that disappeared from Polly's booth.

"I hope Polly intends to apologize to poor Edie after the awful things she said."

"With everything else that's going on, I never had an opportunity to tell her."

Rose straightened. "Well, let's hope Polly steps out of line and you get to toss her out on her butt soon."

"In the meantime, I feel a responsibility to tell Hannah's parents about what happened here today. Do you know how I can contact them?"

"No, but I'll find out and let you know by the end of the day." Rose glanced at her watch. "I've got a few errands to run before Heather's service. I'll see you at the funeral home at one."

"One?" Katie sat up straighter in her chair. "I thought it was at two."

"The newspaper clearly stated one o'clock. Don't be late." And off she went.

Katie grabbed her phone and punched in Andy's number, hoping he'd answer despite the fact the shop wouldn't officially open for hours. Finally, he did.

"Angelo's Pizzeria."

"Thank goodness you picked up."

"What's up, my love?"

"Remember when you penciled me in for lunch? Well, pencil me out. Heather's memorial service is an hour earlier than I thought."

"It's just as well. I'm still stuffed from breakfast. Not that I don't want to be with you," he hurriedly explained. "How about sharing a pizza with me later in the shop?"

Pizza, again? "I'd love to." Had he noted the insincerity in her voice?

"I'll try to make it to Heather's service," Andy promised.

"Okay, see you there."

Katie hung up. She had just enough time to get Donna's merchandise marked and on the floor and change her clothes for the service. She stuffed the note back in its original envelope and thrust it into her purse just as Donna returned.

Grabbing a handful of tags and a pen, Katie moved aside to let Donna sit at the desk. "Let's get those pillows priced and ready for sale. And welcome to the wonderful world of retail."

~~~~~~~

Katie's black skirt was a teensy bit tight. All those pizzas and cinnamon buns, no doubt. She yanked on her jacket to straighten it and pulled in her stomach as she flashed a smile to Mr. Collier across the way. The funeral director glanced at the cherry grandfather clock that stood in the entryway. It was five minutes until showtime. So far Katie, Rose, and Edie were the only mourners in attendance.

Four floral arrangements—two on each side—flanked the empty casket at the front of the room. Katie wandered over to read the cards. The first, a lovely display of white gladioli, was from Rose. The next, pink carnations, from Edie. The third, roses and baby's breath, was from Seth.

And the fourth looked like . . . real Scottish heather? But that couldn't be—it was the wrong time of the year. Katie glanced at the card. "We never had Paris."

Her stomach did a flip-flop and her throat constricted as she read the scrawled signature. "Jeremy." He must have arranged for them to be sent before he'd been killed.

"Yes, I saw it."

Katie whirled to find a dry-eyed Rose standing behind her. "Sad, isn't it? Maybe he really did care about Heather. I wonder if he would have come today."

"We'll never know."

The sound of voices from the doorway drew their attention. Seth had entered, along with several Artisans Alley vendors. Rose hadn't been expecting a crowd, as evidenced by the small room and the double row of six chairs that sat in front of the coffin, but she seemed heartened by the appearance of friends. Would any of Heather's schoolmates bother to attend?

Detective Davenport was next through the door, and Katie clasped the strap of her leather shoulder bag, which held the threatening note. She was not looking forward to their conversation. Maybe she could snag Seth and let him act as a kind of intermediary. But then she wasn't eager for Seth to know the contents of the note either. Nope, this was one time to go it alone. And it would be better to get it over with quick, too.

Davenport did an all-points visual around the room. Katie caught his attention and waved him to join her. The detective made a beeline for her, as always clad in his rumpled suit and ever-present raincoat. Did he wear it year-round?

Katie already had the envelope out of her purse and thrust it at him. "I don't know who sent this and I only opened it this morning, so don't yell at me for not telling you about it sooner."

Davenport withdrew the paper, read it, and frowned. "What have you been up to now, Mrs. Bonner?"

"Nothing."

He studied the envelope's postmark. "Well, you must have annoyed someone on Friday. Who do you think could have sent it?"

"I told you I don't know. And I never want to see it again, so please take it away."

Davenport stuffed the envelope into his raincoat's inner pocket. "You probably obliterated any fingerprints," he grumbled.

"I'm sure whoever sent it handled it with latex gloves and didn't lick the seal, so there's probably no DNA signature either."

Davenport scowled. "You watch too much TV. Have you got anything else to tell me?"

Katie glanced down at a small stain on his tie. "You spilled your soup." She turned and walked back toward Rose and Edie. The two older ladies made up a makeshift reception line, which she joined.

"As least I have closure now," Rose was telling Seth.

"Is the Sheriff's Office any closer to finding out who was responsible for Heather's death?" he asked.

Rose leveled a withering glare at Davenport. "They don't share that kind of information with me."

The front door opened once more and Kevin Hartsfield entered. He flinched as he walked, and Katie wasn't certain if it was because of his bad leg or that he was simply uncomfortable at being there.

"I'll be right back," Katie told Rose, and hurried to meet the newcomer. "Mr. Hartsfield, I'm so glad you could make it."

"Thank you, Mrs. Bonner. It was kind of a spur-of-the-moment decision. Besides me, I'm not sure any of Heather's teachers still live in the area."

"I'm sure Heather's aunt will be very pleased to see you." Katie nodded toward Rose. "Mrs. Nash is the lady in the pink dress."

Hartsfield didn't take his cue and head on over to Rose. Instead, he stared at his shoes, leaning heavily on his cane.

Katie leaned closer. "Is everything okay?"

With his free hand, Hartsfield rubbed his razor-burned chin. "Could we sit down for a minute?"

"Of course." She led him over to twin upholstered chairs against the west wall, feeling the eyes of most of the room upon them. Hartsfield collapsed into his, rested his cane against the arm, and massaged his right knee. He said nothing for a long time. Katie wasn't sure if he looked embarrassed or humbled.

"Is something wrong?" she tried again.

Hartsfield cleared his throat. "I keep thinking about something you said yesterday during our phone conversation."

Again he fell into silence and Katie fought the urge to rip the words from his mouth. She'd tried to draw him out about Heather and then Barbie. He hadn't been forthcoming on either subject. "I don't understand."

"You asked if I knew who fathered Barbie's child, and I wasn't entirely truthful."

That sparked Katie's interest, yet at the same time she hoped she wasn't about to hear—

"It was me."

—a confession.

Swell.

Katie studied Hartsfield's careworn face, looking for any feature he might share with Donna. She didn't find one. Donna was definitely her mother's daughter.

"It was wrong. She was my student. I was her teacher and—"

And nowadays he'd be thrown in jail to rot.

"—and we were both in need of . . . affection, if nothing else. Her parents . . . my wife . . ."

Katie bit her tongue. In her view, there was no excuse for exploiting a child, no matter how much that child looked like an adult. And worse, Hartsfield had let Barbie fend for herself, never taking responsibility for the life he helped create.

"I'm not looking for pity," he continued.

And you won't get it from me, she thought.

"Except for my sister, I'm all alone in this world. My wife and I couldn't have children, and by the time we stopped trying, they said we were too old to adopt."

"I didn't think that was relevant anymore."

"It isn't—if you have enough money, and we didn't, so that was the excuse we were given. And then Ellie got so sick . . ."

Despite his sob story, Katie found it hard to feel sorry for the man and had to force herself to stay quiet. After all, this was a funeral parlor, and she didn't want to upset Rose.

"What is it you're trying to tell me, Mr. Hartsfield?"

"Not tell—ask." He looked into her eyes—his own watery. "Would you act as intermediary and ask my daughter if she'd be willing to meet me?"

Katie leaned back in her chair. "I'll be honest with you. Donna is pretty bitter about her situation, and I think she has a right to be. She's lived a life of relative poverty and now with her mother gone, her difficulties have increased exponentially."

"I'm not a rich man. As you know, I've got my own financial problems. And I can't change what happened in the past. But maybe the future could be brighter—for Donna *and* for me."

"And Fawn?" she asked.

"Fawn?" he repeated, bewildered.

"Your granddaughter."

Hartsfield's eyes widened. "I didn't know." His shoulders slumped and he looked away, falling quiet again.

The sound of the outside door opening once again shat-

tered the funeral home's terrible quiet. This time it was VJ
Ingram who entered. Dressed, as ever, in baggy cutoffs and
a T-shirt, he looked completely out of place. Had something
happened at Artisans Alley? Had Vance sent him?

VJ made eye contact with Katie, his expression one of
guarded sheepishness. He motioned for her to join him.

Katie rose from her chair. "I'll speak to Donna, Mr.
Hartsfield, but I can't promise anything."

"I understand that. Thank you, Mrs. Bonner."

"If you'll excuse me." Katie crossed the room to meet
VJ, who hovered just outside the viewing room. In his
hand, the boy clutched a wrinkled paper sack.

"Is something wrong at Artisans Alley?" Katie asked.

VJ shook his head. "Uh, no, Miz Bonner. I—uh—need
to talk to you. Kinda in private."

Katie glanced in Rose's direction and found her still en-
gaged in conversation with Seth. Katie nodded and led VJ
down the corridor, outside one of the empty rooms.

"What have you got to tell me?"

VJ's usually pale complexion was tinged pink, and he
stared at his worn Nikes. "My Dad made me come over
here. Right after he grounded me."

Grounded? Only yesterday Vance had bragged that VJ
never got into trouble. "Why are you telling me this?"

"Because . . . because . . ." Instead of explaining, he
shoved the bag at her.

Katie took it and a wave of relief swept through her. She
didn't have to look inside to know she held the last copy of
Star Whores in her hand. "You took it? Why?"

VJ squirmed inside his enormous clothes. "I wanted to
show the video to my friends. Malcolm Gilman said his dad
had an old beta machine in his basement and—" VJ's head
dropped lower. "How often do we get to see some girl get
banged?"

Katie figured it was a regular rite of passage for all teenaged boys, but refrained from commenting on the depth of her disgust.

"How did you get into Artisans Alley?" she demanded, her voice hushed.

VJ's cheeks went a shade darker. "I kinda borrowed my dad's keys. I've been with him lots of times when he closes and I've seen him punch in the security code. It isn't that hard to remember."

Katie frowned. *Note to self: Change Artisans Alley's security code tonight!*

"Anyway," the boy continued. "I'm real sorry, Miz Bonner. And I'll have lots of time to ponder my mistake." That last sounded like a direct quote from Vance.

"How long will you be grounded?"

"Three months," he nearly wailed.

Katie had never heard such a heartbroken voice. She winced at the length of the punishment, which seemed a bit excessive. She'd talk to Vance about it later. In the meantime, she stashed the bag in her oversized purse. Unbeknownst to him, VJ had just made Mark Bastian's day, and Katie was also glad Davenport hadn't seen the exchange take place.

"I appreciate your returning my property," she said.

VJ began to back away. "Okay, well, I'll see ya later, Miz B."

VJ continued to shuffle backward until he ran into the opening door. "Whoa! Sorry," he said, and ducked past the young woman who entered.

If VJ was the last person Katie expected to see at Heather's service, Donna Gordon was the next to last. She'd donned a dark denim coat and, as a nod to decorum, had removed the studs in her nose.

"Donna, what brings you here?"

"I know Ma would've come. She still considered herself Heather Winston's best friend. I thought I should come in her place." Donna looked inside the room toward the casket and leaned forward. "I've never been to a funeral home before. What am I supposed to do?"

Katie gave Donna a quick rundown on funeral etiquette. "Mrs. Nash is the one in the pink dress."

"I thought people were supposed to wear dark clothes," Donna said.

"Mrs. Nash wants to celebrate her niece's life—not mourn her death."

Donna took a step forward, but Katie's outstretched hand stopped her. "Your mother's high school math teacher is here. He'd like to meet you."

Donna's gaze swept the room, landing on Hartsfield. Her lip curled. "My sperm donor? I don't think so."

"You know?" Katie asked, shocked. "But you told me—"

"What was I supposed to say?" She exhaled a shaky breath. "My ma was my best friend. She never kept anything from me."

"Then what was she really doing at the Webster mansion on Tuesday night? Have you told Detective Davenport?"

"That jerk? I wouldn't give him the time of day. He thinks Ma's death was an accident, but I know better." Donna nodded, her gaze fixed with determination. "And— one way or another—the person who killed Ma is going to pay."

Twenty-four

Katie gaped at Donna. "Please don't do anything foolish. Think of Fawn, if nothing else. If something happened to you, she'd be all alone."

Katie absentmindedly looked in Hartsfield's direction, but Donna still wouldn't acknowledge him. Instead, she actually patted Katie's hand. "Don't worry. I'm not as trusting as my mother. And I can take care of myself."

Famous last words.

Donna looked back at the crowd still surrounding Rose. "I guess I'll wait a few minutes before I talk to Mrs. Nash."

"Some of your pillows are already in her booth."

"Oh, yeah? Then I guess I'll have to thank her." Donna's eyes wandered over to the casket, and she pursed her lips as though in an effort to keep from crying. Was she thinking of her own loss, which was still so fresh—and the fact she had no money for a proper burial for her mother?

She cleared her throat. "I noticed you had a bunch of old dolls on top of your file cabinet. Do they sell well?"

"We don't sell commercially made product. I bought

them at an auction the other night. I'm going to clean them up and try to find them all new homes. All except the wooden one. That one I'm keeping."

She tilted her head in surprise. "Why that one?"

A blush warmed Katie's cheeks. "I guess because it looks like it needs to be loved."

Donna's gaze flickered back to Katie, and her lips quirked into a smile. "What time do you want me to bring the rest of my stuff to Artisans Alley?"

"How about five thirty?"

"Can do." Donna's gaze wandered. "Think I'll go look at the flowers. I saw an ad in the paper this morning for a job at a florist. Maybe I could learn flower arranging. See you later." And with that, she crossed the room without looking at Hartsfield, who apparently had no clue he was in the same room as his daughter.

With Rose still occupied, Katie found herself at loose ends and wished Andy would show up. She let her mind wander. If Donna was arriving at Artisans Alley at five thirty, perhaps she could convince Bastian to meet her at six. They needed to talk.

She left the room and took out her cell phone, making sure Detective Davenport was well out of earshot before she punched in the number. Voice mail picked up and she left a message for Bastian to call her.

Katie returned to the parlor and glanced at her watch. Shouldn't the service have started by now? Or had Rose asked Mr. Collier to wait awhile on the chance some of Heather's peers might show? But when the door opened again, it was Burt Donahue and his wife Sylvia who'd arrived. The arrogant auction house owner paused at the entryway, assessing the crowd before him, while his meek wife stayed a step behind.

Katie stepped forward. "Mr. Donahue, I'm surprised to see you here. You said you'd never met Heather Winston."

"Rose has been a good customer of mine for more than

a decade. Being here is just a business courtesy," he said blandly.

That was a rather coldhearted explanation. Katie hoped he wouldn't be as blunt when speaking to Rose. At the same time, she wondered if Donahue had already inspected the Webster mansion property.

"Will you stay for the service?" Katie asked.

"No. We're meeting my son and daughter-in-law over at the mansion within the hour."

Bingo! It was a good thing Fred had collected the key before she'd had to leave for the service.

Donahue turned his head toward his wife but didn't bother to look at her. "Stay here." He strode off, his gait almost a swagger. Sylvia took a step backward, as though trying to blend into the woodwork, but not before Katie saw anger flash across her features. Katie hadn't thought Sylvia capable of that emotion—or any other, for that matter.

"Is something wrong, Sylvia?"

The toad of a woman clutched her handbag tighter. "We shouldn't have come here. That young woman had no business being on our property, let alone dying there. Our mistake was renting to lowlifes. That won't happen when we open Donahue's Shamrock Inn. We'll host a strictly high-end clientele."

Her words had tumbled out—more than Katie had heard her utter before. But it seemed her font of conversation had run dry, and Sylvia seemed to withdraw into herself and reverted to her usual submissive demeanor.

Katie's phone chimed. She retrieved it from her purse and retreated farther into the hallway, stabbing the green call button.

"Katie, it's Mark Bastian."

"Thanks for returning my call so quickly. I have your . . . property, and I'd like to return it."

"Katie, you're a lifesaver," he said, and she heard the gratitude in his voice.

Katie turned her back on Sylvia and lowered her voice. "Can you come and get it tonight?"

"Name the time and place."

"How about Artisans Alley at six? Do you know where it's located?"

"The old applesauce factory that used to be part of the old mansion site?" he asked.

"Yes."

"I know the place. Fine. I'll see you then."

The connection broke and Katie replaced the phone in her purse.

Sylvia was staring at the crown molding near the ceiling, trying to look as though she hadn't been eavesdropping. But Katie hadn't mentioned a name. There was no way Sylvia could tell who she was talking to or what it was about.

Stop being paranoid, Katie chided herself.

"Excuse me," Katie said as she sidled past Sylvia and reentered the parlor.

Donahue had already finished his brief conversation with Rose and charged toward the exit. "Sylvia!" His wife fell in step behind him.

Katie scowled. How had Donahue achieved so much business success with such poor people skills?

Mr. Collier approached Rose, and those assembled made for the dual row of chairs. Katie sat beside Seth and behind Edie, leaving an empty chair on the end in case Andy showed up. Hartsfield also sat up front, and Donna took a chair in the row behind, as far away from him as she could.

Collier cleared his throat. "We'll begin today's remembrance with a short prayer." They all bowed their heads. Behind them, the door opened and closed quietly. Collier finished with, "Amen," and Andy slipped into the empty chair beside Katie.

"What've I missed?" he whispered.

"Plenty."

A dry-eyed Rose approached the podium, took in all their

faces, and smiled. "I suppose you've all been wondering why I chose to wear such a vibrant pink dress to Heather's service. It's because I wanted this to truly be a celebration of her life, not her death. Most of you didn't know my niece. I'd like to tell you about her."

Rose spoke for almost twenty minutes, recalling with love and humor a life that had ended more than two decades before. How sad that so few had gathered to remember Heather.

Katie looked over her shoulder at the closed door. Though she'd just spoken with him, she'd hoped Bastian might show up. He was probably busy coordinating Rick Jeremy's funeral. Thanks to the director's celebrity, there'd be far more than ten people in attendance.

At last Rose left the podium, and a bagpipes rendition of "Amazing Grace" filled the small room. Had Mr. Collier pressed some remote control to start the music? It was a tune sure to break the hearts of anyone who'd lost a loved one. Tears stung Katie's eyes as she remembered the last time she'd heard a similar recording at her beloved aunt Lizzie's memorial service. Andy reached for her hand and squeezed it.

When at last the music faded, Mr. Collier approached the podium and spoke. "Mrs. Nash would like to invite you all to a reception at her home." He gave the address and directions, although Katie was sure everyone, with perhaps the exception of Donna and Hartsfield, knew where Rose lived.

Everyone stood, but only Davenport made a beeline for the exit. Katie hurried to catch up with him. "Detective, you haven't mentioned how your investigation is progressing."

"There doesn't seem much point in pursuing it now that Rick Jeremy's dead."

"You think he killed Heather? Then why was he assassinated?"

"Hollywood types always make enemies. I'll wait and see what the RPD comes up with, then decide how to proceed."

"And what if they don't come up with anything? Heather deserves justice!"

Davenport sighed, thrusting his beefy hands into the depths of his raincoat pockets. "Mrs. Bonner, Heather Winston's been dead for twenty-two years. It's a cold case and now the prime suspect is dead. No one can guarantee justice will be served, and I'm sorry to tell you, but sometimes people *do* get away with murder. That's just the way it is."

Katie clenched her fists to keep from hitting Davenport. With that attitude, she'd be surprised if he ever solved a case. She had to work to keep her voice level. "What about the note I received?"

"Jeremy probably sent it before he died."

"And what if it wasn't him?" she demanded.

Andy and Seth approached, each wearing an expression of concern. "Is there a problem here?" Andy asked, in full protective mode.

Davenport shook his head. "Not with me. Good-bye, Mrs. Bonner. Tell Mrs. Nash I'll be in touch if I have some news." He turned. The three of them watched the door close behind him.

Seth spoke first. "I hope high blood pressure doesn't run in your family, Katie, because you look like you're ready to have a stroke."

Andy loosened his tie. "Ready to murder that cop, more like. What did he do this time?"

"That's just it—he never does anything!" Katie exploded.

"It's not your job to take up the crusade," Seth warned her.

Andy nodded. "Agreed."

Katie exhaled through her nose, hoping her snorts of frustration didn't make her look like Polly. Donna Gordon stood nearby, nervously eyeing the door.

Seth pulled Katie down the hall to clear the exit and give

them more privacy, and Donna fled the building before she could bump into her biological father.

"Katie," Seth said, his voice somber. "I know you're upset with the detective, but let it go for now. You know Rose means a lot to me. I've got friends within the Sheriff's Office. I'll ask them to make sure Davenport follows up on any leads he's got, but only if you promise you won't keep digging into this."

"Hear, hear," Andy agreed.

"I'm not investigating Heather's murder. I'm only trying to give Rose some peace of mind."

"Which looks a lot like you're poking your nose into things you shouldn't."

"Oh, Andy—go make a pizza!" Katie cried in exasperation.

He leaned forward to kiss her. "That's exactly where I'm going. Keep talking sense into her, will you, Seth? And I'll see you around seven for dinner, right?"

Katie exhaled another sharp breath, sorry for snapping at him. "Okay."

Andy leaned forward again, planted a quick kiss on her lips, and then turned to follow the queue out of the funeral parlor. Seth and Katie brought up the rear. Rose had already put on her rain bonnet and coat and was in the parking lot, heading for her car as Katie and Seth left the building.

"Are you going to Rose's?" Katie asked.

Seth nodded. "It's the least I can do. I never knew Heather, but she was my cousin."

They hadn't spoken about Seth and Rose's connection in quite some time.

"I didn't think you and Rose had ever talked about the past."

"We don't need to. Concentrating on the present is much more important. And I want you to promise me that's what you'll do, too."

"Okay," Katie said, grudgingly.

Seth clasped her hand and walked her to her car. "I'll see you at Rose's house."

Katie nodded and got into her Focus. But instead of starting the engine, she sat for a few minutes, thinking about everything that had transpired during the previous hour. Truth be told, she felt exhausted and couldn't face dealing with anything else that evening. After she closed Artisans Alley and dealt with Donna, she would spend an hour or so with Andy at the pizzeria before heading back to her apartment to soak in the tub and then go to bed early.

With that decision made, she withdrew her cell phone from her purse and punched in Mark Bastian's number. Voice mail picked up. "Mark, it's Katie. I've had a change of plans. Don't come to Artisans Alley tonight. I've got to be in the city tomorrow anyway. I'll deliver your missing item then. Please call back and let me know you got this message."

Next, Katie dialed Artisans Alley's number. Vance answered on the second ring. "Hi, Vance, it's Katie. Can you look out the window and see if there's a crowd looking over the old Webster mansion?"

"Is there a reason you care?" he asked.

"Well, sort of. I haven't mentioned my suspicions to anyone else, but . . ."

~~~~~~

Only six mourners trooped out to Rose's house for cookies and punch. Edie Silver had assembled quite a spread. She'd obviously visited the McKinlay Mill Bakery, but Katie didn't doubt that she'd baked a few batches of cookies herself. Rose had assembled every picture she had of Heather—some framed, some in albums, but most of them lying flat on the coffee table or propped up against china cups on the shelves above her sideboard. Time crept on, and Katie kept looking at her watch, anxious to get back to Artisans Alley before it closed.

After everyone else had departed, Edie announced she'd be spending another night with Rose. Katie hugged them both good-bye and hopped into her car, her guilt about Rose assuaged as she drove the mile or so back to Artisans Alley. But it worried her that Bastian hadn't yet returned her call.

Katie pulled into Artisans Alley's back lot, parked her car near Polly's, and walked around to the front of the building to enter through the double doors near the cash registers. Vance was giving the five-minute store-closing warning over the public address system. Was it that late already? Somehow she'd lost track of time.

When the last straggling customers had shuffled out, Vance secured the building while Katie cashed out. A couple of minutes later, he met her in her office. "I've been thinking about it ever since you called earlier. You really should talk to Detective Davenport," he said, concerned.

Katie locked the day's receipts in the safe and turned to face him. "He's the last person I'd share my suspicions with."

"Why not tell Andy or Seth Landers?"

"Because they're both always nagging me to mind my own business."

"And you ought to listen." He shook his head ruefully. "Come on, let's go change the security code. And this time I promise Vance Junior won't learn it."

It took only minutes for them to decide on and change the password. Katie liked having Vance as her backup—in business and in personal matters.

By the time they'd completed the end-of-day tasks, it was almost five thirty and Vance was putting on his jacket to leave when Katie heard a knock at the door outside the vendors' lounge. As expected, Donna stood on the top step, surrounded by boxes and black plastic trash bags. Katie let her in as Vance left for home. "See you tomorrow," he called over his shoulder, then paused. "Unless you want me to stay."

"No, go home. I'll be fine. Besides, Andy's right next door if I need him."

"Promise me you'll call him when you're ready to leave."

"I will."

"Katie!" He used his worried-parent voice.

"I will. I promise."

Vance frowned but turned and headed down the steps.

"What was that about?" Donna asked.

"Nothing," Katie said with a dismissive wave of her hand. "Here, let me help you with that." Katie and Donna dragged the stuff into the vendors' lounge, piling it on the big Formica table. "If you've got an inventory list, I'd be glad to tag everything and put it out on display tomorrow."

"That's okay, I've got lots of time tonight."

"Unfortunately, I need to leave before six."

"Oh, well. Okay," Donna said, sounding miffed.

"Let's see what you've got."

"More pillows and some other things my ma made." Donna opened the biggest carton, pulling aside a swath of cotton batting that had acted as a cushion.

Katie gasped. Nestled on a bed of old baby blankets were five of the wooden dolls Polly had been selling in her booth. "Your mother made these dolls?"

"Yeah, and the ones Polly Bremerton's been selling as antiques, too. I was glad to hear you wanted to keep the one you bought at the auction."

"You put those dolls up for sale?" Katie asked, aghast.

Donna shook her head. "Ma did, along with a bunch of other stuff. We needed the money and Polly told her to get rid of the prototype doll. She wanted Ma to throw it away, but we figured if we could get a couple of bucks for it—why not?"

Why not indeed.

And then something occurred to Katie. "You weren't by any chance at the auction the other night, were you?"

"Me? Oh, no."

"Because someone was bidding hard against me to get these dolls."

Donna's complexion became quite rosy and she wouldn't meet Katie's gaze.

If Donna hadn't been there, then perhaps a friend of hers—or her mother's—had been there. The person had dropped out of the bidding as soon as the dolls had hit the fifty-dollar mark. Had Barbie arranged for that in advance? What other box lots had belonged to the dead woman?

Katie sighed. It wasn't worth pursuing. She turned her thoughts back to the conversation at hand.

"Did you take the clothes from the dolls in Polly's booth?" Katie asked.

Donna bristled. "So what if I did. She still owed Ma a hundred bucks. Polly told me that since Ma was dead, the deal was negated. I figured if I had the clothes, I could sell *these* dolls."

"Did you put nooses on Polly's dolls and hang them in her booth?"

"Hang them?" she asked, confused. "Why would I want to do that? I just left them in her cabinet."

"But you did break into the cabinet, right?"

Donna squirmed. "Well, yeah. But Polly didn't pay for those clothes—they belonged to Ma, and now they're *mine*."

Donna was probably no taller than five foot five and Polly was at least six foot and could easily have hung the dolls in her booth—and without the use of a step stool or ladder. It would've suited her to bolster her cries of victimhood.

A board creaked somewhere in the main showroom, but Katie ignored it. Something more insidious lurked at the edges of her mind. Barbie said that some lunatic had threatened her granddaughter. Even Polly wasn't that sick . . . was she?

"Did Polly threaten Fawn?" Katie asked.

"I don't know. But she was really mad at Ma. Ma wanted

her hundred bucks, and Polly said she wouldn't pay until more of the dolls sold. And she wanted Ma to *give* her these dolls, too. Ma said no. She came in here one day and saw the dolls selling for two hundred bucks. Polly only paid her twenty-five each. Ma heard there's a doll show next month in Buffalo and she decided she was gonna take them there. I think Polly found out."

Katie's stomach tightened. Had Barbie met Polly at the Webster mansion to talk about it? Had Polly pushed Barbie over the railing, killing her? Surely she wasn't that malicious . . . And yet Polly was a bitter, angry woman who looked for slights and mistreatment—real or imagined. She'd threatened Fawn and mistreated her own grandchild.

The board creaked again. Polly's car had been parked out in the lot when Katie arrived, and yet she hadn't seen her inside Artisans Alley.

"You can come out now, Polly. We know you're there," Katie called.

Sure enough, Polly stepped into the doorway, her face pinched with anger. But it was obvious from Donna's frightened expression that she hadn't known Polly was there. She backed away, putting the table between her and the furious woman.

"I was here first." Polly swung her glare from Donna to Katie. "You can't let her sell those dolls to compete with me."

"There are much larger issues to discuss, Polly. Like what are you doing here after hours?"

"I was working in my booth—tidying up," she said defensively.

"The lights have been off for over half an hour."

"Those doll clothes belong to me," Polly said, ignoring Katie, and rushed to grab one of the dolls from the box.

Donna leapt forward, wrenched it from her, and hurried around the table. "They're mine!"

"Ladies, ladies!" Katie pleaded.

A rapping on the outside door drew all their attention. Mark Bastian peered through the glass.

Oh no!

"Go away!" Katie hollered.

Bastian opened the door and stepped inside anyway. "Am I interrupting something?"

"No," Donna said.

"Yes," Polly hollered.

"You didn't get my message, did you?" Katie asked.

A disconcerted Bastian didn't close the door. "Uh, no. But if I could just have my property, I'll leave you ladies to your discussion."

"It's in my purse. I'll get it," Katie said and took a step toward her office.

"No!" Donna wailed. "Don't leave me alone with this psychopath. She killed my mother."

"Liar!" Polly hollered.

Bastian's gaze darted from Polly to Donna and finally back to Katie. "Do you need help?" he muttered to Katie under his breath.

"I can handle them, but *you've* got to get out of here. *Now!*"

The door opened wider behind him. Sylvia Donahue poked her head inside. "I was hoping there'd still be someone here. Can I use your phone?"

"Come on in—join the party," Donna said, chagrined.

"Mrs. Donahue?" Bastian asked, inching backward toward Donna and Katie.

"What a coincidence to see you after so many years," the older woman said.

"Do you two know each other?" Katie asked.

"We met only once—years ago," Sylvia said. "This young man did some repairs for us over at the mansion."

Bastian's rigid stance said he wanted to be anywhere other than with this woman. "What are you doing here, now?"

"We've been looking over the mansion. We're going to buy it back," she said.

"Where's your husband?" Katie asked, craning her neck to look beyond Sylvia to see if Burt was waiting on the step outside.

"He's home. *Safe* at home."

That was an odd choice of words. But with Burt in the next town, Katie felt she could relax a bit.

"Why would anybody want to buy that horrible old place?" Donna asked. "At least two people have died there."

"There's a lot of history in that old house," Sylvia said. "Not all of it savory, as you well know. I'm hoping we can finally lay all the ghosts to rest."

"Ghosts?" Katie repeated, fear creeping back into her gut. A whirlwind of isolated facts began to coalesce in her mind as panic churned through her. She grabbed Bastian's arm, shoving him toward the door, but he dug in his heels.

"I have another appointment and I really need you all to leave *right now*," Katie said. "Perhaps I could meet with you all some other time."

Sylvia's wide mouth flattened into an imitation of a smile. She shut the door, turning the dead bolt. "Another time won't do." She stared at Bastian. "You see, I need to know exactly what you've told the police about the dead girl."

He met the older woman's gaze. "I didn't tell them anything because I don't know anything for sure. But I can guess."

"Burt killed Heather, didn't he?" Katie blurted, instantly regretting it.

"Don't be stupid," Sylvia said. "He doesn't have the guts for anything other than bullying people. She died having a seizure."

"How do you know?"

Sylvia's smile sent chills up Katie's spine. "I was there."

"What were you doing at Barbie's apartment?" Katie asked.

"My louse of a husband called me there. The girl was foaming at the mouth, turning blue. He was afraid she'd die on him—or should I say *under* him."

"Heather was having an affair with Burt?" Bastian asked, shocked.

Katie shook her head. "From what I understand, Dona-hue's always thought of himself as an entrepreneur. I'm betting he was Jeremy's secret backer. He loaned you guys the money to make *Star Whores*. After the fire, he demanded immediate repayment—plus repairs to Barbie's apartment."

Bastian nodded. "We were broke and scared."

"Barbie had the reputation," Katie continued, "but it was Heather who used sex to bribe Donahue to keep him from cutting off your financing."

"The stinking little tramp," Sylvia muttered, an ugly scowl crossing her wrinkled features.

Bastian ignored her. "Heather wanted to be the next Marilyn Chambers. She had plans to leave McKinlay Mill forever and go to New York or LA. Honest, Katie, when she turned up missing, Rick and I believed that's exactly what she did."

"Why didn't you tell the police this years ago?" Katie asked.

"We were two stupid college kids."

"I don't get it," Donna said, turning her puzzled gaze on Sylvia. "Why did your husband call you when Heather had one of her fits?"

"Because she's a nurse," Katie answered.

"Was a nurse," Sylvia corrected.

"But Heather didn't die of a seizure," Katie continued. "She was wrapped in plastic and sandwiched between the walls in Barbie's apartment. She clawed at the plasterboard, trying to escape, before she died of suffocation."

"Too bad." Sylvia's cold glance rested on Bastian. "I gambled that Mrs. Bonner was calling you from the funeral parlor. I wanted to be here to thank you for killing Barbie."

"I didn't kill her," Bastian protested.

Donna pointed at Polly. "She did."

"I did not!" All eyes turned toward her, and Polly shrugged and lowered her voice. "It was an accident."

"Shut up!" Sylvia shouted.

Katie whirled on Sylvia. "Why do you care how Barbie died?"

"Because it saved me the trouble of killing her myself. I've already taken care of Jeremy Richards. And now there's only one person left who knew the truth." Sylvia withdrew a snub-nosed revolver from her jacket pocket and aimed it at Bastian.

Twenty-five

Polly's eyes widened in indignation, her cheeks flushing to an ugly red. She leaned forward. "What kind of a stupid statement is that, Sylvia? You can't kill all four of us and hope to get away with it."

Shut up! Katie wanted to scream.

Sylvia blinked, taken aback. Had she been so intent on getting rid of Bastian that she hadn't considered the other witnesses?

"Well, well—" she sputtered. "Now that you all know, you'll have to die, too."

Polly threw back her head and laughed.

"I've got more than enough bullets, and I'm a crack shot," Sylvia continued. "I earned marksman status in the army." She straightened, her sagging bosom thrust forward with pride.

Katie remembered Donahue's NRA belt buckle and assumed he was the marksman. Yet for all Sylvia's bravado, the gun wobbled.

"Put that thing down, you old fool," Polly ordered.

The gun ceased moving. "I'll shoot!" Sylvia warned.

"Nobody threatens me!" Polly stepped forward and reached for the gun.

A shot rang out.

Everyone froze. Time appeared to stand still as well, as the next few seconds seemed to take eons to unfold.

Polly's mouth dropped open, her eyes going wide as a scarlet stain blossomed across the front of her crisp white blouse. She staggered forward a step, grabbed Sylvia by the jacket, and fell forward onto her.

Sylvia screamed and the spell was broken.

"Run!" Katie shouted, and dashed into the darkened showroom, leaving her pumps behind. Donna and Bastian followed her, heading for the main doors. The emergency lights were scant, but Katie knew the way. Bastian and Donna struggled to keep up. But when she reached the doors to the lobby, Katie realized they were locked. Frustrated, she yanked at the handles.

"We've got to get out!" Donna cried.

"Is there something we can use to break them?" Bastian said, looking around.

"They're plate glass."

"Any other exits?" he hollered.

"On the east side, but we'd have to double back and it's locked, too."

Donna began to whimper.

"Got any other ideas?" Bastian demanded.

"There's an emergency exit upstairs. There're windows and—"

Something heavy crashed across the showroom. Sylvia must have extricated herself from under Polly's bulk.

"Come on," Katie hissed, and pulled Donna through the first booth and threaded her way through the darkened recesses toward the back staircase.

"You can't get away," Sylvia shrieked. "I won't let you!"

Katie paused at the bottom of the stairs. She grabbed Donna by the shoulders. "There's an emergency exit three booths north of Polly's. Get out and call the Sheriff's Office from the pizza parlor next door. Go!"

"What about you?" Bastian asked.

"I can't leave Polly."

"She'd leave *you*!" Donna cried.

Katie gave the girl a shove. "Go!"

"But—"

"I know my way around here in the dark and Sylvia doesn't. Go!" Katie insisted.

Bastian didn't need any prodding. He grabbed Donna's arm and hauled her up the stairs.

Katie took off down the aisle, intending to circle back to her office. Pounding footsteps overhead made her pause halfway down the aisle. She needed a diversion to give Bastian and Donna time to find the exit. Casting around, she grabbed the first breakable item she could find—a glass vase—and crashed it against a booth wall. The noise reverberated through the eerie darkness.

The gun roared from somewhere behind her and Katie darted into the closest booth, banging her shins against an unbudgeable crate, snagging her panty hose. She bit down on her hand to keep from crying out, but what if Sylvia had heard the clanging metal?

What on earth had caused her to separate from Bastian and Donna? Donna was right. Polly would never have gone back to save anyone else. It was her own stupid arrogance that had gotten her shot in the first place. There's no way she could still be alive, and yet Katie couldn't abandon the woman on the slight chance that she wasn't dead.

A creaky floorboard gave Sylvia away. She had to be within ten feet of the booth where Katie hid. The security light was three booths over, and it was too dark to see exactly what was stacked on the nearby shelves, which formed a barrier between her and the aisle. But what if Sylvia was poking her head into every booth as she passed? Had she just fired at a shadow?

Katie fumbled in the darkness to identify the objects around her. Nothing seemed heavy enough or blunt enough to use as a weapon. Ceramic bowls, plates, trinket boxes. Damn! Right about now a big solid bird bath would fit the bill. Why couldn't she have ducked into a booth that held iron sculptures? Instead, she clasped a large, heavy bowl and raised it, ready to crash it down on Sylvia's graying head.

Katie held her breath as tentative footsteps neared.

Creak, creak.

Katie's hands trembled. The blood seemed to have left her arms, making her fingers tingle.

Creak, creak.

The footfalls passed her by.

Katie exhaled and lowered the bowl.

No more footsteps sounded above. Had Bastian and Donna gotten out? Andy would be furious to find she'd stayed behind. If Sylvia didn't kill her, Katie was sure Andy would.

A loud crash and the sound of muffled cursing from somewhere down the aisle told Katie that Sylvia had tripped over something in the dim light.

Katie bit her lip. Should she venture out, head back the way she'd come, or go for the stairs and freedom? But that still left Polly possibly bleeding to death.

With exaggerated care, Katie replaced the bowl on the shelf and tiptoed to the booth entrance. She stuck her head out and peered down the aisle.

Nothing.

So far so good.

She took another few steps forward and smacked her toe into something hard and wobbly at the entrance to another booth. Nerves ajangle, she reached down to steady what turned out to be a bowling pin painted to look like a demented circus clown.

Aha! The perfect weapon.

Well, sort of. It wasn't as good as Superman's outfit for deflecting bullets, but it would make a nice club.

Katie hefted the ninepin and took another step forward. She was now behind Sylvia but couldn't count on the element of surprise.

Avoiding the center of the aisle—and the most creaky boards—Katie tiptoed back toward the main showroom. She'd take a circuitous route to where the floor changed from wood to concrete, one Sylvia wasn't likely to know, and head back to the vendors' lounge. If her luck held, she might be able to haul Polly outside, and if she were dead, Katie could escape without harm.

Katie crept past the cash desks. Just inches to go and no more noisy—

Another floorboard groaned under her foot.

The sound echoed through the cavernous showroom. She hopped across the last board and quickened her pace.

Six booths to go and she'd make it to the vendors' lounge.

Could Polly still be alive?

Five booths to go.

How long would it take for the deputies to arrive?

Four.

The parking lot was empty. Running in her bare feet across it would make her an easy target.

Three.

Sylvia stepped into the glow from one of the overhead security lamps. She shook her head, clucking her tongue. "I'll bet you didn't know I once had a booth in this place, did you, Mrs. Bonner?"

Blood—Polly's blood—stained Sylvia's light-colored jacket.

Keep her talking—keep her talking.

"What did you sell?" Katie asked.

"Anything that looked handmade that we couldn't dump at the auction house."

Ezra must have needed the booth rental money if he'd rented space for that kind of flotsam and jetsam.

"It must've been hard on you, every time you arrived and left here, always seeing the Webster mansion across the Square, knowing you'd left Heather there to die—and that she was still there."

Sylvia laughed. "It never entered my mind." Her eyes narrowed. "What happened to the others?"

"They got away. They're probably calling the Sheriff's Office right now. That's what I told them to do."

"And you stayed behind all alone to play hero?" she asked and laughed.

Heroine, Katie absently thought. She swallowed. "There's no point in shooting me now, Sylvia. If Polly doesn't make it—"

"I've had a lot of experience with dead patients, and I can tell you, she's definitely no longer alive."

"Then you know that Mark Bastian will tell the cops everything. That you killed Heather, Jeremy, and Polly. You're already looking at a long stretch of time in a jail cell, Sylvia."

"Then I've nothing to lose by shooting you, too." Sylvia raised the gun and aimed. "Good-bye, Mrs. Bonner."

Twenty-six

Katie swung the ninepin just as the gun exploded. The bullet hit the pin and knocked it out of her hands. The force sent Katie spinning, and she smacked into the booth wall. A purple- and teal-colored ceramic clock in the shape of a fish fell to the floor and shattered. A shelf kept her from falling. Katie squeezed her eyes shut, expecting another blast from the revolver.

None came.

Seconds ticked by.

Katie dared to look back to where Sylvia had stood, only to find the woman lying on the carpet in a crumpled heap.

"Sylvia?"

No answer.

Katie took a step forward. "Sylvia?" she tried again.

The woman didn't appear to be moving.

What if she was faking? What if—

The overhead lights flashed on. Only Vance had the keys to get in, and the main switch was just inside the front entrance.

"Vance?" she called, but her voice sounded funny—shaky.

"Katie? Where are you?"

"Booth fourteen."

A horde of heavy footsteps tramped into the showroom. Guns drawn, five sheriff's deputies launched themselves at Katie.

"Don't shoot, don't shoot!" she cried, raising her hands in surrender.

They took in the scene of destruction but didn't lower their guns. Vance elbowed his way through the group. "She's the bad guy." He pointed to Sylvia's supine figure.

A deputy brushed past Katie, kicked the fallen gun away, and then crouched beside Sylvia, placing a hand on the side of her neck. "I got no pulse, and a lot of blood here."

Katie turned to face Vance, her hands still in the air. "What're you doing here?"

"Well, you didn't think I was going to just go home after you'd set yourself up as a target. I kept watch from my car in the parking lot and called nine-one-one as soon as Sylvia showed up."

It was the first part of his explanation that Katie reacted to. "I was *not* a target. Or I wouldn't have been if Bastian had left when I asked him to."

"Save it for Detective Davenport." It was Deputy Schuler, whom Katie recognized as the first officer on the scene after Ezra Hilton's murder the year before. He turned away and spoke into the microphone on his lapel. "Situation under control. Better call for the meat wagon."

Katie winced at his word choice. "You might have to send for two. Sylvia shot Polly Bremerton before she came after us."

Vance's face paled to match the white of his neatly trimmed beard. "Polly's dead?"

"Sylvia said she was, but I was hoping she lied. She's in

the vendors' lounge." Katie pointed. "Through there, by the back door."

Schuler and another deputy took off.

Katie met Vance's gaze. "Polly saved our lives."

To say Vance looked skeptical was putting it mildly. Despite the fact it was the control freak in Polly that had gotten her killed, that was the way Katie would tell the story. She'd let Polly, in death, have the last word.

~~~~~~~

The medical examiner knelt beside Sylvia's body, yet it was the ninepin in his hands that held his attention. "I'd say it was a ricochet. The bullet hit the bowling pin and was deflected. Just her bad luck"—he glanced at Katie—"and your good fortune that it happened like that."

Katie almost smiled. "Kind of like a bullet bouncing off Superman, huh?"

Davenport gave Katie a sideways glance and scowled. "It could only happen to you, Mrs. Bonner."

"Why, Detective, it almost sounds as though you wished I'd died," she chided.

The paunchy cop bristled. "Not at all. But you wouldn't have been in danger if you hadn't meddled in things that don't concern you."

They'd had this argument before, and his views made no more of an impression on Katie now than they had in the past. "What happens next?"

Davenport stared down at the dead woman. "We bring her husband in for questioning. See if we can get him to confess his part in Heather Winston's murder."

Katie frowned. "I don't understand why Sylvia didn't just leave well enough alone. I mean, there was no tangible evidence that Burt Donahue was even connected to Heather. There was no reason for Sylvia to kill Jeremy."

"It was probably Barbie Gordon's death that spurred her

on. She might've thought Jeremy or Bastian was out for revenge, and maybe her husband would be the next target."

"Maybe," Katie conceded, still unconvinced.

Davenport bounced on the balls of his feet, looking almost jovial. "Four murders solved. Not bad for a night's work."

Yeah, and Katie had no doubt the detective would take all the credit for it, too. Then again, what difference did it make? Her bigger concern was that the media would make a big deal out of two more deaths at Artisans Alley. She could see her day off tomorrow spiraling out of control as she played spin doctor.

Polly's body had already been removed. Sylvia seemed to be of greater interest, and the lab team had been taking their sweet old time taking photos and measurements. It was after ten and Katie felt like she'd been awake for a week.

"Almost done," said the ME, straightening.

"Can I let my vendors in tomorrow? It's our regular setup day," she told the detective.

"I don't see why not," Davenport said.

"Thanks."

The ME signaled to his subordinates to remove Sylvia's body, and Katie and Davenport stepped aside. Davenport actually smiled—an unnerving sight. "That's it, then. All your troubles are over now, Mrs. Bonner. It's time for you to get back to real life."

Real life. The question was, did Katie have one?

Twenty-seven

Twenty-four hours later, the bell on the door tinkled, her-
alding Katie's arrival at Angelo's Pizzeria. Andy tossed
dough in the air in time to a reggae beat while Richie, his
teenaged helper who manned the ovens, did a hip-hop shuffle. Neither seemed to care they'd gained an audience, and
Katie was content to watch the show until the phone rang,
interrupting their unchoreographed routine.

"Aw, damn," Andy said.

"I'll get it," Richie said and grabbed the receiver.

"You're late tonight," Andy said, stretching the oval of
dough into a more rounded shape.

"I've been hosting Gilda's bridal shower, remember?"

"Oh, yeah. How'd it go?"

Katie hoisted herself onto the counter, swung her legs
over it, and faced Andy. She withdrew a peppermint from
her jacket pocket and unwrapped it. "Bridal Bingo was a
huge success."

She popped the peppermint into her mouth and immediately scrunched it between her molars.

Andy winced. "You know I hate when you do that."

Katie swallowed the shards of candy. "So shoot me."

"After what happened last night, I don't see how you can joke," he muttered with a scowl.

Katie didn't want to discuss that.

"And weren't all your lady friends creeped out to be partying in a building where two people died the night before?"

"If they were, a couple of glasses of champagne punch took care of that." She changed the subject. "Rose and Edie did a fabulous job decorating Artisans Alley's lobby. Gilda got all kinds of funny gag gifts and we toasted her with champagne. It was fun!"

"I wasn't talking about the party. I was talking about everything *else*." As predicted, he hadn't been pleased to learn of her showdown the evening before with Sylvia. "So, are you going to tell me all the juicy details of your day?"

"You'd keel over from boredom."

"I'll risk it," he said, and tossed the dough high with a flourish, deftly catching it once again.

"While Rose and Edie worked on the lobby, I spent three hours with the never-charming Detective Davenport giving my official statement on what happened at Artisans Alley last night."

"Have they nabbed Donahue yet?"

Katie poked her tongue at a wad of gummy candy stuck on one of her back molars. "In a cheap motel near Cincinnati. He said he was on his way to visit relatives. Yeah, right."

Andy laughed, ladled sauce on the dough, and sprinkled cheese on top. Next he arranged pepperoni, broccoli, and mushrooms on it before he picked up a paddle and scooped up the pie. Richie traded a slip of paper for it, and Andy started on the next order.

"What about your new friend, *Mark*?" He couldn't have said the name with more disdain.

"We're going to have lunch later this week—after Jeremy's funeral. That's when I'll—" She paused, looked to see that Richie was otherwise occupied, and lowered her voice. "Reunite him with his property."

Andy changed the subject. "Did you get Donna all straightened out?"

"Her merchandise is now scattered through a bunch of crafters' booths. She ought to do all right."

"I meant with her father."

Katie shrugged. Witnessing Polly's murder had had a profound effect on the young woman. It had at last sunk into Donna's brain just how alone in the world she and little Fawn were. She'd asked Katie to set up a meeting between her and Kevin Hartsfield. He had that empty apartment just sitting there—and Donna and Fawn needed somewhere to live. Maybe the three of them would never forge a loving relationship, but just talking to one another was a start.

"How's Rose?" Andy asked.

"Relieved. She was worried they'd never solve Heather's murder. Edie's going to join her on the trip to Florida to bury Heather's remains next to her parents. Rose will have real closure now."

"Good for her," Andy said and finished off yet another pizza.

Now for the bad news. "Um . . . thanks to all my time being taken up with the Sheriff's Office, and what with all the bridal shower stuff, I lost out on both apartments I was supposed to look at today."

"Oh." Andy removed his plastic gloves and moved to stand beside Katie. He placed a hand on her back, tracing circles with his palm, his awkward attempt to give comfort. "Well, don't think about that right now. I've got a surprise for you."

"Not another pizza," Katie whimpered.

Andy scowled. "What's wrong with my pizzas?"

"Nothing, they're great. It's just . . . I've eaten so many of them in the past few months that I think I'm turning into one. Or at least my thighs are turning into mozzarella cheese."

"Your thighs look fine to me," he said and kissed her nose. "And so does the rest of you."

"Not that you've seen it lately," she muttered.

"Well, my surprise may just remedy that. Richie!" He waved a hand at his helper. "Watch the shop for a few minutes, will you?"

"Sure thing," the boy called.

"You—" He grabbed Katie's waist, pulled her off the counter, and covered her eyes with her hands. "Don't peek until I tell you." He grabbed her arm and dragged her forward.

"Where are we going?"

"Upstairs. I've got something to show you." Andy led her to the back of the shop and pulled her up the steps.

Katie sighed. At last. The scent of fresh paint, his refusal to let her even go upstairs to close the window on that rainy day the week before. Now he was no doubt going to solve all her problems by unveiling the spruced-up apartment and handing her the keys to her new home.

Had he had time to go over to her apartment to gather a few of her belongings? That's what she'd have done. Maybe bring a couple of pieces of furniture over. Perhaps he'd added a pretty wallpaper to the bedroom. Maybe hearts, exquisite little flowers, or a trailing ivy pattern. And if he hadn't . . . well, she'd add one.

The door creaked open. A light switch clicked on. Andy pulled Katie over the threshold. "Don't peek!" he warned.

Katie scuffed across what had to be new carpet. Andy's voice hadn't echoed, which meant there must be furniture in the room, too. A rush of anticipation made Katie want to jump out of her skin.

Andy let go of her arm and stepped away. "You can look now."

Katie opened her eyes and her mouth gaped.

"Surprise!" Andy called.

The walls had been painted an icy blue. Cheap, short-napped carpet in a darker shade covered the hardwood floor in what had been the apartment's living room. Lined against the far wall was an industrial-strength folding table with a computer, fax machine, and telephone lined up like they'd just come out of their boxes. A case of computer paper sat under the table and a beige file cabinet was stuffed into another corner. A couple of utilitarian metal folding chairs were the only seating.

"It's not finished yet," Andy said. "I've still got to get a desk, some shelves, and a safe. But you're looking at the world headquarters for Andy's Cinnamon Buns."

Katie's lip began to tremble. Andy sidled up, threw his arm around her shoulder, and beamed. "Aw, I knew you'd get all choked up." He wiped away a tear before it could cascade down her cheek. "Starting tonight, we can eat our pizzas up here, too!"

Katie turned on him, her eyes blazing. "What have you done?" she cried.

"Don't you like it?" He seemed genuinely confused.

"I thought you were fixing this place up for me!"

"Why would you think that?"

"Because you wouldn't let me come up here. You kept it all such a secret."

"You said you wanted to see more of me. Now we've got a nice place to come to get away from the shop."

"But not *away* from the business!" she cried. Didn't he understand *anything*?

Andy looked puzzled.

Katie's shoulders sagged and she sank into one of the cold metal chairs.

"You don't like it," he said, crestfallen.

"I do," she said, with all the enthusiasm of a death-row prisoner contemplating his last meal. "I'm just a little"—a *lot*!—"disappointed."

A little disappointed? *Ha!* She hadn't even considered he might be doing anything other than feathering a nest for her. "Do you realize that as of Friday I have no home?"

"I told you—you can live with me."

"We've been over this a million times. I will *not* give up my cats—not even for you. And I don't want to and can't afford to board them for any length of time."

"I'm not asking you to. I'm going to hate myself for even suggesting this, but . . . they can stay here until you find a place."

Katie squinted up at him, trying to gauge his sincerity. "Really?"

Andy smiled. "Yeah." He grabbed her hand, pulling her into a snug embrace.

Dear, sweet Andy didn't realize the Pandora's box he'd just opened. "What about my stuff?" Katie asked, all innocent.

"You can put it in storage."

"Not the upholstered pieces. I've heard about mice infestations in those places. Can I bring them here—just until I find a place?"

Andy pulled back, scrutinizing her face. "Uh . . . sure." But he didn't sound entirely convinced.

Katie nestled her cheek against his shoulder, closed her eyes, and enjoyed the sensation of his arms encircling her.

Yes. First the cats.

Next, the upholstered pieces, including Katie's bed frame and mattress.

Then perhaps a dresser with just a few clothes in it.

Add a couple of gallons of paint—in warm colors . . . pretty new curtains . . . some new appliances . . .

Possession was nine-tenths of the law, after all.

Andy heaved a weary sigh and kissed the top of her head. "Aw, hell. Welcome home, Katie."

Recipes

Katie's Banana Bread

2 ½ cups flour
1 cup sugar
3 ½ teaspoons baking powder
⅓ cup oil*
¾ cup milk
1 teaspoon vanilla
1 egg
1 cup chopped walnuts (optional)
1–2 cups mashed bananas (the more you use, the moister it
    will be)

Preheat oven to 350° F.
    Spray 2 loaf pans with cooking spray, dust with flour.
    Measure all ingredients and place them in a large bowl.
With an electric mixer, blend on medium speed and scrape
the sides of the bowl often. Pour into the pans. Bake 55–60
minutes until a toothpick comes out clean. Cool on a rack.
Slice to serve.

(*For fewer calories, you can substitute unsweetened applesauce for the oil—it'll taste just as good!)

Freezes well.

Katie's Peanut Butter Cookies

1 cup shortening
1 cup peanut butter
1 cup sugar
1 cup brown sugar
2 eggs
2 ½ cups all-purpose flour
1 teaspoon baking powder
1 ½ teaspoons baking soda
½ teaspoon salt

Preheat oven to 375° F.

In a large bowl, combine shortening, peanut butter, sugars, and eggs. Mix well.

In another bowl, sift together the flour, baking powder, baking soda, and salt. Slowly stir into the sugar-butter mixture until a dough forms. Chill the dough for at least an hour.

Shape the dough into 1¼-inch balls. Place about 3 inches apart on ungreased cookie sheet. Flatten in a crisscross pattern with the back of a fork. Bake until light brown, 9–10 minutes. (For chewier cookies, bake at 300° F for 15 minutes.) Cool on baking sheets for a minute; transfer to a rack to cool completely.

MAKES ABOUT 3 DOZEN.

Andy's Cinnamon Buns

3 ½ to 4 cups all-purpose flour
1 package active dry yeast
½ cup warm water (105 to 115 degrees)
¾ cup lukewarm milk (scalded then cooled)
⅓ cup butter, softened
⅓ to ½ cup sugar (the more, the sweeter)
½ teaspoon salt
1 egg

Cinnamon Mixture

½ cup sugar
2 tablespoons butter, softened
2 teaspoons ground cinnamon
¼ teaspoon cardamom powder
½ cup raisins (optional)
½ cup chopped walnuts (optional)

Glaze

1 cup powdered sugar
1 tablespoon milk
½ teaspoon vanilla

Dissolve the yeast in warm water in a large bowl. Stir in the milk, sugar, butter, salt, egg, and 2 cups of the flour. Beat until smooth.

Turn the dough onto a lightly floured surface. Knead in enough remaining flour to make a moderately soft dough that is smooth and elastic, from 3 to 5 minutes. Place in a greased bowl; turn greased side up. Cover and let rise in a warm place until the dough has doubled in size (about 1 ½ hours—the dough is ready if an indentation remains when touched).

Punch down the dough. Turn the dough onto a lightly

floured surface, then roll the dough into a rectangle, about 9 by 18 inches; Once rolled out, spread with butter. Mix the butter, sugar, cinnamon, and cardamom powder together in small dish. Sprinkle over rectangle. If you are adding raisins and/or chopped nuts, sprinkle over the cinnamon mixture before rolling up. Roll up tightly, beginning at wide (18-inch) side.

Seal well by pinching the edges of roll together. Stretch the roll to make even. Cut the roll into 1½- to 2-inch slices. Place a little apart on a greased pan or cookie sheet. Cover and let the dough rise until double in bulk (about 35–40 minutes). Heat the oven to 375 degrees. Bake until golden brown, 25–30 minutes.

Glaze: Mix the powdered sugar, milk, and vanilla until the glaze is smooth and of desired consistency. If too thick, add a little more milk. Spread rolls with glaze while warm.

MAKES 12.

◆ ◆ ◆ ◆ ◆ ◆ ◆ ◆ ◆ ◆ ◆ ◆ ◆ ◆ ◆ ◆ ◆ ◆ ◆

NOW AVAILABLE
If you liked the *New York Times*
bestselling Booktown Mysteries, you'll love
the Victoria Square Mysteries by

Lorraine Bartlett
A Crafty Killing

The first book in the Victoria Square Mysteries

Young widow Katie Bonner discovers the body of
Ezra Hilton, who ran the local artisan coopera-
tive like his own fiefdom. The entire co-op is in
a disgruntled uproar, and it seems like the detective in charge of the investigation does everything
except investigate the murder. Everyone from the
village's lawyer to the quilt shop owner had mo-
tive to want Ezra dead, and it's up to Katie to find
out who before more of her vendors die.

◆ ◆ ◆ ◆ ◆ ◆ ◆ ◆ ◆ ◆ ◆ ◆ ◆ ◆ ◆ ◆ ◆ ◆ ◆

M511T1111